W

A
w
a
ra
w
sa
Se
w
al
b
to
po
as
th
ar

WHERE THE RAINBOW ENDS

WHERE THE RAINBOW ENDS

by

Shirley Worrall

Dales Large Print Books
Long Preston, North Yorkshire,
BD23 4ND, England.

British Library Cataloguing in Publication Data.

Worrall, Shirley
     Where the rainbow ends.

     A catalogue record of this book is
     available from the British Library

     ISBN   978-1-84262-807-2 pbk

First published in Great Britain in 2009 by
D. C. Thomson

Copyright © 2009 by Shirley Worrall

Cover illustration © Roberto Pastrovicchio by arrangement
with Arcangel Images

The moral right of the author has been asserted

Published in Large Print 2011 by arrangement with
Shirley Wells

Dales Large Print is an imprint of Library Magna Books Ltd.

Printed and bound in Great Britain by
T.J. (International) Ltd., Cornwall, PL28 8RW

Chapter One

February 14, 1873

'Matron! Matron, you'll 'ave to come quick!' Elizabeth looked up from her register and suppressed a sigh. Young Doris was a good girl and a hard worker, but chaos had a habit of dogging her every step.

With only the date written, Elizabeth Johnson laid down her pen.

'What is it, Doris?' she asked, rising to her feet.

'By the gate, Matron. There's a trunk and I 'eard a noise.'

When Doris was in one of her excitable moods, there was no point trying to get any sense from her, so Elizabeth followed her to the front door.

Dawn was breaking on this cold, wet February day, and the streets of Liverpool were reluctant to come to life. Rain had made puddles at the front of the orphanage, but Elizabeth paid them no heed because she suddenly realised the reason behind Doris's babbling.

A child's cries could be clearly heard by now.

'Oh, my!'

'It's coming from the trunk, Matron.'

Elizabeth ran the last few yards to the gate and lifted the heavy lid of a huge, brass-hinged trunk.

'Run and fetch Doctor Stapleton, Doris, and be sharp about it!'

Who could do such thing? And how long had these children been here? Left in this trunk on such a morning, the poor mites would catch their deaths.

Judging by the noise, the young girl was healthy enough. Elizabeth was concerned about the boy, though. He looked too pale, and it wasn't natural to sleep through such a din.

'Now, now,' she soothed, stroking the girl's hot face, 'there's no need for that noise, is there? Let's get you both inside by the stove.'

The children looked to be about the same age, possibly a year old, and had similar colouring. The boy was a paler imitation of the girl. She had glossy, auburn curls and dark green eyes.

Her cries stopped abruptly and Elizabeth silently congratulated herself on her way with young ones. But her soothing manner wasn't responsible for the sudden quiet. The young girl's eyes were on the sky.

Elizabeth looked up and saw the brightest rainbow she had ever seen. Every colour was

8

sharp and clear.

The young girl stretched out her hands as if she could grasp it and pull it down to earth.

'Come along,' Elizabeth said, gathering the children to her. 'You can look at your rainbow from inside where it's warm and dry. We'll all catch our deaths if we're not careful.'

Later, when Dr Stapleton had pronounced both children well, Elizabeth found a letter tucked inside the trunk.

To whom it may concern at the orphanage. I entrust my late sister's children to your care. Both are clean and healthy. Thank you.

It was written in a good, clear hand and neatly folded with the children's birth certificates, from which Elizabeth learned that the children, Amelia and James, were twins. They were fourteen months old. The mother's name was given as Mary Penrose. The father wasn't named.

At the tap on her door, Elizabeth folded the letter.

'Yes?'

Doris stepped inside.

'The little ones are settled now, Matron. They're both asleep. I reckon the little girl wore herself out with all that yellin'.'

'I think you're right. Thank you, Doris.'

Elizabeth recalled the rainbow and despaired. At the time, she had seen it as a sign, as if God were saying, 'Take care of the little ones'. But that was fanciful.

At present, one hundred and twelve children lived at St Joseph's; there wasn't really room for any more. Yet what could she do? The council would have to approve the extra funding necessary, and that was that. Over Elizabeth's dead body would they close this orphanage to any child.

'Mel, you're not listening to me!'

'Sorry.' Smiling, Amelia linked her arm through Ivy's.

She and Ivy had arrived at St Joseph's within a month of each other and now, seven years later, they were inseparable.

'What did you say?'

'What were you thinking about?' Ivy asked. 'In another world, you were.'

It was time for bed, and they were walking up the stairs, but Amelia wasn't sleepy.

'I was wondering if we'd see that lady again tomorrow. The one in the fine clothes who came out of that big house.'

'The house near the church?'

'That's the one. If Matron hadn't hurried us on, I would have spoken to her.'

'What about?' Ivy scoffed.

'Well, I don't know,' Amelia admitted, and both girls burst out laughing.

Amelia thought the lady had looked friendly, though. A half-smile had played on her lips as she'd waited patiently for the children of the orphanage to pass her on their way to church.

Matron had apologised to her and hurried the children on, but she hadn't appeared to mind the delay.

She had been wearing a blue dress, the like of which Amelia had never seen before. Her dark hair had been tied at the back of her head and not a single strand had strayed.

'One day,' Amelia told her best friend, 'I'm going to wear fine clothes like that. And I'll live in a grand house like that one, too.'

'Oh, yes?' Ivy laughed. 'You'll be lucky. Your fine lady will have lots of money. She wasn't left at St Joseph's with nothing, was she?'

'I wasn't, either,' Amelia pointed out. 'Me and James were left in a trunk. A huge thing it was, according to Doris, with brass handles and everything.'

'And where is this famous trunk?' Ivy asked doubtfully.

Amelia had no idea. She'd heard the story of how she and James had been found at the gate, but she had never actually seen the trunk.

'I'll ask Matron tomorrow,' she said suddenly. 'That trunk's mine by rights. I'm eight years old now and I should have what's mine, shouldn't I?'

'And what will you do with it?' Ivy teased.

'Keep all your fine clothes in it?'

'One day, Ivy, I shall do just that!'

Elizabeth looked at the young girl standing before her. She had no real favourites among the children, but Amelia Penrose held a special place in her heart. In Amelia was proof that St Joseph's was doing an excellent job.

James Penrose was a quiet, biddable, easygoing boy, but his sister was different. She was fiercely protective of her brother, proud, stubborn, fun-loving, clever – oh, yes, she was clever all right. The child was for ever asking questions. Never had Elizabeth known a girl more inquisitive or eager to learn. It was hard to believe she was only eight.

'It's about my trunk, Matron,' Amelia began firmly. 'The trunk me and James was in when you found us.'

'Yes?' Elizabeth prompted.

'Well, it's mine, isn't it? I'd like it, please.'

The girl stood there with her head held high. Those auburn curls that the staff couldn't tame and wouldn't cut were as stubborn as the girl herself.

'It belongs to you and James, yes,' Elizabeth replied. She knew, though, that James would be happy enough to go along with Amelia's wishes.

'You have no room for it,' she added, 'but we've kept it safe for you.'

That trunk was all the girl had in the world and Elizabeth could understand the relief that flashed across the child's face.

'Come along,' Elizabeth said briskly, taking a bunch of keys from her desk. 'I'll take you to see it.'

As Elizabeth strode along the corridor, Amelia skipped by her side.

The storeroom was always locked and rarely used, and it took Elizabeth a few moments to find the right key.

'There's a lamp somewhere,' she murmured. 'Ah, here we are. Careful, child, until we have the lamp lit.'

'Oh!' As soon as the small, dusty room was bathed in light, Amelia spotted her trunk.

Elizabeth smiled as the girl slowly ran her fingers over the brass handles and hinges, and then tried to move it.

'But I can't lift it,' Amelia cried.

'No.' Elizabeth laughed. 'You'll find it easier when you're grown, but you'll always need a friend to help you.'

Elizabeth had no worries on that score. People flocked to Amelia; she would always have friends.

'It has a false bottom,' Elizabeth explained. 'Here, look.'

Amelia gazed in awe as the secrets of her trunk were revealed to her.

'Was it my mother's trunk, Matron?'

'I would say it must have been.'

In truth, they had no idea. All they knew was that Amelia's mother was dead and either the woman's brother or sister had brought Amelia and James to the orphanage.

Amelia, like so many of the children here, had no past, but so long as there was breath in Elizabeth's body, she would have a future.

'She must have been a special lady,' Amelia murmured, 'to own a trunk like this.'

'Yes,' Elizabeth agreed softly. 'I'm sure she was a very special lady. You'll be special, too, Amelia Penrose, so long as you work hard at your lessons.'

'I do, Matron!'

'Yes,' she agreed, smiling.

Amelia was already special. The child was as bright, as beautiful and as surprising as the rainbow they had seen on the day the children had arrived at the orphanage.

As eighteen-year-old Amelia stepped out of the boarding-house she gazed up at the huge moon. She'd been working all day and was ready to drop into her bed, but she was hoping she would see Miles Carter.

The streets were quiet at this late hour. They were cold, too, and she pulled her coat tighter.

Her heart was all aflutter. Last night, she had thought Miles was going to kiss her. If

14

Mrs Whaley's heavy footsteps hadn't sounded on the staircase, she was convinced he would have. Instead, they'd jumped apart guiltily and Amelia had hurried on her way.

She was paid to work at the boarding-house, not talk to the guests, and upsetting Mrs Whaley would earn her no thanks.

She'd hated working at the boarding-house and had longed for better things, until eight weeks ago when the handsome American sailor, Miles Carter, had arrived.

From the first time he'd smiled at her, she had skipped about her duties and wouldn't have traded places with Queen Victoria herself.

Miles's steamship was being repaired and he, along with two others from the crew, was staying at the Whaleys' boarding-house until his ship was declared fit to return to America.

Amelia hadn't shirked her duties, but she had spent far longer than she should have chatting to him.

He'd told her all about his home in America, about his father, his two brothers and his sister-in-law who ran the family business. It was like learning of a different world and Amelia couldn't get enough of it. She loved hearing of the scrapes he and his brother had got into as children. Miles had a real family, and it sounded wonderful.

Amelia was about to go back inside when

she heard the sound of laughter. She would have known his laugh anywhere. Miles was always laughing.

Seconds later, he and another American rounded the corner.

'Why, if it's not the prettiest girl in the world!' Miles declared. 'And what might you be doing out in the cold, Amelia Penrose?'

Amelia was grateful to the dark night for hiding the flush of colour that burned her face.

'I wanted some air,' she lied. 'I was just about to go back inside.'

'Not so fast,' he said. 'I'd like a word.' He turned to his companion and said, 'I'll be up in a while.'

They stood watching his shipmate walk into the boarding-house. As soon as he was out of sight, Miles grabbed her hand.

'Come round here,' he said and, laughing, they ran round the corner.

They stopped in the alleyway and Amelia stood with her back to the wall, her hand still in his.

'I've been doing a lot of thinking,' Miles said, and his unusually serious tone had Amelia's heart racing with a mixture of fear and excitement. Fear that he might be leaving in the morning, and excitement because he clearly considered her important – someone with whom he could share his thoughts.

'I'm giving up the sea,' he said, 'and going home to stay. I'll help my father and brothers.'

Amelia felt a huge lump in her throat. She had known, of course, that he would soon be leaving for America, but in her dreams she had waited for him to make his next crossing to Liverpool. Now he wouldn't be coming back. Ever.

'I'm tired of the sea,' he explained, 'and I want to settle down.'

'I see,' she said.

The moon skipped behind the clouds before emerging again.

'Now–' He paused for what seemed a lifetime to Amelia. 'The thing is,' he said in the American drawl she loved so much, 'I can't bear the thought of leaving you behind, Amelia. You must know how I feel about you?'

She had hoped and prayed and, some-times, even believed he felt the same about her, but she hadn't known.

'I love you,' he said.

'Oh, Miles, and I you!'

'Would you marry me? Could you leave here, come to Seattle and share my life?'

'Marry you?' She was struggling to speak and she felt sure that Mr and Mrs Whaley would hear her thundering heartbeat all the way back at the boarding-house. 'Yes. Yes, Miles, I'll marry you.'

His hands, large and strong, cupped her face. Then he kissed her.

The following afternoon, as Amelia ran, with her coat billowing out behind her, she wondered if anyone in the whole of Liverpool could be as happy as she was right now.

She was eighteen years old, she was in love with the most wonderful man in the world, she had a half-day to herself, her very best friend had a half-day – oh, yes, life was good!

Her boots clattered noisily on the roads as she raced, smiling all the way, to Albert Dock.

She soon spotted her friend, and she ran across the road to her, narrowly missing being knocked over by one of the huge dray horses.

'Look, where you're going, Mel!' Ivy cried, laughing.

'Oh, Ivy!' Amelia hugged her friend tight. 'He asked me. Last night, Miles asked me!'

'What?' Ivy shook her head, bemused at such excitement, but used to it. 'Miles asked you what?'

'He proposed, Ivy. We're getting married!'

Amelia's happiness had kept her awake for most of the night and she still couldn't quite believe it. Each time she thought about his proposal and the way he'd kissed her, her stomach flipped over.

'Married?' Ivy echoed. 'But, Mel, you hardly know him.'

'I know him better than I know myself,' Amelia retorted.

'But he's so – different.'

'Of course he's different. He's American!'

'But when? And where will you live?'

Amelia linked her arm through Ivy's as they began walking through the crowds.

'In three weeks' time,' Amelia explained. 'Miles's ship will be ready then and we'll be leaving for America straightaway.'

'You're going to America?' Ivy was appalled.

'Yes. Miles's father has a business there. A general store – oh, and a livery stables, too. His brothers and his sister-in-law all help to run it. Miles is giving up the sea and settling down.' She gave Ivy's arm a squeeze. 'With me, Ivy.'

'America? But what about us? Me and James, I mean? We'll never see you.'

'You will!' Amelia laughed at her friend's long face. 'Not so often, but don't you see? With Miles and me helping run his family's business, we'll have money. We'll be able to come and visit.'

'Whereabouts in America?' Ivy asked, frowning.

'Seattle!' Amelia even loved the sound of her new home.

'What's it like there?'

19

'Miles says it's all new,' Amelia told her. 'Last June, the whole town burned down and–'

Ivy shuddered.

'Can you imagine?' Amelia rushed on. 'The whole town, well, almost the whole town, was burned down. Miles said the fire started in a paint shop, and it swept south, destroying buildings, the docks – everything in its way.

'But now Seattle's almost been rebuilt. It's so modern and lots more people have moved there. Builders for a start, I suppose. It sounds a wonderful place and I can't wait to see it!'

Ivy said nothing as they walked along.

'You could try to be pleased for me,' Amelia said, disappointed in her friend.

'I suppose I am, if that's what you really want. It's just that it seems such a long way away.' Ivy thought for a moment. 'I know how much you hate working in that boarding-house. Are you sure you're not marrying Miles just to get away from there?'

'Of course I'm not!'

It was typical of Ivy to put a damper on things, Amelia thought crossly. So what if she wanted to escape the boarding-house? Who wouldn't? It was all right for Ivy. She had accepted long ago that she would end up in service and that suited her. Amelia couldn't accept it. These days, with the twentieth century only a decade away, there were opportunities aplenty for those who looked for them.

Besides, she loved Miles. She had loved him ever since she'd first laid eyes on him, ever since he'd spoken to her in that wonderfully romantic accent of his.

Miles was like her; he wanted to get on – to make something of his life.

'What does James say about it all?' Ivy asked.

'He doesn't know yet. Miles only asked me last night and you're the first person I've told. I'll tell James on Tuesday night. He said he'd call to see me.'

'Will I see you married?'

Amelia, too happy to stay cross for long, laughed at the expression on Ivy's face.

'Of course you will, you silly thing. I couldn't get married without you there, could I? As soon as I know what time it's to be, I'll let you know.'

James helped himself to another sandwich. For all Amelia complained about Mr and Mrs Whaley, they'd put on a good spread for her wedding. He knew his sister was fond of Helen and Arthur Whaley, though. They could be demanding employers at times, but they were fair and both would speak their minds. The Whaleys liked Amelia, too, and Mrs Whaley had been dabbing her eyes during the ceremony.

Walking towards him was another woman who had shed a tear during the service, and he certainly hadn't expected that from Matron.

'What do you think of your new brother-in-law, young James?' she asked him.

'He would always be 'young James'. Just as she would always be 'Matron', he supposed.

'I like him well enough,' James replied, adding with a smile, 'And I admire any man brave enough to take on my sister.'

Matron laughed at that.

'They make a handsome couple,' she said.

James followed her gaze to where Amelia and Miles were talking to Ivy. In truth, Amelia was talking, leaving Miles little to do except nod now and again.

Matron was right; they made a handsome couple. Miles was an inch taller than Amelia, and wiry where she was slim. According to his sister, who couldn't stop talking about the American, Miles's eyes were a light grey – 'the colour of the sea on a misty morning,' Amelia had told him dreamily.

James hadn't noticed his eyes, but, yes, he was a handsome fellow with thick, blond hair.

'We'll miss her,' James murmured.

Ivy, especially, would miss her, he knew that. The two girls had been best friends for as far back as James could remember.

'We will,' Matron agreed softly. 'I'm used to her calling on me once a month or so. You'll have to take her place, James. I mean it. Don't be a stranger.'

'I won't,' he promised.

He knew that a special bond existed between her and Amelia. He didn't fully understand it, but he knew it was there, and he was touched by her words. His company would be poor compensation for his sister's, but he vowed to keep in touch. Matron had been their rock during those years at the orphanage, and he would never forget that.

'Her ship leaves in the morning, then?' Matron asked.

'Yes. Ivy and I are going to see them off.'

'That will be nice for them. And how are you finding your job, James?'

'It suits me well enough.'

He couldn't complain. There were jobs far worse than hotel work. That was something of which he reminded himself every time he carried suitcases up those stairs.

Elizabeth left James and sought out the newly-weds.

'It's time I was leaving, Mr and Mrs Carter,' she told them.

'Mrs Carter!' Amelia laughed, her green eyes shining with happiness. 'I hope I soon get used to that.'

To Elizabeth, she would always be Amelia Penrose. More than that, she would always be her rainbow girl.

'Thank you for the sheets and pillowcases, Matron,' Amelia said, clasping Elizabeth's hands in her own. 'They're lovely. They'll be in my trunk and on their way to America in the morning. We'll treasure them.'

'Yes, thank you, ma'am,' Miles said. 'They're much appreciated.'

'You're very welcome,' Elizabeth told them. 'So you're taking your trunk to America?'

'Of course.'

Elizabeth smiled at the expression on the young girl's face. A team of six wouldn't take that trunk from Amelia.

'I hope you're strong enough to lift it, Miles,' she said with amusement.

'I believe I'll have to be, ma'am. I tried to dissuade Amelia – I thought it would be better to leave it with James, but–'

'Stuff and nonsense!' Amelia cut him off. 'Wherever I go, my trunk follows!'

Miles shrugged in defeat and they all laughed.

Ivy stood by James's side and gazed up at the huge ship. People were crawling all over it, as well as on the quayside, and she doubted she would be able to pick out Amelia and Miles.

She was wearing new boots and her feet were sore and blistered. They were cold, too.

'What an adventure for her,' James said.

To Ivy's surprise he sounded envious.

'Do you wish you were going?' she asked.

'Oh, yes. Don't you?'

'I can think of nothing worse. They're all foreigners.'

James laughed at that.

'Of course they're not. Everyone speaks English.'

He thought for a moment.

'I'd like to visit,' he said, 'and see what it's like. It's such a big country – they've got deserts and mountains. Yes, I'd like to see it, but I wouldn't want to live there.'

'She'll be living with strangers,' Ivy pointed out.

'No. She'll be living with her husband and his family.'

'I suppose so.'

Ivy knew she should be happy for her friend, but it was difficult. She would miss Amelia so much.

She wasn't like Amelia. Ivy didn't make friends as easily. She wasn't as pretty as Amelia, or as clever or exciting. Oh, she would miss her!

They had grown up together and shared everything. Ivy hadn't had a single thought that Amelia didn't know.

'Did you enjoy the wedding?' James asked her.

'I did, yes.'

She wished she could wake up to find there had been no wedding, and no ship about to take Amelia away. But it had been a lovely day.

'She looked prettier than ever,' she said, smiling, 'and it was good of Mr and Mrs Whaley to put some food on for afterwards.'

'It was,' James agreed.

Ivy still couldn't make up her mind about Miles Carter. He was handsome, polite and charming, yet Ivy couldn't really warm to him. In Amelia's eyes, the man could do no wrong, but Ivy thought he was weak. He had only been a sailor for two years, yet he was already tired of it. If he was so keen to settle with his family and run the business, why had he left in the first place?

Perhaps she was being unkind simply because he was taking Amelia away. After all, given the chance, James would take off to visit America, and he wasn't weak, far from it.

'There they are!' James cried, pointing.

Ivy looked up, spotted Amelia, and waved frantically. It was impossible to miss Amelia and those auburn curls.

Amelia was shouting, but they couldn't make out the words.

Minutes later, the huge steamship was edging away and beginning that long journey. It would take almost two weeks to reach America.

'I hope the sea stays calm for them,' Ivy said.

'Yes,' James agreed.

Ivy's arm was aching, but she kept waving until long after Amelia was out of sight.

She finally dropped her arm, just as the first tear fell. This was it, then. No more would she spend her free time with her best friend. She felt bereft.

'There, don't cry, Ivy.'

'I'm sorry, James, it's just that—' She took her handkerchief from her pocket and blew her nose.

'I know,' James said. 'I'll miss her, too.'

Ivy sniffed and nodded. Of course he would. She was his sister, the only family he had.

'We've still got more than an hour,' he said. 'Let me buy you a cup of tea and something to eat.'

'That would be nice. Thanks.'

They stood watching the ship for a few more minutes, then began walking away.

Ivy kept dabbing at her eyes. Life would never be the same again and, right now, she didn't think she would be able to bear it.

'She'll write letters,' James reminded her.

'It's not the same, is it?'

'No, but it's better than nothing.'

'Yes,' Ivy agreed on a sob, 'it's better than nothing.'

Tears blurred her vision as they walked

on. She tried to think of other things but, suddenly, she was crying as if she would never stop.

'There, there,' James said gently, rubbing her back.

'I wish Miles Carter had never been born!' she burst out.

Surprisingly, James smiled at that.

'We'll miss her,' he said, 'but it's not as bad as it seems right now. We'll write to her and we'll hear all her news. Perhaps we'll visit her one day. Perhaps she'll visit Liverpool. None of us knows what the future holds, Ivy, but it's never as bad as we fear.'

Blowing her nose again, Ivy nodded her agreement.

'Come on,' James said, tucking her arm through his, 'let's go and have that cup of tea.'

Weeks later, on a Thursday evening, as the Carters sat around a polished table in the dining-room, Amelia saw her new family together for the first time. Her first glimpse of her new home had come as something of a disappointment. It was smaller than she had imagined. Smaller than Miles had led her to believe, too.

The general store, with Miles's father's name prominently displayed out front, consisted of two large rooms – one open to the public that sold everything from hardware to fabrics, and one where goods were stored and records were kept.

To the side of the shop was the living accommodation. It was on two floors, and it was a good size, although still not as large as Amelia had thought.

The livery stables that, according to Miles, provided the bulk of the family's income, was half a mile away.

Perhaps, Amelia thought, she was simply too weary to appreciate it. When she had met her family properly and settled in, then enjoyed a good night's sleep in her new home, she would see it in a different light.

She was certainly travel-weary. After the initial excitement, the thrill of crossing that mighty ocean had lessened considerably. The waters had been rough at times and many people had suffered from seasickness. Amelia had been lucky in that she had merely been bored. Day after day had passed when all she had seen was sea – mile upon mile of grey, uninteresting sea.

She wasn't used to having time on her hands, either, and the luxury had soon worn off. There simply hadn't been anything for her to do.

Then, early one morning, as she'd been standing at the ship's railings, Miles had sought her out, slipped his arm around her shoulders and pointed.

'See?' he asked.

'I see the sea.'

But then, miraculously, she had seen a dark spot on the horizon.

'Oh, yes!' she'd cried, and the rush of excitement had caught her all over again.

'New York,' Miles had said with satisfaction. 'Not much longer now.'

After days of train travel, through the most stunning countryside at times, Amelia was exhausted. She found it difficult to believe that doing nothing could be so tiring. Of perhaps the excitement of seeing her new home for the first time had worn her out.

The train took them non-stop from Chicago to Tacoma, and it was there that they had arrived late last night, after travelling through fertile countryside with industry flourishing on all sides. It fascinated Amelia to see so many new villages being built along the line of the railroad.

Last night, they had stayed in the large and very beautiful Tacoma Hotel. In one direction was the harbour, and in the other, spectacular hills and valleys. Amelia immediately fell in love with Tacoma.

A two-hour boat journey had brought them to Seattle. The sky was overcast, and there was a damp chill in the air, but Amelia was taken with it at once.

She met with her new family briefly, but they were all busy. Amelia hadn't been expecting special treatment, but she had thought they might have found the time to welcome Miles and his new bride.

'You'll get to meet them properly at supper,' Miles promised her. 'Now, let's get this confounded trunk upstairs.'

He hadn't stopped complaining about her trunk once. If Amelia had had any idea of the journey involved, travelling across the width of America, she might have left it in England. But, no, she couldn't have done that. Besides, it was here now. They had arrived and it was too late to worry about the problems her precious trunk had caused.

'We've had four new horses arrive today,' Jacob, her father-in-law, explained, a large piece of steak on his fork, 'which is why we three–' he nodded at Miles's brothers '–have been away from the store all day. It's been left to Constance here to look after everything.'

'I see.' Amelia nodded her understanding and took this to be some sort of apology for not welcoming them.

'We'll be glad of the extra help,' he went on, 'now that you and Miles are here. Constance is a grand girl, but we can't expect her to take care of the house and the store.'

'You can cook, can't you?' Constance asked.

'Of course,' Amelia replied. 'I can help in the store, too. I'd be happy to.'

'You'll start off doing the cooking and

31

cleaning,' Constance said firmly.

Amelia looked at Miles, expecting him to argue, but he was tucking into his steak and potatoes as if he hadn't eaten in days.

She didn't know what to make of her new family.

Jacob Carter sat at the head of the table, a large man with a grizzled beard and weathered, wrinkled skin. He looked a friendly, if distracted character, but he didn't smile often.

On being introduced to his new daughter-in-law, he had shaken Amelia by the hand and looked her up and down as if she were a horse he was thinking of buying.

'I'm very glad to meet you, ma'am,' he'd said, still shaking her hand in a strong, firm grip.

'And I, you,' Amelia had replied warmly. 'I've heard so much about you and your sons from Miles. I've been looking forward to meeting you all.'

Jacob had seemed satisfied with her response, had shaken his son's hand in a congratulatory manner, and had then suggested that as soon as their belongings were put in their room, Miles went on down to the stables to help his brother.

Amelia had gone with him, met his brothers, and then walked back to spend the rest of the day organising their room.

'It's been used as a storeroom,' Constance

told her, 'so it'll need a bit of a clean.'

Constance must be keen on under-statement, Amelia decided. The room had been dirty and dusty, but she'd soon swept it and washed it clean.

She had enjoyed unpacking their things, making up their bed, and adding a few personal touches to their room. She'd washed the curtains, but they still looked grimy and were badly worn. As soon as they had settled in, she would make new ones.

'Are all the girls in Liverpool as pretty as you, Amelia?' Theodore asked, and his eyes that were so like Miles's twinkled with humour.

'Much prettier,' Amelia said, blushing a little.

She knew he was only teasing her, and she welcomed the humour, but the frown on Constance's face said she would do best to ignore it. Constance certainly didn't take kindly to her husband teasing his sister-in-law.

'They're nowhere near as pretty,' Miles said firmly through a mouthful of potato.

Theodore and Constance made an odd couple, Amelia thought. Theodore, according to Miles, had always been the ring-leader. It was he, older than his brothers by a couple of years, who, instead of setting them a good example, had got the three of them into mischief. Even now, at almost thirty, he looked as if he had a ready smile and a sense of fun.

Constance, on the other hand, looked older than her twenty-six years. Her hair was a dull brown, already tinged with grey, and she had it scraped back from her face in a severe style. She gave the impression of being too busy to smile. Of course, she'd had a hectic day looking after the store as well as cooking this meal.

Tomorrow, Amelia would help her and, hopefully, get to know her sister-in-law. She dearly hoped the two of them would become good friends.

Seth, the youngest of the brothers, had a ready smile, too. He looked just like Miles and Theodore in that he had the same fair hair and those grey eyes, but he was quieter. He seemed a little shy with Amelia.

During the meal, the men talked of horses and business. Miles was eager for news, of course, and Amelia found their discussion interesting. She had dozens of questions, but she would save them for Miles. It seemed that she and Constance were expected to remain silent.

She caught Constance's gaze and smiled at her, but Constance either didn't notice, or chose to ignore the smile.

As she climbed into bed that night Amelia was tired, but her head was far too full to sleep.

'Constance says I'm to have breakfast ready for everyone at seven-thirty tomorrow,' she told Miles.

'Does she indeed?'

'I hope I do everything right, Miles.'

'Of course you will.' She heard his smile in the darkness. 'Don't worry, Constance will be there to show you where everything is. And don't let her order you around. As my wife, you've as much right to give orders as she has.'

That was exactly what Amelia had thought.

'I'm not sure she wants me here,' she said quietly.

'What? Of course she does. Why wouldn't she?'

'I don't know,' Amelia murmured. 'Perhaps she's been used to doing things her way and doesn't want a stranger in the house. A woman, I mean.'

'And perhaps she doesn't want a pretty one like you in the house,' Miles said knowingly. 'Theo's always had an eye for a pretty girl,' he added with amusement.

He reached for her hand.

'It's been a bit strange today, that's all,' he said, yawning. 'We're tired and everyone's been busy. You've had no time to get to know anyone. Life will settle down, you'll see. You'll soon feel part of the family.'

Amelia knew he was right. What had she

expected on her first day? She was living in a new country, in a new home, with a new family. Of course things would seem strange.

'What did you think of the stables?' he asked her.

'Oh, Miles, I loved it! I loved the horses and the way their coats gleamed.'

'We'll have to get you up on their backs,' he said, adding, 'Constance fancies herself a horsewoman.'

Amelia had never sat on a horse and the idea didn't appeal to her. However, if Constance Carter could ride them, so could Amelia Penrose.

Amelia Carter, she corrected herself with a small smile.

'Come here,' Miles murmured, pulling her close.

With his arms tight around her, Amelia gave a sigh of contentment, and drifted off into a deep sleep.

The following morning, Amelia was in the kitchen in plenty of time to help with breakfast, but Constance was already waiting for her.

'Good morning, Constance.'

'Morning. Everyone's in a rush this morning so you can set the table and then do the eggs. You can cook eggs, can't you?'

Despite suspecting again that Constance resented her presence, Amelia had to smile.

'Yes, I can cook eggs.' She'd soon lost count of the number of eggs she had cooked every morning at the Whaleys' boarding-house.

'Good. When we've cleaned up, I'll show you where everything is so that you can do breakfast by yourself tomorrow.'

Amelia went into the dining-room and set the places exactly as they had been put out the previous evening. That was her first mistake.

'We'll eat in the kitchen when the men have finished,' Constance told her, sweeping the extra cutlery up into her hand. 'Apart from the old man, they'll all be off to the stables. They'll be in a rush and will need serving quickly.'

'I see.' Amelia had imagined the family starting the day together, and was disappointed. It was like being back at the boarding-house rather than being part of a family. But she supposed they would sit down together this evening.

They worked quickly, preparing and serving breakfast, and then sat in the kitchen to eat.

'How long have you and Theodore been married?' Amelia asked.

'A year last fall,' Constance told her, and Amelia remembered hearing how the Americans called autumn the fall. She loved the expression and the way it reminded her of falling leaves.

'We've known each other all our lives,' Constance added.

'Have you always lived in Seattle?'

'My, you're one for questions! Yes, I have. My parents were among one of the first families to settle here back in the Fifties. Not the first year – then there were only a few log cabins on the beach at Puget Sound.'

'And what about the fire last year?'

'We were lucky. This place–' she waved an arm to encompass the building '–missed it. Trade was good while everyone started rebuilding. Now, you do read and write, don't you?'

'Yes, of course.' And very well, too, Amelia wanted to add.

'Good, I've made a list of your duties.'

'My duties?' Amelia was appalled. The way Constance spoke, she might have been an employee rather than a member of the family. The last thing she wanted was to get on the wrong side of her sister-in-law, but Miles had said she wasn't to let Constance give orders.

'Miles was expecting me to help with the business,' she explained carefully, 'so I'll have to talk to–'

'No doubt the old man will be telling Miles want he expects from him now he's back,' Constance cut her off. 'And if he

38

doesn't, Theo will.'

Amelia had been right in the first instance; Constance resented her presence. She didn't want her here at all.

'I'll have to talk to Miles,' Amelia said firmly. 'Obviously, I'm more than willing to do my fair share around the house, but—'

'This has nothing to do with Miles,' Constance said, interrupting her yet again. 'There's no room here for anyone with fancy ways and big ideas.'

'We don't have big ideas,' Amelia said, 'but Miles has come home to help run the family business. He's expecting me, as his wife, to assist him in that direction.'

Constance rose to her feet, and picked up her empty plate.

'Listen to me, Amelia Carter,' she said, her voice low but edged with steel. 'This isn't a family business, as you call it. This business belongs to Jacob Carter. If you've had ideas about coming here to lay claim to any share in it, you've made a big mistake.'

Amelia listened to her, her knuckles white as she gripped her knife and fork.

'The old man's all for having you here – he's a great believer in family, is Jacob. But when Jacob goes, the business passes to the eldest son. That's my Theodore.'

Amelia was furiously angry at being spoken to in this way, and also deeply hurt that the friendship she had longed for was nothing more than a dream. The last thing Constance wanted was a friend, it seemed.

'And when that day comes,' Constance went on coldly, 'my Theodore has big plans for the business. Plans that don't include his kid brother or his fancy English wife!'

Chapter Two

April 1893, Seattle

Amelia jumped down from the young bay gelding, patted his neck and walked him back to his stable. The sky was overcast, as it often was in Seattle, but it was a pleasantly warm day. A perfect day for riding.

Amelia, however, couldn't say she had enjoyed the morning's outing. There had been too much on her mind, like the money missing from the savings tin in their bedroom. She had her suspicions, and intended to confront Miles when he returned from Tacoma that evening.

Miles believed in living for the moment, but Amelia was determined to put any spare coins in the tin. She wanted to save enough so that, one day, they could open a business of their own. That would take a long time, though. There simply wasn't any spare money to be had. Even so, Miles shouldn't have taken what little money she had managed to save without discussing it with her. There had been almost forty dollars in that tin.

The gelding snorted impatiently and Amelia began to rub him down.

Usually, her sister-in-law exercised him but, as Constance was pregnant and had been feeling peaky for the last few days, Theodore had put his foot down. Theodore wasn't the perfect gentleman, but Constance had looked poorly enough for him to insist that Amelia helped out at the stables.

For Amelia, it was a gift. She loved the horses and, given the choice, would have spent all day with them.

When she had finished rubbing down the gelding, she walked back to the house.

She was on her way to the kitchen when Constance stopped her.

'You'll have to take over here,' her sister-in-law told her. 'I'm going upstairs for a while.'

'Are you feeling unwell again?' Amelia asked curiously.

'I'm going to lie down for an hour, that's all.'

Constance must be feeling very ill indeed. She never allowed Amelia to work in the store unless it was unavoidable. She certainly looked ill. Her complexion was a sickly grey and there was a thin film of perspiration on her forehead.

'I'll be back in an hour,' Constance said, heading for the back, 'and make sure you keep a note of everything you do. Do you hear me?'

'Of course. Relax, Constance. I do know what I'm doing.'

'Hm.'

With that, Constance was gone, leaving Amelia to the delights of the store.

Not only did Amelia know what she was doing, she could have done it a whole lot better, and this knowledge never failed to frustrate her.

If only she could give her plans free rein. But she couldn't, and there was no point wishing.

It was Jacob and Theodore who ran the business – mainly Jacob. Theodore, it seemed, was content to go along with his father's ideas. But they were tired ideas.

Seattle's population was increasing rapidly, and if they didn't move with the times they would find trade dwindling. As the population increased – and it had increased at an amazing rate in the three years Amelia had lived there – people were becoming keen to set up business in Seattle. Business meant competition.

They needed to attract women to the store, too. It was possible to buy fabrics – it was possible to buy almost anything – but the fabrics weren't chosen with any thought and they certainly weren't displayed to their best advantage.

The place needed a good clean, too. If it were up to Amelia, she would close the store for a week – that suggestion alone would be enough to send Jacob to an early grave, she thought with amusement. But she would empty the store completely, give it a good clean and then display the goods so that potential customers could see what was available.

But it wasn't up to Amelia. The men, when she had dared to voice her ideas, had merely laughed at her.

'Fancy British ways,' they had scoffed. Either that or they would try to explain, as if speaking to a dim-witted child, that the nation was in the grip of a depression. It was soul destroying.

'The business keeps us all,' Miles often said. 'What more can anyone want?'

It didn't keep them as well as it could, or should, and unless they moved with the times, it wouldn't keep them at all. But Amelia knew she was wasting her breath. Miles was happy enough with his lot.

Amelia tried to be, but she wasn't content. She loved her husband, and she got along well enough with the family, apart from Constance, who had been suspicious of her from the start, but she longed to drag them all from their ruts and wake them up to the fact that Seattle was being swept along on a tide of progress. Progress was exciting, but fickle. It had no time for dallying.

She tapped her foot impatiently. Business should be booming and, as yet, she hadn't seen a single customer.

At that, the door opened and in walked Daniel Gray. Left to his own devices, he would spend half the morning talking. He was a great one for gossiping and a poor one for spending.

'Good morning, Mr Gray,' Amelia greeted him briskly. 'What can I do for you today.'

'I wanted to see Jacob,' he said, looking about him as if he expected to spot Jacob in his hiding place.

'He's gone to Tacoma with Miles and Theo,' Amelia explained. 'They'll be back this evening. Anything I can help you with?'

'Nah!' Chuckling at the very idea of being helped by a woman, Daniel touched his forehead and left.

Minutes later, Daniel's son, Frank, entered the store. Unlike his father, Frank seemed pleased to see her.

'And to what do we owe this pleasure?' he asked, smiling.

'Constance is busy elsewhere,' she explained. No need to tell him that Constance wasn't feeling well. 'What can I do for you,

44

Frank? Or, like your father, would you rather talk to the men?'

'I'd much rather talk to you,' he teased her. American men, she had discovered, were far more forward than their British counterparts.

'I've come to collect the foodstuffs,' he went on. 'Theo said it would be ready for me this morning.'

'Oh, right.'

Amelia checked in the book and, sure enough, saw Frank's order for the animal feed. The sacks were in a pile out the back, and she checked them off against the list.

'All here,' she said with satisfaction.

'I expect I'll see Miles this evening, then,' he said, as he was about to leave.

'Oh?' Amelia asked, brows drawing together.

'Er, yes.' Frank realised he had probably said too much. 'Some of us had, erm, planned to meet up,' he explained, his skin flushed scarlet now.

'Gambling!' Amelia was furious. That, she suspected, was responsible for her missing savings. They had been gambled away.

'Now, then, did I mention gambling?' Looking aggrieved, Frank hurried out of the store before she could question him further.

Amelia had had her suspicions for some time now, and she wasn't best pleased about it.

She knew, though, that her husband would give her one of his smiles and laugh it off. She was the one who wanted their own business, not Miles. She was the one who wanted something better for the future, something for their children.

Not, she thought dully, that there were any children to consider. After three years of marriage, she was beginning to wonder if there ever would be. It was a thought that broke her heart.

Young Tommy was a year old now and Constance was about to present Theodore with their second child. It didn't seem fair...

Jacob and Theodore were back around seven that evening, but there was no sign of Miles.

'I think that's Miles's business, don't you?' Jacob murmured when she questioned this.

She nodded and smiled, but no, she didn't think it was Miles's business, not when there was the matter of the missing cash to discuss with him.

Amelia finally heard Miles arrive in the early hours of the morning. She had tried to sleep, but her anger had kept her tossing and turning. She was sitting up in bed when she heard him stumble on the stairs.

When he walked into their bedroom, the light from her candle showed her his sheepish expression. Why am I so desperate for children, she thought with exasperation, when I have Miles? Miles could be more trying than half a dozen children.

'You still awake, sweetheart?' he whispered.

'I am. Where have you been?'

'A spot of business—'

'A spot of gambling, more like,' she retaliated, keeping her voice low so as not to wake Theodore and Constance in the next room. 'Miles, how could you? You took our savings! You knew we had put that money aside for our future.'

'I only borrowed it,' he whispered.

'Pah!'

'I did!' Grinning from ear to ear, he dug into the pocket of his jacket, pulled out some dollar bills, and dropped them on the bed. 'Savings repaid with interest, sweetheart!'

Amelia grabbed the cash and counted it.

'A hundred dollars!' she whispered incredulously.

'You didn't think I'd risk our savings, did you?'

She had thought exactly that.

'What if you'd lost it, Miles?'

'I didn't, did I?' He blew out the candle and climbed into bed beside her.

Amelia lay on her back, a smile on her face and the dollar bills clasped tightly in her hands. In the morning that cash would be hidden away somewhere safe – safe from

Miles. She had never shown him the secret compartment in her trunk. The only people who knew about it were Matron, her twin brother, James, and her best friend, Ivy.

As she held the money tight, she wondered what James and Ivy were doing right now. First thing in the morning, she would write to them both...

May 1893, Liverpool

James wished they could have made a day of it, maybe even taken in the music hall this evening, but he and Ivy only had a half-day, and that was almost gone.

As James walked her home, past the docks that were a bustle of activity, he was reminded of the day they had waved goodbye to Amelia.

Letters came from America frequently, and were full of amusing anecdotes about the Carter family. So much so that James felt as if he would recognise any one of them in the street. Amelia's father-in-law, Jacob, was a man set in his ways who fought against change, or progress, as Amelia called it. Then there were Miles's brothers, Theodore and Seth. They were chalk and cheese, according to Amelia. As for Constance, Amelia's sister-in-law, there was little love lost there.

'Have you heard from Amelia?' James asked as they walked.

'Not since the last one I showed you. The one where she wrote about Constance having a baby,' Ivy replied.

Silly of James to ask, really. If Ivy had received a letter, she would have mentioned it. He was making conversation, that was all.

Strange that he should need to. Usually, he and Ivy didn't stop talking when they met up.

'Is everything all right?' he asked, frowning. He hadn't noticed anything amiss but, thinking about it, Ivy had been unusually quiet this afternoon.

'Yes, fine.'

She gave him a smile that didn't quite reach her eyes.

'Amelia doesn't write as often as she used to, does she?' she went on. 'I suppose she's got her own life now.'

James stopped walking and turned to look at her.

'You do miss her, don't you, Ivy?'

'I do,' Ivy admitted. 'It's three years now and I still find it hard to accept that she's on the other side of the ocean.' She nodded past the ships to the water. 'But there,' she went on, 'we all have to get on with our lives, don't we?'

They walked on, lost in their own worlds. James supposed that Ivy's thoughts centred around Amelia. His own were on Ivy. There was definitely something bothering her.

'Tell you what,' he suggested, 'we've got a night off next week. We'll go to the music hall, shall we? My treat. A late celebration for your birthday.'

'That would have been nice,' she said slowly, 'but–'

James waited.

'I've arranged to do something else,' she said at last.

'Oh?'

'Yes. Perhaps we'll do it – some other time.'

'Er, yes.'

'I've arranged to do something else' – what did she mean by that? It was unlike Ivy not to tell him what she was doing. Come to that, it was unlike him not to ask.

Something was stopping him.

Ivy was – well, James supposed she was his best friend. They had a history, a background. They knew each other well. They had grown up together.

So why, given all that, did he suddenly feel as if she were a complete stranger to him?

They said little as they walked and were soon parting at the railings that stood black and cold outside the house where Ivy had worked since leaving the orphanage.

'Be seeing you, Jimmy,' Ivy said.

'Yes.'

He stood to watch her skip down the steps around the back of the house. She would have been into her room, changed out of her best clothes and ready for an evening's work by the time he finally walked on.

James couldn't shake off his feelings and when, three days later, a letter arrived from Amelia, his spirits dripped even lower. That had nothing to do with his sister's letters, as he hadn't even read it, but it had more to do with the fact that he couldn't show it to Ivy. How could he when he didn't know when he was seeing her again?

He saved the letter until he was in bed that evening, when all was quiet and he could read it properly.

Nothing changes here, she had written, *and nothing ever will if Jacob has anything to do with it. Never have I known a man so against progress. All he talks about is the depression. Another store has opened and, although it's not as big as ours, it could be considered a rival if the owners work hard...*

James had to smile. He could imagine his sister's frustration as she tried to make her father-in-law see the error of his ways.

Constance hasn't been feeling well lately and, while I feel for her, it does mean I'm allowed to exercise the horses and work in the store more often.

The news ran on...

What do you reckon to the new fellow who's working with Ivy, then? Her last letter was full of young Alex. Have you met him? Is she smitten, do you think?

Alex? James tossed the letter down and went to stand before the window to peer out into the darkness.

His heart was racing as he picked up the letter again. *Is she smitten, do you think?*

James didn't know what to think. He had heard Ivy mention Alex, of course, but he hadn't paid any heed.

'He seems a nice enough chap,' was all Ivy had said.

She had said a lot more to Amelia, it seemed.

On Monday morning, James set off to the orphanage to see Elizabeth Johnson. He liked to keep in touch with her, as did Ivy, and, besides, he wanted to know if Matron had any theories on this Alex.

She was standing on the front steps when he arrived, a deep frown on her face, but that cleared as soon as she spotted him.

'James, what a delightful surprise!'

'Is something wrong, Matron?' he asked. 'You look … troubled.'

'Only the usual,' she said, tapping her foot. 'Too many children and not enough funds. Come along inside, young James.'

Minutes later, James was sitting opposite Matron with a cup of tea in his hands.

That was why Matron was so popular, James thought. No matter how busy she was, she always had time for people.

He wondered how old she was. It was twenty years since he and Amelia had been abandoned at the gates of St Joseph's orphanage and they had always thought Matron was old. She must be nearing sixty now, he supposed.

Her hair had once been dark, he recalled, but had been a silver-grey for many years now.

'Have you heard from Amelia?' she asked him.

'Yes.' Smiling, he took Amelia's last letter from his pocket and handed it over.

She smiled as she read it and James knew exactly how she felt. Amelia wrote as she spoke and it was almost like having her in the room with them.

'She sounds well enough,' Matron said, handing back the letter.

'Yes,' James agreed, wondering how he might approach the matter uppermost in his mind.

But Matron was talking about Amelia and he couldn't have got a word in if he'd tried. All that was required of him was to nod in the appropriate places.

He was on his feet, about to leave, when Matron mentioned Ivy.

'I wonder if Ivy and her Alex will be wed?'

'Wed?' James repeated, taken aback both by the comment and by the way his stomach suddenly churned.

'It's more than three years since she saw her best friend married,' Matron pointed out quietly. She looked at him for a moment. 'Why, you've gone quite pale, young James.'

'Well…' But he was lost for words.

'Ivy's twenty-one now, the same age as you and Amelia,' she went on, seemingly oblivious to his discomfort. 'I expect she is thinking of marriage. After all, she can't wait for ever, can she?'

Wait for what, he wondered, as he walked away from the orphanage.

He wished he hadn't called there now. Matron had made him feel much worse. The thought of Ivy marrying that Alex – well, it made him sick to his stomach.

It was two weeks later, when he knew Ivy had an afternoon off, although he didn't know what she planned to do with it, that James went to the house to confront her.

If she came out of the house with Alex, then so be it. That was unlikely, though. It was doubtful their time off would coincide. At least, that's what he hoped.

He had a long wait and people were beginning to look at him suspiciously as he paced up and down the street. His patience was finally rewarded.

Ivy stopped when she spotted him, gathered herself, and then began walking towards him.

'Hello, James,' she said. 'How are you?'

'I'm well, thanks. You?'

'Yes, very well, thanks.'

She stood in front of him, waiting for him to speak.

'I thought I'd see if you were doing anything today,' he said hesitantly.

'I'd just planned on walking,' she said.

'Do you mind if I walk with you?'

'Please yourself.'

James fell into step with her. Why was she being so distant with him? Was her mind full of Alex?

Ivy had changed in the three years that Amelia had been in America, he realised. She was bolder and more self-confident now that she no longer lived in Amelia's shadow. Was she prettier? James couldn't say. She looked especially pretty today, though. Her blonde hair, tied up at the front, shone in the pale sunshine.

'I heard from Amelia,' James said at last, taking the well-read letter from his pocket.

He handed it to her. He would see what she made of the *Is she smitten?*

She coloured slightly when she read it, but handed it back without comment.

'I haven't replied yet,' he said hesitantly. 'Wasn't sure what to say – about you and Alex, I mean. Still, I suppose you can tell her that yourself.'

'I can,' she agreed.

Why was it, James wondered, that they always ended up at the docks? Today the sea was a dark, moody grey.

'Are you and Alex walking out?' James asked at last. 'Of course, it doesn't matter to me, but I thought that, when I wrote to Amelia—'

'If it doesn't matter to you,' Ivy snapped, 'then there's no point me telling you.'

James looked at her. She had never snapped at him like that before. Whatever was wrong with her?

'I'd like to know where I stand,' he said firmly.

'*You* would like to know where *you* stand?' She threw back her head and laughed at that, but it was a laugh that held no humour whatsoever. 'Wouldn't we all, James Penrose!'

'Ivy, what on earth do you mean?'

She rounded on him then.

'For your information – although, as you say, it doesn't matter to you – I am not walking out with Alex. My choice, not his. He's nice, kind and thoughtful – in fact, I must be mad not to grab him with both hands.'

'So if—'

'And if we're talking about where we stand,' she cut him off furiously, 'perhaps you'd care to tell me where *I* stand. For the last three years, I've been spending all my free time with you. Not courting, obviously.

56

We've never got around to that. And probably never will!'

'Courting?'

'Yes, courting!' she cried. 'Will we ever get around to that? Or should I go back and talk to Alex?'

'Courting,' he said again. 'Is that what you–? I mean, would you like that?'

The silence seemed to go on for ever.

'Yes, I would, James,' she said, and her voice was soft again although her face was still scarlet.

'So would I,' he said, and his heart felt like singing. It was him she wanted, not Alex.

'Then perhaps you'd like to buy me a cup of tea,' she suggested, slipping her arm through his, 'and tell me how long it might be before I start thinking about my bottom drawer...'

June 1893, Seattle.

Amelia was in bed, trying to sleep, when she heard the crash. At first, she thought Constance – for there were only the two of them and young Tommy in the house – must have dropped something. Then she heard the screams.

She was down the stairs in an instant and bending over her sister-in-law who was sitting at the bottom of them, screaming.

'The baby!' Constance shouted. 'It's coming!'

'What? Calm down, Constance.'

The baby cannot be coming, Amelia decided. For one thing, the doctor had told them it wasn't due for another three weeks. For another thing, the men had gone to bring four horses to the stables and wouldn't be back until the day after tomorrow. It was the middle of the night – no, this baby could not come. Not now, Amelia couldn't cope.

'So you know better than the doctor?' Amelia chided her sister-in-law.

'I know it's coming. I was lying on my bed when the pains started. I thought I'd come downstairs and have a drink but–' Constance broke off as pain tore through her. 'I fell on the stairs,' she gasped.

She grabbed Amelia's hand. Her fingernails were biting into the skin.

With a strength she didn't know she possessed, Amelia dragged Constance into a sitting position and then held her upright. In between the pain that had Constance screaming out, they managed to get her lying down on the floor in the sitting-room with cushions beneath her head.

'I'll go and fetch–'

'No! Don't leave me!'

'I have to, Constance. I need to fetch the doctor.' As she spoke, she remembered that Dr Brown wasn't in town. She saw the Constance knew it, too.

'I'll get Edith,' she insisted. 'She'll know what to do.'

'Don't leave me,' Constance pleaded. 'Please, don't leave me! I'll die – I know I will.'

'Stop talking daft,' Amelia said sternly. 'I don't know what to do, Constance. I have to get help.'

'It'll be all right.' For a moment, Constance seemed to calm herself. 'There's no time to get help. The baby's coming!'

There followed the longest hours of Amelia's life.

Constance and Theo's second son, a big, healthy-looking boy, eventually entered the world, but Constance knew little about it. The pain had been too much for her and she had slipped into unconsciousness.

Amelia did all she could for the child. When he was clean, wrapped in blankets and screaming loudly from the drawer of the dresser, she quickly checked on Tommy, who had managed to sleep right through his mother's screams, and raced out into the street and ran for all she was worth.

Dawn was slowly breaking but there were few signs of life on the streets of Seattle.

Edith had raised eleven children of her own and everyone turned to her in times of trouble. If Dr Brown couldn't come up with a cure for a particular ailment, Edith was sure to have just the thing.

The door was soon opened and, struggling for breath, Amelia explained the situation.

'You get back to her,' Edith told her, 'and I'll be close behind you. Try not to worry. Constance is a tough one. A fighter.'

For the next few days, Constance fought for her life, but when Dr Brown returned, he managed to reassure Theodore and the rest of the family that she would pull through.

'It's just a matter of time,' he said calmly. 'Her body needs a chance to recover.'

Whether he felt as confident as he sounded, Amelia never knew, but he was right.

A week after her ordeal, Constance was sitting up in bed and asking for her new son.

Amelia had tears in her eyes as she saw mother and son meet properly for the first time. Constance lay back against the pillows, her sleeping son cradled in her arms and a rare smile on her face.

'I'll never forget what you did for me, Amelia,' she said softly. 'If it hadn't been for you—'

'I did nothing,' Amelia replied.

'You stayed with me,' Constance argued. 'You didn't let me give up hope. You didn't let me die.'

'Oh, I wasn't about to let you die,' Amelia said with a smile. 'Theo would never have forgiven me.'

Constance laughed at the truth of that, and gave Amelia's hand a squeeze.

'Thank you,' she whispered.

July 1897, Seattle.
Amelia knew Miles well. She loved him, but she was aware of his faults. He could be weak and he lacked ambition. How could she persuade him that the future was theirs for the taking?

She gazed at the newspaper on her bed. It was the 'Seattle Post-Intelligencer', July 17 edition, and the headline had her heart racing every time she saw it. *Gold! Gold! Gold!* it read.

Residents of Seattle had woken to the sound of the newspaper boys hawking that extra edition of the newspaper. It had been printed before the steamer *Portland* had even passed up the sound.

When it finally tied up at Schwabacher Wharf, Amelia, along with around five thousand others, had been there to watch. And what a sight it had been!

A whole line of miners, sixty-eight according to the newspapers, had wrestled sacks, boxes and suitcases full of gold down the gangplank. Between them, they had carried more than two tons of gold.

By noon that same day, every ticket had been sold on the *Portland's* return trip north to the Klondike River.

Amelia's trunk contained less than fifty dollars. She'd had to give Miles the other fifty to pay off gambling debts. No way could they afford to travel to the Klondike by steamer.

She bit on her lower lip. Already, she was planning the journey, yet she hadn't convinced Miles they should set off to seek their fortune.

'What's that you've got?' Miles came into their room, taking her by surprise.

'I've been reading about the gold strikes,' she said lightly.

'You and everyone else in Seattle.' He flopped down on the bed, his head resting on his hand as he scanned the newspaper's story. 'No-one can talk about anything else,' he went on. 'All I've heard is gold, gold, gold. Everyone's packing up and leaving.'

He was right. Farmers and bank clerks, ministers and policemen – everyone was heading for the Klondike.

'I've been thinking about it myself,' he admitted slowly, taking Amelia by surprise.

'Thinking about heading off to search for gold?' She hardly dared to believe it.

He nodded.

'Oh, Miles!' Amelia jumped to her feet. 'I've been thinking of nothing else. Let's do it. Let's go!'

'What? Oh, come on, sweetheart,' he said, smiling indulgently, 'it's no place for a woman. I was thinking of–'

'Going on your own?' she cried. 'Not on your life, Miles Carter. I'm your wife. Where you go, I go. Besides, lots of women are going. Everyone's going. And why not? There's a fortune to be made. Of those miners on the *Portland,* no-one had less than ten thousand dollars. Think of that, Miles.'

'I have been,' he said slowly.

'We've still got fifty dollars,' she said. 'We can do this, Miles.'

He walked to the window and stood there, looking down on Seattle's streets.

'I could do it,' he said at last. 'I'm not sure about you, though. It's no life for a woman.'

'You'll not leave me here!' Amelia said firmly.

She stood by his side at the window and slipped her arm around his waist.

'I'm fit and strong, Miles. We've no children to think about–'

She would miss Tommy and young Fred desperately, but they were Constance and Theo's children, not hers. It seemed now that she and Miles weren't to be blessed with children of their own.

'I know that.' He was nodding slowly.

'We've got that fifty dollars,' she rushed on, 'and if we fill my trunk with essentials from the store, we'll be able to sell them on the journey.'

He laughed at that.

'We can't take that old trunk of yours, Amelia!'

'I won't leave it behind!' But they could argue about that later.

After giving it some thought, Miles suddenly turned, caught her in his arms and danced her around their bedroom.

'Let's do it,' he cried, laughing. 'Let's go to the Klondike and make our fortune. We'll be rich, Amelia. Rich!'

Chapter Three

April 1898, Chilkoot Pass, Alaska

'We're turning back, Amelia, and that's my final word! We'll turn back while we're still able.'

'If you think,' Amelia retorted, folding arms that screamed in agony, 'that I've come all this way only to turn back, you've got another think coming. You can turn back if you like, Miles Carter, but you'll do it without me!'

She turned from him and began the painful process of putting one foot in front of the other.

It was two months since they had left Dyea to begin the hazardous, seemingly impossible journey through what had to be the closest thing to hell on earth – the Chilkoot Pass.

They had endured all that the inhospitable area could throw at them, the snow, the blizzards, the frigid temperature – and the avalanche.

Tears that were a mix of distress and physical pain blinded Amelia as she climbed onwards. The avalanche had been the bitterest blow yet. Some said it had claimed the lives of forty miners, and others believed the figure was closer to seventy. Those poor men had been so close to the summit, too. In sight of the Canadian flag, even. Now they were gone, and their dreams of riches gone with them.

Many had already turned back and yes, perhaps they were the wise ones. But it wasn't in Amelia's nature to give in although, right now, she wished it was. She would give all she had to be back in their room in Seattle.

She looked back and saw Miles behind her, and behind him was a long line of men, hundreds of them, and a handful of women who moved doggedly and slowly forward.

All along the pass were discarded belongings. The authorities had insisted that stampeders take enough supplies to last a year, but people simply couldn't carry such an amount.

The pass was too steep for animals past a certain point, and they had to haul their hundreds of pounds of supplies on their backs. They moved up and back on the trail, making multiple trips over each section, shuttling loads further and further up the trail.

Anything the miners considered not essential had been sold or simply abandoned on the wayside.

They were close to the summit now, but Amelia didn't look up. The worst part was yet to come. They had a thousand-feet climb in that last half mile.

The bitter wind froze the tears on her face, yet she forced her legs forward. She was as close to death as it was possible to be while still breathing. But they would make it. They had to!

Rumours were rife on the journey. All those on the Chilkoot Pass now wished that, instead of leaving Dyea on this awful route, they had left Skagway and taken the White Pass. The White Pass, according to rumours, was an easier route, a route passable with horses and mules. Yet, according to the same rumours, many pack animals had died, either of starvation or exhaustion.

'Turn back, for the Lord's sake, Amelia!' Miles cried out.

'Never!' she shouted back.

The greatest challenge lay ahead, but

Amelia couldn't turn back now. They had come so far; it would kill her to give in and go home.

The final ascent consisted of a staircase carved in the ice. Once they had done that – and they *would* do it – came the descent to Lake Bennett. Surely that would be easier?

'Josh?' Amelia staggered across to a man they had befriended weeks ago. 'You should be way ahead of us by now,' she said, concerned.

'You turning back, Josh?' Miles guessed, having followed Amelia.

'I am. You can keep your gold,' he said, 'and I'll keep my life. I'm selling as much as I can and heading back.'

'But we're almost there,' Amelia urged him.

Josh nodded up at the towering summit.

'No, Mrs Carter. This has been the worst experience of my life. I never knew such a land as this existed. Getting to the top is going to be even worse.'

'It's the avalanche,' Amelia persisted. 'It's unsettled everyone – all those poor men who died.'

'I'm going back,' he said firmly.

Miles dropped down at Josh's side.

'And we'll join you.'

'We will not, Miles!'

So many were thinking along the lines of Josh and Miles that the pass had become a moving marketplace, dotted with buyers and sellers. Those turning back were selling what they could and those trudging on bought at a good price.

'If you've any sense at all, you will join us,' Josh said, speaking to Amelia. 'There are dozens of us heading back. It's the only sensible thing to do, woman.'

'Give up?' Amelia scoffed.

'Mrs Carter,' Josh said slowly, 'it'll take a lot more than stubborn pigheadedness to reach that summit. You're a strong, brave woman, I'll not deny that, but, if you don't mind me saying so, you're also very foolish. This godforsaken land is no place for a man, never mind a young woman. You'll give your life, and for what? A silly dream.'

Amelia threw back her aching shoulders.

'I do mind you saying so, Josh. We knew the hardships that lay ahead–'

But they hadn't. None of them had known how inhospitable and hostile this land was.

'I won't go back,' she said.

'I'm with Josh,' Miles said. 'It's foolish to go on and risk our lives trying to get to that summit. We'll turn back, Amelia.'

'For what?' she cried. 'To work in your father's store? To help with the business until Theo takes over? And who's to say Theo will have a need for us then? He has two sons – it'll all belong to them one day. There's nothing to go back to.'

'We are turning back, Amelia!'

She couldn't defy her husband. But she couldn't turn back, either.

'I won't, Miles,' she said quietly.

'You'll be on your own, then,' Miles told her.

She nodded.

'So be it!'

With that, she began climbing ever upwards.

She concentrated on the pain rather than the fact that she was defying her husband. She couldn't think about that now. Nor could she think about the way she and Miles had drifted apart on this terrible journey. The hardships should have brought them closer together instead of driving them apart.

A few minutes later, she heard Miles muttering and cursing behind her.

Amelia smiled to herself. He was with her, he still cared for her. As soon as they reached Lake Bennett, they would be just fine.

June 1898, Lake Bennett, Canada.
Sitting outside their tent, Amelia felt some of the exhaustion leave her, banished by the spark of hope. She had bought a stove for twelve dollars and, less than an hour later, sold it for twenty-two dollars.

They had saluted the Canadian flag, said a relieved farewell to the Chilkoot Pass and were now camping out at Lake Bennett.

As far as the eye could see there were thousands of tents, probably ten thousand in all. While people waited for the lake's ice to melt, they lived on what, to Amelia, was a marketplace. There was money to be made here and the stove was her best sale yet.

The ice was breaking up fast and all they heard were tales of drownings and boats being wrecked. The Mounties had been kept busy as they went out in three or four boats on a line to rescue people trapped in vessels that were either caught or crushed by the ice. Outfits had been lost and people drowned. It was all due to people going on the ice too soon, but Amelia could understand that. Everyone was eager to leave for Dawson.

As impatient as she was, though, Amelia knew they must wait a while longer. Having risked their lives on the Chilkoot Pass, there was no point killing themselves on the last leg of the journey.

Squabbles broke out all the time. Amelia had seen one man tear his tent up and then saw his boat in half! Tempers ran high as people dreamed of the gold they could be digging.

'You'll be Mrs Carter!'

Startled, Amelia looked up – and up – to find herself gazing straight at a man who quite took her breath away. He was a tall, strong-looking man who seemed perfectly at ease with himself. All around her, people had been living on their nerves for far too long. This man looked as if he had never known a moment's worry.

'I am.' She scrambled inelegantly to her feet. 'And you are?'

He looked her up and down and Amelia felt herself colour. Given that she was wearing blue jean overalls, a sweater and top boots, she was surprised he hadn't mistaken her for a man.

'Sam Hunter, ma'am. I heard you'd been asking after me,' he explained.

'I have, yes! I want – that is my husband and I want to get to Dawson as soon as possible. My husband and a friend are building a boat, but I wanted to speak to you first. I hear you're the best river boat pilot there is. How much do you charge your passengers, Mr Hunter?'

'Sorry, ma'am, but you're wasting your time. I don't take women on my boat.'

'What?' He had already taken a stride away from her and she had to dash after him. 'Why not, for heaven's sake? My money's as good as anyone else's, isn't it?'

'It is, ma'am, but as I said, I don't take women.'

'But why?'

'Because it's not a Sunday outing,' he said frankly. 'I don't know how much you've heard about the journey, but several people have lost their lives. Have you any idea how long the trip takes? Three weeks! Do you have any idea what it's like on the Five Finger Rapids?'

'I don't, Mr Hunter, but I do know what it's like crossing the Chilkoot Pass. I believe that if I can cope with that, I can cope with anything.'

'You have a reputation, Mrs Carter. By all accounts you're a brave, strong and determined lady.' A reluctant smile touched his lips. 'A fine businesswoman, too, I've heard. If I ever need to buy a stove, I'll know not to buy one from you.'

'The gentleman was willing to pay my price,' she said defensively.

'Then everyone is happy.'

'Mr Hunter,' Amelia said calmly, 'as I said, my husband and his friend are building a boat. The thing is—'

'They've never built a boat before?' he guessed, and Amelia nodded.

'Mrs Carter,' he said, speaking equally calmly, 'most of the people here have never built a boat. And most of them have never even been on the water. People seem willing to accept that when upwards of two thousand boats leave here, there will be disaster, yet few believe themselves to be in any personal danger.'

Amelia agreed with him, which was

exactly why she wanted to employ his services. If anyone could get them to Dawson safely, this man could.

'I believe you're right,' she said.

'You can believe it or not,' he told her, 'but I still don't take women on my boat. Women and boats have no place together. Good day, ma'am.'

He touched his forehead and began walking away from her.

'We'll pay you double,' she called after him.

'Sadly, you won't,' he called back with a slight chuckle.

Amelia could have stamped her feet in frustration. Instead, she forgot about Sam Hunter and went inside their tent.

It was true, she could pay him double the usual fare. On the journey, she had bought and sold wisely. Thanks to some prudent purchases, she and Miles were far better off financially than when they had started.

She opened her old trunk, something she always did when she was troubled, and emptied the contents into a neat pile.

My, how Miles had grumbled about dragging that trunk across the Chilkoot Pass! Yet the trunk had served them well. Their belongings had remained safe and secure.

Their cash, too, was safe, right at the bottom of the trunk in the secret compartment. With it was her birth certificate, their marriage certificate and letters she'd had from home – short, quick notes from her brother, letters full of questions about America from Matron, and long, chatty pages from Ivy. Thank goodness Ivy and James were wed, she thought with amusement. Her brother was a poor letter writer and Amelia was glad Ivy was now doing the job for both of them.

Amelia didn't need to count the cash, she knew to the nearest cent how much they had, but she did so anyway.

It was while doing this that she had an idea.

She locked the trunk, jumped to her feet, left the tent and went in search of her husband.

Miles and David, a quietly spoken man they had met on the trail, were busy working on their boat.

Miles spotted Amelia and came over to her.

'It's going to take too long,' he complained.

She had known he would say that.

'I know.' She slipped her arm around his waist and looked up at him. 'The stove I told you about, the one I sold for twenty-two dollars – well, with the other bits and pieces, we've got enough cash to get out earlier, Miles. I've spoken to Sam Hunter, but–'

'Hunter?'

'Yes, he's the best man with a boat for miles,' Amelia explained. 'Runs his own business taking people to Dawson.'

She saw the way Miles's eyes lit up at that idea.

'And we can afford it?' he asked hopefully.

'Yes, but there's a problem. He won't take women on his boat.'

'What? Confound the man. Why not?'

'Because he says it's no place for a woman. And he's adamant.'

'There must be others who will,' Miles said quickly.

'Not that I know of,' Amelia told him, 'but listen, Miles, I've had an idea.'

'Oh?'

Amelia had to laugh.

'Must you always look so worried when I have an idea?' she teased.

'Sorry.' He pulled her to him and gave her a squeeze. 'I just want to get to Dawson. I had no idea it would take this long.'

'That's all everyone wants,' Amelia agreed. 'But Sam Hunter – when I spoke to him earlier, I was wearing – well, these clothes,' she said, stating the obvious, 'and looking like this, I'm surprised he didn't mistake me for a man. And that's my point, Miles! I could pretend to be a man for as long as the trip takes – about three weeks, I gather.'

'Do what? Oh, sweetheart!'

Miles erupted into laughter until the tears ran down his face.

Amelia was disappointed that he hadn't taken her idea seriously, but it was so good to see him laugh again. When she had first met him, he'd always been laughing. These days, it was the devil's own job to raise a smile from him. Not, she admitted, that anyone had laughed on that godforsaken Chilkoot Pass.

But that was behind them now. They had grown close again in the short time they'd been camped at Lake Bennett.

'I could do it, Miles.' She was grinning as she spoke. 'I'd wear your clothes, make sure my hair was hidden under a hat and scarf, not say anything–'

Miles rubbed the tears of laughter from his face.

'Oh, sweetheart,' he said again.

'We'd get to Dawson before a lot of the others,' she pointed out quietly.

She would leave him to think on that. Having been coaxed and cajoled all this way, Miles was getting impatient to reach Dawson.

Amelia was, too, but for different reasons. With so many men eager to make their fortunes at the gold fields, there was money to be made. A precious few would find riches by digging, but anyone attending to those men's needs could make a fortune, too.

That night, Amelia was drifting off to sleep but she knew Miles was wide awake.

'Perhaps it could be done,' he said at last. 'And as you say, we'll be in Dawson quicker. Have a head start on the rest.'

'Exactly,' she replied, smiling in the darkness. 'Talk to Sam Hunter tomorrow, Miles, and find out when he's planning to leave. Don't tell him who you are, though. Use another name.'

'I will,' Miles agreed.

Two weeks later, Amelia and Miles were on board Sam Hunter's boat along with a dozen more paying passengers. At long last, Amelia knew they were almost there.

Most of the ice had melted now and Amelia, despite wearing Miles's clothes and having to keep quiet, was determined to enjoy the experience.

They had been moving for less than two hours when she sensed that Sam Hunter was standing behind her. She didn't turn around, yet she knew it was him. What would she do if he struck up a conversation with her?

'I hope you enjoy the trip, Mrs Carter,' he said softly.

Amelia spun round.

'How did you know–?'

'There's nothing gentlemanly about you,' he replied with amusement.

'I hope you don't plan to throw me off at the earliest opportunity, Mr Hunter.'

'No.' He turned away from her, and she almost missed his reply.

'I'll leave that to the rapids.'

Amelia was slightly miffed at being caught out, but she was also relieved. She would no longer have to pretend, and soon, God willing, they would be in Dawson.

June 1898, Liverpool

The city had sweltered beneath a hot June sun all day. Everywhere had been heavy with heat and dust. Now, as the evening wore on, it was possible to breathe again.

Ivy had settled the twins for the night, or hoped she had, and was ready to sit down with Amelia's latest letter. She had read it once, found it impossible to believe, and she looking forward to reading it again at her leisure.

She gazed down at the twins, Martha Amelia and Albert James, and, as always, her heart melted.

At the time, she and James had been completely taken aback when presented with twins but, with James being a twin, she supposed they shouldn't have been so surprised. Ivy had been shocked and delighted and not a little frightened. The thought of caring for one baby had worried her, but two…

Yet, they were delightful! Although Martha and Albert were only eighteen months old, already it seemed that young Albert was the headstrong one, whereas Martha was a gentle and biddable as the day was long.

Martha took after her father. Albert, Ivy thought fondly, took after his aunt Amelia. Ivy would be willing to bet that he caused them some headaches in the years ahead.

How she loved them both. How James loved them, too.

James would be home soon, but she had bought a nice piece of fish from the market, so his meal would be quickly prepared. The vegetables were all ready on the stove.

There was time enough to sit down with a cup of tea and Amelia's letter.

It was dated two months earlier, yet had only arrived that morning.

The previous letter, written shortly before this one, had given her and James the shock of their lives. James had opened it and Ivy remembered the way he had called out to her.

'You'll never believe this. Amelia and Miles are off in search of gold!'

Ivy frowned as she read this latest letter. No doubt Amelia would laugh if she knew how she and James worried about her, but this did nothing to alleviate her fears. The journey, and the land into which Amelia and

Miles were venturing, sounded terrifying. People were willing to give their lives for gold.

It had to be bad, worse even than Amelia admitted in her letter, because for the first time, she sounded almost beaten.

I'm too tired to write more. As soon as we reach Dawson, I'll tell you all about it.

Amelia was never too tired for anything.

Ivy wondered, not for the first time, how she and Amelia had become such close friends. They were chalk and cheese. Not for all the gold in the world would Ivy leave the comforts of home. There was enough adventure in life, taking care of the little ones and putting food on the table, without seeking out danger.

I never knew such a frozen, godforsaken place existed, Amelia had written, and Ivy shuddered.

She was still wrapped up in the letter when she heard the back door open and close.

'Jimmy? That you, love?'

'It is.'

He smiled as he came into the kitchen and planted a kiss on her cheek, but he looked dreadful.

She really had believed he was getting better, but he was limping badly and his face was ashen.

It was two weeks now since the accident.

He had been on his way home when one of the brewery horses had run out of control, smashing barrels and kicking James into the cart.

They'd had the doctor out to look at his leg twice, and James had been off work for over a week.

This morning, the deep gash had looked worse than ever when she'd bathed it and dressed it for him.

Ivy had no idea where the money would come from, but he would have to see the doctor again. Knowing she would have a fight on her hands over it, she decided to leave that particular discussion until later.

'Twins asleep?' James asked, dropping on to the chair at the kitchen table.

'I wouldn't go that far, although they're quiet for the moment. We've got a letter from Mel,' she told him, pointing at the table. 'Your dinner won't be long.'

'Have they struck gold yet?' he asked with a smile.

'Read for yourself.'

He said nothing as he read the letter and when she turned from the stove, she saw his brows drawn together in a frown.

'That was two months ago,' she said quietly. 'I hope they're all right, Jimmy.'

'Of course they are.' But she could see that he was worried. 'Once they've got this journey out of the way, they'll be fine. Who knows, maybe they'll be rich enough to come and visit us.'

Ivy smiled; perhaps they would at that. And wouldn't that be grand? Amelia would adore her nephew and niece.

They'd eaten – at least, Ivy had eaten and James had pushed his food around the plate until declaring he hadn't much of an appetite – and Ivy had washed the crocks and put them away. She was about to sit down with some mending.

James eased himself down into the armchair, wincing as he did so.

'Jimmy,' she began, preparing herself for an argument, 'your leg's getting no better, love. We'll have to call the doctor again.'

'Don't talk daft,' he said impatiently. 'It'll be fine.'

'That's what you said last week,' she reminded him, 'and, if anything, it's worse.'

'We'll see.'

'I mean it, Jimmy. I'm worried about it.'

'There's nothing to worry about, love. We'll give it a couple of weeks.'

She picked up one of his socks to mend, but she couldn't let the matter rest.

'It's making you ill,' she protested.

'I'm tired, that's all.'

'You're ill,' Ivy corrected him. 'Which is why you're seeing the doctor again.'

'We can't afford it, Ivy,' he said, his tone letting her know that the discussion was over.

'We can't afford to have you off work, either,' she argued. 'Better to pay the doctor and make sure it gets better than to be off work for another week because you refused to see him.'

'We'll leave it another week,' he said firmly, and he picked up the newspaper, effectively putting an end to the conversation.

Ivy could see his point. What with a week's wages lost and the doctor's bills, money was very tight indeed. She was right, though. Whereas they could scrape together enough for him to see the doctor again, they would really struggle if he was too ill to go to work. If he took any more time off, he might find himself without a job to go to.

She wasn't too worried on that score, though. He had worked at the hotel for Mr Carshaw since leaving the orphanage, and this was the first time he had been ill.

Mr Carshaw thought very highly of James. Only last Christmas, he had described him as 'honest, reliable and hard working'.

No, it wasn't the job that worried her right now. It was the fact that this cut to his leg was making him ill in himself. That didn't seem right.

'I'll get some water heated up,' she said, getting to her feet, 'and I'll bathe that leg for you again. We'll put some salt in the water.'

'Right,' he agreed, 'but then that's it, Ivy.

That's enough fussing for one day.'

Ivy would leave it for this evening, but first thing in the morning – assuming James had the strength to get to work – she would go to see Matron. If anyone could persuade James to see sense, it was her!

June 1898, Dawson, Canada

Amelia had news for Miles, and hoped and prayed that, this evening, he would come home in a better mood.

After a journey at times terrifying and at times exhilarating, they had arrived in Dawson. They were, once again, on firm land. The five-hundred-mile Yukon River journey from the lakes to Dawson was behind them. They had survived the White Horse rapids and the Five Fingers rapids and, along with thousands of others, had arrived in Dawson.

Sadly, Miles's temper had deteriorated on reaching the town.

A lot of people were disappointed when they reached Dawson only to find that local miners had claimed all the gold-bearing creeks months ago.

People milled about the town, or they gave up and went home. That thought made Amelia shudder. After such a journey, she couldn't have borne the thought of going home.

Besides, if Miles could but see it, there was

money to be made here. Not the vast fortunes that had kept the miners optimistic on the journey, perhaps, but there was work for the taking and, just as important, opportunities aplenty.

Some men were working other miners' claims, or working in the saloons or hotels. Others, Miles included, insisted on looking for gold in a nearby creek.

A lot of people lived on their boats while they decided what to do, but Amelia and Miles didn't have an option. Instead they had rented a small building – too grand to be called a shed and too ramshackle to be called a house – and, from there, Amelia was cooking for the miners. They were willing to pay a high price for the luxury of having good, nourishing food in their stomachs.

She was standing in their doorway when she saw Miles returning. He walked slowly, head down, shoulders hunched.

The sight brought a flash of irritation to Amelia. Perhaps they would never find gold, but the future was far brighter here than it had been in Seattle.

She loved her husband, but he had developed a habit of always looking at the bleak side of life. He couldn't, or wouldn't, look on the bright side, and she occasionally lost patience with him.

'Let's walk,' she said, reaching for his hand. 'I've something I need to discuss with you.'

'And I've something I need to discuss with you,' he replied firmly.

'You first, then,' she said lightly, as they set off down the main street. She could guess what was coming – Miles still wanted them to go home.

'We've a bit of money put by now,' he said, 'which means we can go back to Seattle. We can go by steamship. If we leave now, before the river freezes over again, we'll soon be back. When we're there, we'll be able to set up in business.'

'Doing what?' she asked.

'I don't know,' he admitted.

No, he wouldn't have thought that far ahead. All he wanted was to get back to Seattle. Perhaps she couldn't blame him for that. Everyone's hopes had been dashed to discover there were no mining claims to be had. On top of that, he missed his family.

'We don't have to go back, Miles,' she said gently. 'That's what I want to talk to you about. You see the building at the top of the street?' She nodded at a large wooden building. 'We can rent that.'

'What would we want to do that for?' he demanded.

'So that we can let out rooms,' Amelia explained. 'These men want food and lodgings and are willing to pay a good price.'

'A boarding-house?' Miles scoffed. 'I thought you wanted better than that. Or have you forgotten living like a slave in Liverpool?'

She hadn't forgotten, and yes, she had complained about the work at Mr and Mrs Whaley's boarding-house. This would be different, though. This would be hers. Well, it would belong to both of them.

'I don't mind working hard for us,' she pointed out.

'Well, I do. I'm not staying in this awful place just to run around after people who think they can order you about just because they're guests.'

'See sense, Miles,' she said urgently. 'It would be our own business. Far better than helping run your father's store just so Theo can profit from it.'

'I'd rather do that, and live in Seattle, than struggle for a few dollars in this awful place.'

It wasn't so awful, not really. It was different from anything they had ever known; it was filled with people either hopeful or despairing and it was overrun with dogs that people no longer had a use for. It was also a place where people had money and were willing to spend it.

'It wouldn't hurt to give it a try for a few months, would it?' she coaxed.

'Yes, it would. A few months and the river will have frozen again!'

Miles grabbed her arm, turned her back, and started walking towards their home.

'I'll hear no more on the subject,' he said firmly.

Amelia took a deep breath, then changed her mind and kept quiet as she walked beside him.

Where was the good in that, though? She had to tell him and now was as good a time as any.

'The building I was telling you about,' she began, and she was nervous as she awaited his reaction. 'An agreement had to be reached quickly, Miles. You see, several people were interested in taking out the rental. It was going to the first person to sign the lease and hand over the money.'

'Good,' he said with satisfaction. 'Then it's gone to someone rash enough to sign the lease.'

'That person was me,' she said quietly.

He stopped walking and turned to look at her, his face like thunder.

'You? You signed that lease?' His voice was deep with fury.

'Yes.' She swallowed hard. 'It's ours, Miles. I had to sign it, so it's in my name, but it's ours.'

His face was white, his eyes glittering. Never had Amelia seen him so angry. Never, a small inner voice reminded her, had she given him cause to be so angry.

'That's it!' he said, his voice low but all the more dangerous for that.

'You've defied me once too often – made a laughing stock of me–'

'Miles, no!'

'Yes!' He spat the word at her.

His hands clamped around her arm, his fingers biting into her skin.

'It's high time you were reminded of your place. Of a wife's place–'

Breathless with anger, he suddenly pushed her away as if she were a bundle of rags and stormed off.

Chapter Four

January 1899, Dawson

Miles pulled his thin scarf tighter around his neck, but it was scant defence against the biting cold evening air.

What on earth, he wondered despairingly, was he still doing in this foreign place? He would never forget his first sight of Dawson. The streets had been rivers of mud, and the buildings ramshackle. Then had come the discovery that all the mining claims had been taken long ago.

Now, in the grip of winter, everything in Dawson was frozen solid. He hated it! It was seven months since Amelia had signed the lease on what was now Carter's Boarding House. It seemed longer, and the longer they stayed, the more frustrated Miles became.

The lights from the saloon were beckoning and he was about to go inside when he spotted two children huddled against the building. They looked frozen.

'What are you doing out here?'

'Waiting for our mother, sir,' the young lad answered.

He was around six or seven years old, Miles guessed, and his sister was a couple of years younger.

'She's inside,' the boy explained, nodding at the saloon. 'Singing,' he added proudly.

The little girl, clinging to her brother's arm, said nothing. Her teeth were chattering and tears stained her face.

What sort of mother was it who left two young children on the streets in this weather? Shaking his head, he shouldered open the door.

It was Amelia's belief that if the sale of liquor were properly controlled, there would be fewer fights breaking out over nothing.

'It's entertainment people need,' she said, 'not liquor!'

Liquor wasn't responsible for the fights, he thought grimly. It was the frustration of living in Dawson, knowing you were never going to get a mining claim, seeing people arrive with their dreams and then watching them leave with their pockets empty and their spirits broken.

It was Dawson and this inhospitable land that had men venting their frustrations on their fellow man. It was a place that had sprung up overnight, a place thrown together in a hurry and built on a bog.

Admittedly, companies were beginning to establish themselves. There were butchers, bakers, grocers, clothiers, tobacconists, blacksmiths, gambling halls and no less than twenty-two saloons. There were six sawmills and even they couldn't keep up with the demand for timber.

Some people, fools as far as Miles was concerned, still held on to their dreams, and yes, there was money to be made. Yet, still, he hated it.

What would it take to make Amelia leave this place? All it should take, he thought irritably, was one word from her husband.

Nine years ago, when he had asked her to marry him, he'd thought her the most beautiful woman in the world. He still did. These days, though, he realised that a great deal of that beauty came from within. She had spirit, and it was that spirit that attracted people to her.

The trouble with Amelia's spirit, Miles decided, was that it could be very wearing for those around her.

The saloon was crowded and Miles was

weaving his way to the bar when a woman started singing.

A friend had described a woman who had been singing in the streets for cents people might throw, and he guessed it must be her. She was probably around forty. Maybe older. Her hair was a dull black, her skin was pale and her lips ruby red.

Miles was no expert, but he reckoned her dress had cost a pretty penny. It had certainly cost a lot more than the poor excuses for clothes her children were wearing.

He was all set to march over and tell her what he thought of her when he saw a few men throwing coins her way. Perhaps she would buy her children some new clothes.

'Bella, give us another song!' one man called out.

She certainly had a way with the men, and her flirting paid off. She was soon ready to leave with a pocket full of coins.

Miles reached the door at the same time.

'That was good,' he said.

'Good for him and his business,' she retorted, 'but not so good when you have to put food on your children's plates.'

As soon as the door was open, the children raced up for a hug from their mother. There were tears in her eyes as she held them close, and Miles was glad now that he'd held his tongue.

'You know Carter's Boarding House?' he

asked on an impulse, and when she nodded, he said, 'I own that – me and my wife.'

'Ah.' She ran a keen eye over him. 'So you'll be Amelia Carter's husband.'

One day, Miles vowed, people would look at Amelia in awe and say, 'So you're Miles Carter's wife...'

'I am,' he said shortly. 'And we've been thinking about employing someone. Perhaps you'd be interested?'

'Depends on the money,' she replied.

Everything in Dawson depended on the money, he thought grimly. A fifteen-cent meal in Seattle would set you back two dollars fifty in Dawson. With so many looking for work, wages were painfully low. Yet the demand for food and clothing had sent prices soaring. It was a mad place.

'Enough to put food on their plates,' he said, nodding at the children. 'Come back with me,' he suggested, 'and see what you think.'

When they arrived at the boarding–house, Miles introduced Bella to his wife.

The two women looked each other up and down. Amelia stood with her hands on her hips, and Bella, looking out of place in her showy dress, had her arms folded. They looked about to go into battle, he thought.

Then Amelia's attention was on the children and her expression softened immediately.

'Aw, you're cold, you poor little mites. Come along in here and sit by the stove.' She took them by the hand into the kitchen. 'Hungry, are you?'

The boy glanced at his mother briefly before nodding shyly.

'We'll get you something to eat,' Amelia promised, ruffling the girl's curls.

'We're not after charity,' Bella said hotly. 'Your husband said you might have employment.'

'Employment?' Amelia repeated, looking at Miles in amazement.

'We mentioned a waitress,' he reminded her.

'Yes, but that's if and when we open the dining-room to non-residents. Besides–' She broke off, but Miles knew what she was thinking as she looked at Bella, and it wasn't complimentary.

'Let's get these children fed,' she said instead, adding sternly for Bella's benefit, 'and it's not charity. My guests are always offered food.'

February 1899, Liverpool
For once, Ivy couldn't blame the twins for her slow progress; she was dawdling. She felt sick with worry and didn't know where to turn.

Still, no use thinking of that. Matron had asked to see her and Ivy refused to be

94

anything other than her usual cheerful self.

Later, perhaps she would be able to think of something to solve her problems. If she pawned her wedding ring... Her stomach churned at the very thought of parting with her ring. After James and the twins, it was the most precious thing in the world to her.

But what alternative was there?

She stood for a moment, looking up at the building that had been her home for so many years. How she had longed to leave the orphanage and have a house and family of her own. Yet how safe that dear old building looked now. If only she and Amelia were children once again, talking long into the night, planning and dreaming, not a worry in the world.

Matron came into the hall to meet her, and then Doris was there. Amid the chatter and laughter, Doris told the twins about the latest additions to the orphanage.

'Chickens,' she explained. 'Come along, children, we're about to feed them and collect the eggs.'

Without so much as a backward glance at their mother, Martha and Albert went off with Doris.

'They'll soon be back for their milk and biscuits,' Matron said fondly. 'Come along, Ivy, and tell me all your news.'

'I've a letter from Amelia,' Ivy said, grateful that at least they could chat about that.

'How is she? Still running her boarding-house?'

'Yes, and it's doing well, by the sounds of it,' Ivy said.

They were soon in Matron's sitting-room, with a cup of tea and a slice of fruitcake.

'And how's young James?' Matron asked.

'He's fine,' Ivy replied. 'His leg still causes him pain at times, and makes him limp quite badly, but I think it's as good as it's going to get now.'

'And what about you, Ivy?' Matron's sharp eyes missed nothing. 'Why do you look as if you haven't known a moment's sleep this year? What's troubling you, girl?'

How many times had Ivy heard that question over the years? Enough to bring a sudden sharp sting to her eyes.

'Nothing. I'm fine.'

Matron sat back in her chair.

'In any case, I'm sure I can guess. With James being off work for so long and needing the doctor, I imagine you're struggling for money. Am I right?'

The words were so unexpected that Ivy, all set to deny it, suddenly burst into tears.

'I'm at my wits' end,' she sobbed, 'and I don't know where to turn. I daren't tell Jimmy. I take care of the money, you see. Always have. He gives me his wage and I make sure the rent's paid and food is put on the table. But we got so short, and now...'

Fresh tears came.

'I don't know how I'll find the money for the rent,' she said, rubbing frantically at her wet face.

'I guessed things might be difficult,' Matron said quietly, 'which is why I asked to see you, although I had no idea it was this bad. Right,' she went on briskly, 'firstly, you'll accept a loan from me. Secondly–'

'A loan?' Ivy felt what little colour she had drain from her face. A loan from Matron? It was unthinkable. 'I couldn't do that. It's very generous of you to offer, but no. Thank you, Matron, and I don't mean to be rude, but I simply couldn't.'

'You can and you will, my girl!'

'No, I couldn't.' Ivy had never argued with Matron. No child had ever dared. Not that she was a child now, of course. But this was different. She would never live with herself if she had to borrow money from this woman. 'In any case,' she rushed on, before Matron could argue, 'a loan won't help. What I need–'

'I'm well aware of what you need, my girl, which brings me to the reason for asking you here. It's about a friend of mine,' Matron explained.

'Rose Hodge moved to Liverpool with her husband three years ago. She's recently widowed, however, and is busying herself by writing a book. She's very interested in

97

education, which is how we came to meet.'

'And what has this lady to do with me?' Ivy asked curiously.

'Rose insists she needs a cleaner and someone to run errands, but I suspect she also needs some company. She's looking for someone to help out in the house for a few hours a week,' Matron said, adding quickly, 'someone trustworthy.'

'And you thought of me?' Ivy asked, frowning.

'I did,' Matron said. 'I believe you'll both get along well. She's a lovely woman, and there's very little work involved – more a case of providing company.

'Rose is ... well, she's a little different. Eccentric, some would say. She'll get involved with her book and forget to eat and sleep. She needs someone level-headed about the place and I think you're the very person. I'm sure you'll like her, and the twins will be out and about–'

'The twins?'

'Yes, she's happy for you to take the children along.'

'It's a lovely idea,' Ivy said slowly. The extra money would be a godsend. 'But I'm not sure what James will say about it.'

'Don't worry about James. I'm sure he won't object to you providing company to a friend of mine.'

Ivy had to smile at that.

'No,' she agreed, 'but he won't like me being paid, or cleaning–'

'Leave him to me,' Matron said firmly. 'Meanwhile, call on Rose tomorrow. Ten o'clock.'

The twins burst into the room at that point and all hopes of conversation were over. Two years old now, they were into everything.

Ivy left the orphanage with enough money in her pocket to pay the rent and, although it broke her heart to accept this loan from Matron, it at least meant that she didn't have to pawn her wedding ring.

March 1899, Dawson

'Are you all right, Mel?' Bella asked curiously.

Amelia splashed icy water on to her face and straightened up.

'I've felt better,' she admitted. 'Something's making me sick. Heaven knows what.'

'That husband of yours?' Bella asked with a grimace and Amelia, who had spent the last few minutes being violently sick, spluttered with laughter.

Bella shouldn't be so forward as to make disparaging comments about Miles, but Amelia found it impossible to be cross with her.

Dear Bella. She was the only person, other

than Ivy, who had ever shortened her name to Mel.

Every time she did it, Amelia experienced a fierce longing for Ivy.

Bella was a gem, and she never failed to make Amelia smile. Finding Bella was the best thing Miles had done.

'You heard us arguing, then?' Amelia asked.

'I heard him storm off in a rage,' Bella admitted. 'What was it this time? The same old thing?'

'What else?'

Every day, it seemed, Miles told Amelia they were leaving Dawson. All Amelia could do was remind him how well the business was doing. They had opened the dining-room to non-residents and trade was very good.

This morning had been worse than usual, though. Miles had been in a terrible temper.

'I'm leaving, Amelia. With or without you, I'm leaving this godforsaken place!'

'Then it will have to be without me,' she'd replied calmly. 'We can't just walk out, Miles.'

'Watch me!' Without so much as a backward glance, he'd slammed out of the building and into the street.

Amelia had no idea where he had gone, but she suspected his stomach would soon bring him home.

'Are you sure you're all right?' Bella asked again.

'I'm sure. I was the same yesterday morning, yet by lunchtime I was fine. It'll pass.'

'Go and lie down for a while,' Bella suggested. 'I can manage here.'

Yes, Bella would manage. She was a hard worker as well as a good friend.

When Miles had explained how he'd found Bella's children, cold and hungry, waiting for their mother as she sang in the saloon, and then suggested they employ her as a waitress, Amelia had thought he'd lost his senses. But now...

Bella wasn't the best waitress in the world, admittedly, but the men loved her. She always had a word and a cheeky smile for them. Bella brightened up their dark worlds, and business was booming. So much so that Amelia was keen to move to larger premises.

Bella's children, seven-year-old Isaac and his five-year-old sister, Jane, were good workers, too. Sometimes they swept the floors in the rooms and were always careful to collect the gold dust that fell from the men's pockets.

Miles could say what he liked about Dawson but, thanks to the women mainly, the town had a school and a hospital. Dawson might be lacking a lot of things, but it was bright with opportunity.

Isaac and Jane had just started school and

were thriving in Dawson. Their father had died on Chilkoot Pass and Bella was doing a wonderful job of being both mother and father to them. Amelia often thought Bella must be lonely, but she never mentioned her husband and Amelia didn't pry.

'I'm feeling better now,' she told Bella, 'so I'll get off to the kitchen.'

Miles returned around lunchtime, but Amelia didn't have a chance to speak to him. She was too busy cooking for their customers. When the rush was over, there was no sign of him.

'He'll soon be back,' Bella said.

Yes, he would be back and Amelia planned to have a serious talk with him. He had to learn to settle in Dawson, for a few years at least. They couldn't afford to lose the business.

The hours passed and she realised she would have to postpone their talk until the morning. She couldn't sleep, though. The bed was too big and cold without him.

She lay in the darkness, wondering, as she often did, what had gone wrong between them. They were in love; well, she loved Miles. He had his faults, but so did she, she knew that. Did Miles still love her?

She thought he did. When he was in a good mood – usually when he had won a few dollars gambling, she thought grimly – he'd be as warm, loving and affectionate as he'd been on their wedding day.

These days, though, his good moods were rare. He really did hate living in Dawson.

What else could they do? She couldn't return to Seattle to help run his father's business until Theo took over. She couldn't do that.

On that thought, she drifted off to sleep...

Amelia awoke early the next morning and instinctively reached out for Miles.

But she was alone.

She jumped out of bed, her heart racing. Had Miles left early, or had he stayed out all night?

A quick check of their room told her that his clothes were gone. She dressed quickly and raced down the stairs. No-one was about; it was too early.

She went to the safe and opened the cash box. It was empty!

Her heart still pounding, she ran back to their bedroom, opened her trunk and emptied the contents on to their bed. Everything was safe. The small amount of cash she had put aside was safely hidden in the secret compartment.

Moving more slowly now, she returned everything to the trunk. Then she sat on the bed and tried to make sense of it all.

Miles had gone, and she couldn't believe it. Surely he wouldn't take off without a word?

'With or without you, I'm leaving this god-forsaken place!' he had said.

But surely he hadn't meant to leave like that? And how could he take their money from the safe?

The nausea hit her as suddenly as it had yesterday. But there was no time to be ill; she had to find Miles.

She was in the kitchen when Bella arrived.

'Everything all right, Mel?'

'No. Miles has gone, Bella. He's – gone.'

Finally it sank in. Her husband had walked out on her.

'Gone where?' Bella asked, frowning.

'I don't know.' Amelia was shaking. 'His clothes are gone and – and he took the money from the safe.'

Bella gasped.

'All of it?'

'Yes. And now–' Before she could complete the sentence, she had to rush to the storeroom where she was sick.

Bella was soon at her side, washing her face in cold water.

'I'm all right,' Amelia insisted. 'I expect it's the upset. Miles leaving and everything.'

'He hadn't left yesterday,' Bella pointed out dryly, 'or the day before.'

'What do you mean?'

'I could be wrong, Mel, but my guess is that you're pregnant.'

'What?' Amelia stared back at her. 'But

that's impossible.'

She and Miles had been married for nine years and Amelia had assumed they weren't to be blessed with children. She hadn't liked it, but she had accepted it.

Could Bella be right? Was it possible that, after all this time, she was going to have a baby?

'Oh, my,' she breathed, and Bella laughed.

Amelia didn't want to get too excited, but she was fooling no-one, least of all herself.

She might be pregnant. She might be carrying Miles's child.

'But how can I be pregnant,' she said shakily, 'when Miles isn't here? I can't. It's just not a good time.'

'You'd better send it back until it's more convenient then,' Bella said.

'Bella!' Amelia didn't know whether to laugh or cry.

'Miles will be back,' Bella said confidently, 'when his cash runs out.'

That could be a long time, Amelia thought grimly. He had taken almost all of their money.

July 1899, Dawson
Amelia had escaped and was giving herself half an hour in the fresh air. Ivy's letter was in her pocket and she sat on a tree trunk near the water's edge to read it again.

It was good to hear Ivy sounding so happy,

105

but there, Ivy had all she needed – a loyal, loving husband and two happy, healthy children.

The letter was full of Rose Hodge, the lady Ivy worked for. According to Ivy, the woman was for ever badgering Members of Parliament about the education system.

Thankfully, Ivy had written, *James likes her, too. He says she reminds him of you. By the way, James is thrilled to know he'll be an uncle. We're so excited for you, Mel! I'm sure Miles will be making certain you take care of yourself.*

As yet, Amelia hadn't told her about Miles. How could she tell Ivy that Miles had taken off without a word?

Amelia had been confident that, when his temper cooled, he would come home.

Four months had passed, though. Amelia had to accept the fact that she was alone.

Perhaps Miles was planning to return to Seattle. She had written to his sister and told her she was pregnant, but Constance, delighted with that piece of news, had simply written, *Miles must be thrilled.*

Thrilled? Miles didn't even know. Oh, what a mess!

She sat for a while, gazing at her surroundings. From nowhere, it seemed, a rainbow had appeared. As she watched, the colours grew more vivid in the pale afternoon sky until it was startlingly bright.

Matron had told her of a rainbow that had

been visible when Amelia and James were abandoned at the orphanage gates all those years ago.

'The brightest rainbow I ever saw,' Matron had said. 'I always believed it to be some sort of sign.'

What would have happened, Amelia wondered, if she and James had been abandoned elsewhere, if they'd been left to die on that cold February morning, if someone else – not Matron – had taken them in? She shuddered at the thought.

One thing was certain, her own child wouldn't know such a worry. Her child would have everything she could give it.

All she had done for the last four months was wait for Miles to come home and feel sorry for herself. She was pregnant and alone, and nothing had cheered her.

But very soon, she would meet her own son or daughter. Her own flesh and blood.

Laughing, she jumped to her feet. There was work to be done and fretting about Miles would achieve nothing. Whether Miles returned or not, she had a child to care for and care for it she would.

She was almost back at the boarding-house when she spotted, walking along the street towards her, a man she would have recognised anywhere.

She hadn't seen him since he had brought them to Dawson a year ago, but he still had that relaxed air about him, still walked tall as if he hadn't a care in the world.

'Why, Mrs Carter,' he greeted her, lifting his hat.

'Hello, Mr Hunter,' she acknowledged.

They stood for a long moment.

'How are—?'

Before he could complete the sentence, Bella had come out of the boarding-house and was racing towards them.

'Sam!'

Amelia watched in amazement as Bella threw her arms around Sam Hunter and allowed herself to be lifted off the ground and hugged.

'What are you doing here?' Bella cried.

'A spot of business,' he replied laughing.

He returned Bella to her feet and looked from one to the other.

'Do you know each other?' he asked curiously.

'Yes, I'm working for Mel – Amelia,' Bella explained.

'No wonder trade's so good,' he said with amusement.

How, Amelia wondered, could he possibly know if trade was good, bad or indifferent?

'You'll be coming along to eat, then?' Bella asked hopefully.

'I might just do that, Bella.'

'Good. See you later, then.' Bella reached up, kissed him on the cheek and skipped off back to the boarding-house.

Amelia wondered just how well he and Bella knew each other. She would ask Bella later.

'If you'll excuse me, Mr Hunter,' she murmured.

She was about to continue on her way, but a firm hand on her arm stopped her.

'I'd like a word with you some time, Mrs Carter,' he said. 'I've a business proposition to put to you.'

'Me?'

'You,' he confirmed. 'Your reputation is growing. You've come a long way since you bought and sold that stove at Lake Bennett.'

Amelia wasn't sure how to respond to that.

'Perhaps this evening?' he suggested. 'I'll come along and dine first.'

'Fine,' she replied. 'I'll look forward to it.'

She continued on her way, deep in thought. A business proposition? What could that be about?

It was late that evening when Amelia finally sat down in the back room with Sam Hunter.

He had eaten, complimented her on the boarding-house and the food, and chatted to Bella, but Amelia was curious to know about his business proposition.

Sam sat back in his chair, as relaxed and at

ease with himself as anyone she had ever known.

'I'm still doing the river trips,' he explained, 'and, as I'm sure you know, people are still coming here in their hundreds. Fewer people are prepared to build their own boats, thank goodness. They want to get here safely – and quickly.'

'So you're doing well for yourself?' she guessed.

'I am.' He ran a long finger across his chin. 'I believe I could do a lot better, too, with more boats and experienced pilots. I believe the river is a gold mine in its own right. Given three good-sized boats, the trip could be made more quickly.

'I've done some calculations,' he went on, 'and, if you're interested, I'd like to show them to you.'

'Why me?'

'For this venture, Mrs Carter, I need more capital. In short, I need a partner. I thought of you.'

It was ridiculous, but Amelia felt herself flush with colour. She was flattered, plain and simple. She had a great deal of respect for Sam Hunter and she was pleased to know he felt the same about her.

He might not like women on his boat, she thought with amusement, but unlike some men, most men, even, he was bright enough to realise that a good head for business had nothing whatsoever to do with gender.

'I hear Mr Carter has returned to Seattle,' he remarked curiously.

'Yes.' Perhaps Miles had done exactly that. Whatever he had done, that was the story she told people. 'This is my business – the lease is in my name – so my husband leaves it to me. His family has a business in Seattle, you see.'

She was talking too much.

'This partner you mention,' she said, returning them to easier ground. 'How much capital do you need? And what percentage of the profits would this partner receive?'

He smiled at her impatience, before carefully talking through his ideas.

'I'm assuming,' he said, 'that you'll soon be thinking of moving to larger premises?'

'I've been thinking about it,' she admitted.

Now, she was determined to do exactly that. She had to forget Miles and think about her unborn child.

'If that's the case, then why not build something on the very edge of Dawson – somewhere the boats can moor? The passengers would disembark and walk straight into your rooms.'

What an excellent idea!

'It's something to think of for the future,' she agreed.

Three hours passed in a flash, and when

Amelia went to bed, her mind was racing with ideas.

The following Thursday, Sam Hunter was in the saloon, a drink in his hand, when the man standing next to him, a stranger to Sam, struck up a conversation.

Sam was interested in people. The only reason he went to the saloon was to observe and listen.

'I saw you eating at Amelia Carter's place,' the man remarked.

'That's right.'

'She's a rare woman,' he went on, fingering his untidy stubble.

'Indeed,' Sam agreed.

'Better off without that husband of hers, if you ask me.'

'I wouldn't know,' Sam replied. 'He's in Seattle, isn't he? Helping with the family business?'

'Pah.' The man tapped the side of his nose. 'That's what she wants everyone to think.' He leaned closer to Sam, and spoke in a whisper. 'He walked out on her and took all the money with him.'

Sam kept his face expressionless, but that had shocked him.

'Is that what the rumour is?' he asked casually.

'That's the truth.' The man took a swallow of his drink. 'He'll be back, no doubt, when he's gambled the lot away.'

Sam had heard that Miles Carter was fond of gambling, but was it true that he'd made off with all their money? There was no way he could check, but it sounded like something Carter would do.

'If she's got any sense, she'll send him packing,' the man said gravely. 'But how can she do that when she's a baby on the way?'

Without waiting for an answer, the man finished his drink.

'Time I was off,' he said.

With that, he wandered off, leaving Sam to reflect.

Sam had never thought highly of Miles Carter. He was too weak, too fond of the easy life. He was, however, married to the woman with whom Sam was about to go into partnership.

A few minutes later, Sam, too, left the saloon. He had a lot of thinking to do.

Amelia was sitting in her bedroom, brushing her hair. Silly to care what she looked like because Sam Hunter had seen her at her worst, but she wanted to look presentable.

It was amazing but, by the end of the day, she and Sam Hunter would be business partners.

They would buy two new boats that, in addition to Sam's own, would allow them to cater for the high numbers looking to come to Dawson. The new boats would complete the journey more quickly, too.

There were risks involved, of course, but they had gone into it thoroughly and made allowances for everything the weather and the rapids could throw at them. At worst, they would break even after a year. At best, they would own a thriving business.

At least Amelia had the boarding-house to fall back on.

Maybe next year, assuming the partnership was successful, she would be able to build her new hotel. She could picture it already; the finest hotel in Dawson.

Her hair shone, and she tied it neatly at the back of her head. Physically, she had never felt better. Other than those first days of being nauseous every morning, she had felt strong and healthy. This baby she was carrying must be healthy, too.

Sam arrived early, taking her by surprise. The expression on his face took her by surprise, too. Never had she seen him so grim. A harsh frown marred his handsome face.

'Come into the back room where it's private.' She led the way on legs that were shaking.

'Please, sit down.'

He shook his head and remained standing.

'I'll get straight to the point,' he said, looking uncomfortable for once. 'Our business arrangement – I'm sorry, but I'm pulling out.'

'You're what?' She couldn't believe it. 'But why?'

'Does it matter?' he asked heavily.

'Yes. Yes, it does. I think I'm owed some sort of explanation.'

'Very well.' His gaze was unwavering. 'You're expecting a child–'

How did he know that? Oh, curses on Dawson! Everyone knew everyone else's business.

'And the whereabouts of your husband are in question.'

Amelia felt herself colour. There was no point in denying it.

'The only person responsible for any part of my private life is me,' she said calmly. 'You're right. I've no idea where my husband is. That's my problem, not yours. And yes, I'm expecting his child. I don't see that as a problem, however. I'm capable of taking care of myself, Mr Hunter, and equally capable of taking care of my child.'

He twirled his hat in his hands.

'I'm sorry.'

'This is madness,' she cried. 'My private life is exactly that. It won't affect any business arrangements.'

'But it will,' he insisted quietly. 'We're all human, Mrs Carter. Personal problems do affect us.'

Amelia would bet he'd never had a personal problem in his life.

'I won't let anything interfere with business,' she vowed.

He shook his head.

'I'm sorry.'

He was adamant, Amelia could see that.

'I'm sorry, too,' she said, tossing back her head. 'I think you'll regret this decision,' she added.

'Yes, you're probably right.'

His hand was outstretched and, as she shook it, reluctantly, she wanted to weep. Why did she have the feeling that there was something else, some other reason that he was keeping to himself?

'Goodbye, Amelia,' he murmured.

So that was it. More dreams dashed.

Someone else would buy those boats with him. Someone else would profit from the venture. And someone else, she thought grimly, would build that hotel on the water's edge.

She crossed to the balcony to watch him walk down the street, and was shocked by the sense of loss she experienced. It wasn't only the loss of the partnership, and the loss of her dreams – it was more than that.

As Sam Hunter walked out of her life, she had the feeling she had lost something very precious indeed.

Chapter Five

January 1900, Dawson

Amelia stood at the water's edge with her son in her arms. Jack was already three months old, and it was strange to look back and remember the state she had been in before he was born.

Then, all she had thought about was Constance and the difficult time she'd had bringing baby Fred into the world. Amelia had been convinced her sister-in-law would die.

In the weeks preceding Jack's birth, she had been convinced that she would die, too. She had imagined her child alone in the world, just as she and James had been.

Poor Bella, she thought with a rueful smile. She had borne the brunt of this near hysteria. Why her dear friend hadn't given up and walked out, she had no idea.

Amelia had written letters to everyone – to Miles, to James and Ivy, another to Matron, one to Constance – and had made Bella promise to keep them safe and then mail them if she died.

'It's important this baby knows its family,'

she had insisted to Bella. 'If I die, I want every effort made to find Miles…'

She had seen the lawyer, she'd had Miles's name put on the new sign outside the boarding-house – she had been frantic with worry for her unborn child.

Now, gazing down at him, she could laugh at those worries. If only Miles could see him. Would he approve of the name she had chosen? She'd discarded so many names – James, after her beloved brother, and Jacob, after her father-in-law. In the end, though, she'd settled on Jack. Jack Carter. It was a good, strong name and besides, he looked like a Jack.

That thought made her chuckle. How could such a darling scrap of humanity look like a Jack? Yet, he did.

Oh, she loved him with every breath in her body and didn't care a jot that he robbed her of sleep.

This morning, she had thought he'd caught a cold, but she was over-protective, she knew that. The poor mite only had to sneeze to send her into a panic.

'It's lucky we're here and not in England,' she murmured, stroking his face, 'because then I'd have the influenza to worry about.'

According to Ivy's last letter, the epidemic was sweeping the country.

Today, it was bitterly cold, but bright and sunny, the sort of day that had Amelia feeling glad to be alive.

A smart new boat was moored a short distance away and Amelia knew it belonged to Sam Hunter. She wondered if he was in Dawson, and if he would call at the boarding-house.

Although she hadn't seen him since the day he had walked out on their business arrangement, she'd heard a lot about his new venture. It never paid to take too much notice of the rumours that flew around Dawson, but by all accounts, Sam Hunter was prospering.

Hadn't she known he would, though? He had a quick brain, was a hard worker, and, with the right backing, his business couldn't fail. Even allowing for the vagaries of the climate and the dangers of the rapids, it was sure to succeed.

She had heard that George Dickinson had provided the necessary capital. Presumably he was now reaping the rewards of that backing.

Although Amelia knew him by sight, as did most people in Dawson, she had never met Dickinson. She was curious about him.

Her son stirred in her arms and, smiling, she gazed down at him.

'This, Jack,' she told him, 'is the exact spot on which I dreamed of building my hotel. It would have been the best in Dawson – the best for miles around. But, there–' She

119

smiled down at him. 'We've plenty of time. We'll build that hotel one day. You see if we don't.'

It was pointless having regrets about the partnership she would have had with Sam Hunter. Regrets were a luxury she couldn't afford.

Despite being constantly tired, something she had to blame on her over-protective nature rather than Jack himself, Amelia was optimistic about the future. They had entered a brand-new century and everything felt bright with promise.

'Let's get you home and in the warm,' she said, dropping a kiss on his forehead.

He gazed back at her, and Amelia could have wept with love for him. Did he know how much he was loved, she wondered? Did he realise how precious he was?

One thing was certain, he trusted her with his life. Amelia vowed that she would never betray that trust. Her son would have the best of everything.

She walked back to the boarding-house, a smile on her face as she gazed down at Jack. His face was almost hidden, so wrapped up was he, but his eyes were bright and clear, and his tiny mouth was pouting.

He had green eyes, just like hers, but his hair was as blond as his father's.

'Time to get busy,' she told him, pushing open the door to the boarding-house. 'The men will want their stomachs filling.'

As soon as she walked inside, she knew that something had happened.

Bella's young lad, Isaac, spotted her and immediately looked away and made himself scarce. The whole place seemed to have a hush about it, as if the building was holding its breath.

Frowning, she went into the storeroom.

Bella had been straightening out tins so they could make meat pies, but she stopped when Amelia walked in.

She opened her mouth, but wasn't given a chance to speak because the door opened.

Amelia turned round to see who was there.

For a second, she couldn't move. She certainly couldn't speak. For there, standing by the door, was her husband.

He crossed the room to her, his arms outstretched.

Then Amelia was hugging him – one arm around him, another holding their son. She closed her eyes briefly to breathe in his nearness.

'Oh, Miles. You're home at last!'

She half-expected to wake up and find she had been dreaming again. But, no, Miles was real.

She gazed at him and worried that he looked pale and tired. Beaten, she thought. He looks beaten.

121

'Yes.' A half-smile touched his mouth. 'I'm home, sweetheart.'

'I've missed you so much,' she said.

His smile was warmer now, less tired.

'And I you, Amelia,' he murmured, holding her close.

He nodded at Jack.

'Who's this, then?'

She had imagined he'd returned to Seattle where his sister-in-law would have told him that she was carrying his child. Clearly not.

Miles was looking at his own flesh and blood, yet he didn't recognise him.

She found that strange. She had fondly imagined that he would recognise Jack anywhere, but that was plain silly.

'This is Jack,' she said gently. She pulled their baby's blanket away from his face.

'Our son. This is our son.'

The shock robbed him of breath.

'Isn't he the most wonderful child you've ever seen, Miles?'

'Ours?' Miles said in disbelief.

'Yes.' Smiling, she nodded. 'I found out when you left. I'd been sick for a few days, but I hadn't even suspected. It was Bella–' Amelia spun round, but Bella was nowhere in sight. She must have slipped away to leave them alone. 'It was Bella who first suspected I might be pregnant,' she rushed on. 'I wrote to Constance and told her. I thought you were heading to Seattle, you see. I thought she would tell you and you'd come home.'

He shook his head.

'I haven't been home.'

Home, he'd said. To Miles, Seattle was still home.

Before she could ask where he had been, and a dozen other questions, Jack began to cry.

'My son,' Miles said in an awed whisper.

He opened his arms and Amelia carefully handed over Jack.

The sight of them together, father and son, brought tears to her eyes. It had the same effect on Miles, she noticed.

Jack stopped crying to gaze at his father and Amelia laughed.

'He recognises you, Miles!' She felt sure he did.

'I reckon he does,' Miles replied, a proud smile bringing a glow to his face.

Later, when Miles had eaten and taken himself off to their bedroom to rest, Amelia realised she was shaking.

'You all right, Mel?' Bella asked.

'Yes.' But she dropped down on to a chair, feeling as if she needed to get her breath back.

'I can't believe it,' she murmured, laughing at herself. 'It's almost a year since Miles left and I was beginning to despair of ever seeing him again.'

'Oh, I knew he'd be back.' Bella wore the tight-lipped expression that she reserved only for Miles.

She didn't add 'when his money ran out', but Amelia guessed she was thinking it. She wasn't going to quarrel with Bella, but she thought her friend would do well to remember that if it hadn't been for Miles, her children would still be hungry and cold as they waited for her outside saloons.

But, no, she wouldn't argue with Bella. Life was too short and Amelia was too happy. Miles was home!

Beneath the joy of having him home was a small amount of anger. Not because he had taken their money, although that didn't please her, but that he hadn't let her know where he was, or even that he was safe.

But it was no use being angry. That would achieve nothing. He was home now, and nothing else mattered.

Jack would be the making of Miles, she just knew it. Miles would want to give him everything. He'd had his ten months away from Dawson, and now he would settle down and put his heart and soul into their business for his son's sake.

Late that evening, when Jack was sleeping peacefully, Amelia finally found herself alone with Miles.

He sat in the chair by the side of the bed. Amelia patted the space beside her, wanting him to join her.

'What do you think of your son? Isn't he beautiful?'

'He is, sweetheart.' He sat beside her, and held her hand in his. 'He has his mother's eyes.'

'Oh, Miles, I love him so much.'

'I know. I just wish I'd been here when—' He turned to look at her. 'I had to get away. I couldn't bear this place. Can you understand that, Amelia?'

'I suppose so.'

Yet she couldn't, really. Or if she could, she couldn't understand how he could take all of their money or how he could leave without saying a word.

But she had vowed not to be cross. All she wanted was for the three of them to be happy together. A real family.

'I've been thinking, Miles,' she said, 'and I believe we can afford to buy the boarding-house outright. What do you think? It's doing so well – I think we'd be fools not to.'

It wouldn't be easy, but they would find the money somehow and, together, they would go from strength to strength.

'Miles,' she began carefully, 'the money you took from the sale – do you have it now?'

As soon as the words were out, she wished she could take them back. Of course he didn't have the money. She could see the answer in his eyes. She could guess where most of it had gone, too. It was becoming more and more difficult to bite her tongue.

'That's what I need to talk to you about.' He rose to his feet, walked over to the opposite wall, leaned back, gazed at her for a moment, and then looked away.

There was a letter from Ivy lying on the dresser. He picked it up, turned it over and then put it back.

'I had a bit of bad luck,' he explained, looking everywhere but at her. 'There's a man I owe money to. I need to pay him back.'

'How much?' she asked, and even she could hear the coldness in her voice.

'Five hundred dollars,' he murmured, eyes downcast.

'Five hundred dollars?' she gasped. 'No! Oh, Miles, how could you do this? How could you do it to us – to your son?'

'I didn't know about him!'

Amelia was furious. Since Miles had walked out on her, she'd heard people's whispered comments – 'He'll be back when his money runs out'. Even Bella had thought that. Amelia had heard the gossip and ignored it. She knew Miles better than that. Or she'd thought she did.

'Why have you come back?' she demanded.

'Why?' The question surprised him. 'To be

with you, of course. Look, I know what I did was wrong. I had to get away from here – the place was sending me crazy. I shouldn't have done it, I know. And I should have sent word.'

'You should,' she agreed angrily.

'And I shouldn't have taken the money from the safe.' He looked up at her with eyes like a puppy's. 'I only meant to take enough to see me through. I didn't intend to be away this long.'

'And now that you're back, how long do you intend to stay?' she demanded.

He reached for her, but she moved away.

'For as long as you'll have me,' he said quietly. 'I belong with you, sweetheart. I always have.'

Amelia could feel the ice around her heart melting. But five hundred dollars!

Jack chose that point to wake up and was soon screaming at the top of his lungs.

'Let me.' Miles scooped Jack into his arms, stroked his head and gently rocked him. Amazingly, the cries stopped immediately.

'I won't leave you, Amelia,' Miles vowed. 'You and Jack – you're all I have in the world. I love you both so very, very much.'

Amelia reached for his arm and gave it a squeeze, all anger forgotten. She had her darling son, and she had her husband back. What more could she ask for?

Once they had paid off Miles's debt, and if

they could buy the boarding-house – everything would be wonderful.

For a while now, she'd begun to wonder if she hadn't been a little at fault for the problems in their marriage. Signing the lease on the boarding-house before telling Miles about it had been a mistake. At the time, she'd had to have it. Yet Miles must have felt awful. He would have felt excluded. His pride would have been dented, too, knowing that his wife had done something drastic without his consent.

In future, she vowed, they would be a real partnership in every way.

April 1900, Dawson

'My,' Bella muttered, as she burst into the kitchen, 'we'll have the Prime Minister himself dining here next week. You'll never guess who's eating out front.'

'Then you'd better save time and tell me,' Amelia suggested with a small smile.

'George Dickinson.'

'George Dickinson? Here?' Amelia couldn't believe it.

'Sitting out front as if he owns the place,' Bella informed her.

'Well!'

What on earth was he doing here? Apart from going into partnership with Sam Hunter, George Dickinson owned one of Dawson's top hotels.

Amelia prided herself on the quality of the meals she offered, but the lunchtime menu was basic when compared to the fare George Dickinson would be used to. From what she'd heard, he liked to live in style.

Unable to resist, she removed her apron, patted her hair into place and walked through the dining-room to see for herself. Sure enough, George Dickinson was sitting alone at the largest table they had.

He wasn't especially tall, probably a couple of inches shorter than Amelia, but he was a stocky man. He had broad shoulders and a big chest. His dark brown hair was brushed back from a handsome face and his dark beard was neatly trimmed.

He'd be around forty years old, Amelia guessed. As she watched him, his shrewd gaze was taking in his surroundings.

Amelia was surprised to see him on the premises, but she was flattered that he was taking an interest. She decided to have a word with him once he had eaten, and discover what had brought him here.

Back in the kitchen, she and Bella were too busy to think about him. The dining-room was soon crowded, which was unusual during the day. More customers came in the evening after a hard day's work.

Wait until she told Miles about their important guest! Or perhaps Miles would see for himself. He'd gone to the general store and should be back any minute.

He had been home for three months now, yet she still marvelled at the sheer bliss of waking in the morning and finding him lying beside her, and settling down after a busy day and falling asleep in his arms.

When George Dickinson had cleared his plate and was sitting with a drink in front of him, Amelia, again, went out into the dining-room and walked across to his table.

'Mr Dickinson,' she greeted him. 'It's good to see you here. Was everything all right for you?'

'I'm impressed, Mrs Carter,' he said, those shrewd eyes taking in everything about her, just as they'd given the dining-room a close scrutiny.

Amelia glowed at the compliment, and at the fact that he knew who she was. Before she could answer, however, the door opened and in walked Miles. What a handsome man he was, she thought proudly.

'Miles!' She called him over. 'Mr Dickinson had dined here. He was just saying how impressed he is.'

'Excellent,' Miles said, and Amelia could tell her husband was equally surprised to see George Dickinson in their dining-room.

'You'll be Miles Carter,' Mr Dickinson said, in his careful, considered way. 'I think we have a mutual acquaintance in Bill Constantine.'

Amelia saw the way Miles's face lit with recognition.

'Yes.' He sat himself down opposite George Dickinson. 'I haven't seen him for – oh, it must be six months.'

'He mentioned you,' the other man explained. 'He's staying as my guest for a week or two. You must come along and renew the acquaintance.'

Amelia, realising her presence wasn't needed, left the two men alone.

'Guess what, Bella,' she announced as she strode into the kitchen. 'George Dickinson has invited Miles to his hotel to catch up with a man they both know.' She laughed. 'Heavens, Miles will be dining with the Prime Minister next!'

Bella merely grunted a response.

Now that Amelia thought about it, Bella had shown no excitement whatsoever on learning that George Dickinson was sitting at one of their tables.

'Bella?'

Bella sighed heavily, looked as if she was about to speak and then changed her mind.

'What is it?' Amelia asked, frowning.

Bella sighed again.

'George Dickinson – well, I've known him for years,' she explained.

'Believe me,' Bella added, 'he's not a man to trust.'

Amelia sat down at the table.

'Not trust? George Dickinson? But he's–'

'I know,' Bella said grimly, 'but there was a time when he was neither wealthy nor respectable.'

'Were you and he–?' A shocking thought struck Amelia. 'Isaac and Jane. He's not–'

'Heavens, no! I told you about their father. He died on the Chilkoot Pass.'

'Yes,' Amelia agreed, flushing, 'but I wondered if you'd – well, invented him to stop tongues wagging.'

'No. Ben was real.' Bella's smile was wistful. 'He was a good man,' she said softly, adding grimly, 'which is more than I can say for George Dickinson.'

Amelia waited for more, but wasn't surprised when nothing came. Despite her outgoing, flirty nature, Bella rarely discussed her personal life.

'I expect he's changed.' Amelia couldn't believe that George Dickinson was anything other than a highly respectable and successful businessman.

'Maybe he has,' Bella allowed. 'But maybe he hasn't. Watch him, Amelia.'

Amelia laughed off her friend's concern.

'All he's done is dine here and invite Miles to his hotel.'

Bella didn't comment on that.

'Watch Miles, too,' she said. 'Rumour has it that George likes a game of poker.' Her lips set in a thin, tight line, she added, 'I'll bet he cheats at that, too.'

As they busied themselves in the kitchen, Amelia thought over all that Bella had said. Thought about it and dismissed it.

Dawson was rife with gossip, and jealousy was at the root of a lot of it. George Dickinson was a prime target.

She certainly had no worries about Miles. Like her, Miles wanted to give Jack everything. They now owned the boarding-house outright and Miles was working hard. He was a changed man. He had finished with gambling. The lesson had been learned and those days were over.

They were a family now, a real family, and, smiling, Amelia hugged that fact close.

Three days later, on a damp Friday evening, Miles strode along the street with his head held high, a pocket full of cash and a tingle of excitement coursing through his veins.

Who would have thought that George Dickinson would invite him to his hotel for a poker game? Miles had heard about these events, and knew they were by invitation only. And here he was – with his own invitation.

He had met Bill Constantine at a poker game. The man was honest, which was a rare thing at a card table, and likeable, but he was hopeless at poker. Miles had won a good sum of money from him. With any luck, he would do the same again this evening.

It was refreshing to leave the boarding-house for a few hours, too. They worked hard, and their efforts were paying off. Then, when they took a rest, they marvelled at their son.

Miles still found it amazing that Jack had captured his heart so completely. He would do anything for him.

All the same, a man needed a break and tonight, Miles would be having fun. What's more, he was out with Amelia's blessing.

Not that she knew a poker game was involved. Amelia thought he was merely meeting up with Bill Constantine at George Dickinson's hotel.

Miles walked through the main door and was immediately taken into a small room at the back of the hotel.

'Ah, Miles.' George greeted him with a warm smile. 'Drink?'

This was more like it, Miles thought happily as he accepted. Only the select few, usually the wealthy few, received an invitation from George Dickinson, and now, Miles was among that number.

This evening, Miles, George, Bill Constantine, Peter Tavener, owner of one of Dawson's thriving lumber yards, and Edward Letterman, a goldminer, were present.

The atmosphere was warm, friendly and

relaxed. George was a thoughtful host and the drinks flowed, even when they were playing.

Miles's first hand was a flush, and the evening continued in an equally encouraging way.

When he finally bade his farewells in the early hours of the morning, he had made a small profit. He would have liked to have made more, but it wasn't his place to suggest they increase the stakes.

'Next week,' George promised as he was leaving, 'we'll met again. Perhaps raise the stakes. Are you interested, Miles?'

Raise the stakes? Had George read his mind?

'Count me in,' Miles replied happily.

George clearly shared his enthusiasm.

'It makes for a more interesting game,' he said. 'Far more interesting.'

May 1900, Dawson

Most afternoons, Amelia brought Jack down to the water's edge for an hour. She would sit with him on her lap and tell him of her plans.

Today, with the sun on their faces, she spoke again of the hotel she planned to build.

'It'll be the height of luxury,' she vowed, 'and will cater to those who can afford it. We'll have cut glass chandeliers – imagine that, Jack! We'll have silver. Brass bedsteads, too!'

Jack gurgled happily in response.

'We'll have the best of everything – singing and dancing, too.'

She was so wrapped up in her plans that she didn't spot Sam Hunter until he was only a couple of yards from her.

'Mr Hunter!' She got to her feet, clutching Jack in her arms.

'Mrs Carter,' he acknowledged, removing his hat.

He peered at Jack.

'And this must be your son.'

'Yes, this is Jack.'

Much to her surprise, he lightly stroked Jack's cheek.

'A fine young man,' he said. 'You must be very proud of him.'

'We are, yes. Thank you.' Amelia was touched.

For once, she found herself at a loss for words. She would dearly love to discuss business, the business she should have been a part of, but now, it was nothing to her.

'I saw Bella last week,' he remarked.

Bella hadn't mentioned seeing him. Again, Amelia wondered just how friendly Bella was with the undeniably attractive river boat pilot.

She had asked her friend months ago, but Bella's response had been a laughing, 'Not as friendly as I'd like to be,' before she'd changed the subject.

'She tells me you own the boarding-house outright,' he continued.

'That's right,' she told him proudly.

'A wise decision.'

'Thank you. And you?' she asked hesitantly. 'Your venture is successful?'

If he could talk of her business, she could ask about his.

'Very.'

There was an awkward silence.

'I hear you went into partnership with George Dickinson,' she said at last.

'Indeed.' He fingered his hat. 'Bella told me that your husband is ... friendly with him.'

Why that hesitation before carefully choosing the word 'friendly'?

'Yes, he often visits Mr Dickinson.'

He looked at her long and hard, and just as she thought he was about to comment on Miles's friendship with George Dickinson, he suddenly nodded towards the town.

'Each time I visit Dawson, it's changed,' he said lightly. 'There are buildings springing up everywhere, other buildings burning down. What a strange place it is.'

Amelia knew just what he meant.

'It's constantly changing,' she agreed, 'and I think that's why I like it so much.'

Smiling, he nodded his understanding.

137

A gust of wind blew her hair into her face, and she pushed it back into place.

'It's been good to see you, Mr Hunter,' she said, 'but I must get back.'

He nodded.

'Goodbye, Mrs Carter.'

As she walked back to the boarding-house with the sun in her eyes, Amelia wondered what it was he had thought of saying about Miles's friendship with George Dickinson.

Of course, she might have imagined it. She didn't think so, though.

And why, she wondered, did she have the feeling that he wasn't impressed by either man?

That evening, Amelia was stretched out on their bed waiting for Miles. Jack had finally fallen asleep stretched across her and she cradled him with one arm while holding Ivy's letter in her free hand.

As always with Ivy's letters, she read it over and over. This one had arrived yesterday and she had read it at every available opportunity.

In her last few letters, Ivy had sounded low, as if something was troubling her. She despaired, she'd said in one letter, of ever seeing Amelia again.

Amelia never despaired. Often, she pictured the three of them, Miles, Jack and herself, sailing to England on a vast, luxurious ship. Not see her brother and best friend again? That was nonsense, and she never failed to tell Ivy so.

One fine day, they would walk along Liverpool's streets.

This letter was different, though. Ivy's excitement leaped off the page. She was pregnant again!

James is even more excited than I am, if that's possible, she had written.

Amelia had to smile. Reading Ivy's letter, she doubted that it *was* possible.

She was still smiling as she pushed the letter back in its envelope. She thought she heard a noise, but then all was silent.

Miles was late.

Her chat with Sam Hunter this afternoon had made her uneasy, and she planned to find out all she could about George Dickinson.

Eventually, unable to stay awake any longer, she settled Jack down, pulled the blankets up to his chin, dropped a gentle kiss on his forehead and stood back to gaze at him. Confident the movement hadn't disturbed him, she climbed into bed.

She slept well, and didn't hear a sound until the morning.

Miles was lying beside her. She reached out to him and let out a gasp of shock. His skin was clammy, and he was ice cold.

As if he was aware of her touch, he woke up and groaned.

'Miles, you're freezing!'

'I don't feel too good.' He tried to sit up, but only groaned again. 'I'm shivering – my head hurts.'

'What time did you get home last night? What were you doing? Was anyone else ill?' Oh, but what did it matter? 'I'm getting the doctor,' Amelia said firmly.

Dr Brown arrived later that morning. After examining Miles, who was, if anything, worse, he said, 'He has a high fever.'

Amelia could have screamed at him – anyone could see that.

For the next few days, only Amelia attended to Miles.

She entrusted Jack and the running of the boarding-house to Bella's care and rarely left Miles's side. Yet, despite doing all she could for him, his condition only seemed to worsen.

On Friday, he didn't even recognise her.

'Mrs Carter,' the doctor said gently, putting a hand on her shoulder. 'I'm sorry, but I feel you should prepare yourself for the worst.'

'No!'

'Mrs Carter–'

But Amelia swept out of the room with her hands covering her ears. She refused to listen. She refused even to consider the possibility of losing Miles again.

Chapter Six

September 1901, Dawson

It was a year since Sam Hunter had been in Dawson, and the town had changed dramatically. Every time he visited, he was amazed at the amount of buildings that had sprung up.

Today, however, neither his mind nor his gaze were on the buildings. He was watching Amelia Carter, and the sight of her brought a frown to his face. Even from this distance, he could see how much she had changed. She'd always been so proud and spirited. Now, she looked broken.

News of Miles Carter's death had spread rapidly, but that story had been nothing when compared to the gossip that had gripped Dawson immediately afterwards.

At first, Sam had believed it was just that: gossip. But no. Miles Carter had used the boarding-house as a stake in a poker game, and he'd lost.

Sam had a hundred jobs to do, but he decided to forget them for the time being. He jumped down from his boat and walked to where Amelia Carter was sitting with her son on her lap.

'Mrs Carter,' he greeted her, removing his hat.

He had thought she'd been looking straight at him, but the sound of his voice startled her. Belatedly, he realised that she had simply been staring into space.

She jumped to her feet, putting her son to stand beside her.

Sam did a quick calculation and decided that the child holding her hand must be almost two years old by now. He was a find-looking boy.

'Mr Hunter,' she said, recovering herself.

Standing so close to her, Sam was even more shocked. She had always been slim, but now she was little more than a skeleton. It was as if she was simply wasting away.

'How are you keeping?' Sam asked, although he could tell the answer to that one – badly.

'Very well, thank you,' she answered. 'And you?'

Sam thought back to their first meeting. That had been more than three years ago, when she had persuaded him to take her and her husband across the rapids. He had been half in love with the woman ever since.

Yet, what he'd loved about her seemed lost for ever. The light had gone from her eyes, and the passion was absent from her voice.

'Yes, I'm well, thank you. And young

Jack?' he asked, smiling down at the boy. 'He's growing at a pace. I guess he must be almost two now.'

'He'll be two next month,' she said, managing a smile.

Even when she spoke of her son, there was no life in her voice.

'I was sorry to hear about your sad loss,' Sam said quietly.

She nodded, as if she'd heard the phrase countless times before. He supposed she had.

'Thank you.'

Over the years, he'd seen every expression on her face – excitement, anger, sadness, laughter. Now there was nothing.

He had expected more of her. A lot more. After all, it was eighteen months since she'd lost her husband and Jack needed her more than ever.

Yet, he couldn't begin to understand how she must feel. Watching her husband die of typhoid fever would have been a bitter blow in itself. How much worse it must have been for her, in the midst of her grief, to discover that she'd lost everything else. To learn that her husband had gambled away their business and left her with nothing.

He could understand how difficult life was for her, but he couldn't understand how she still grieved for the husband who had thrown away her future. What sort of man was it who risked everything his wife had worked for on a deal of the cards?

Sam didn't like to speak ill of the dead, but it had to be faced: the man had been a wastrel. Miles Carter hadn't been worthy to wash his wife's boots.

'How is Bella?' he asked, moving on to easier ground. 'Is she still at the boarding-house?'

'She is.' Smiling that weary smile, Amelia nodded. 'But, as I'm sure you know, it's no longer Carter's Boarding House.'

'I heard.' It now belonged to George Dickinson. There was another man Sam had no time for.

He wondered how things would have turned out if, instead of changing his mind at the last minute, he had put his doubts aside and gone into partnership with Amelia Carter. At the time, it had seemed a dangerous thing to do. She had an amazing business head on her shoulders, which was why Sam had approached her in the first place, but there were too many other considerations. She had been expecting a child, she'd had no idea where her husband was, let alone when, or if, he would be back, and, on top of that, Miles Carter had been a habitual gambler.

In the end, Sam had decided that going into business with Amelia was too risky. He had pulled out of their arrangement and, instead, had gone into business with George Dickinson. Sam had needed capital to buy two more boats, and George had provided that capital. The business, as Sam had hoped, had soon become a huge success.

All the same, from the moment they had put pen to paper and finalised their partnership, Sam hadn't trusted the man. There were too many rumours, too many people willing to call him a cheat.

Now Sam wondered if George had won Carter's Boarding House fair and square. Somehow, he doubted that. If Miles Carter had been a wastrel, George Dickinson was a dubious character at best.

Thankfully, Sam had recently managed to buy George's share of the business and he no longer had to deal with the man.

There were still thousands coming to Dawson and, despite the vagaries of the weather and the cost of boat repairs, Sam was making a tidy sum. He worked hard, he employed good men, and any profit was his. That was the way he liked it.

'Perhaps I'll dine there this evening,' he said now.

'And perhaps I'll serve you, Mr Hunter.'

How it must hurt her to be paid a wage to work in her own boarding-house. He looked for the hopeless despair he expected to see on her face, but there wasn't even that. There was nothing.

'I'm sure your next venture will be more successful, Mrs Carter,' he said.

'My next venture?'

'You're a businesswoman, a good one,' he reminded her. 'You won't be content to work for George Dickinson for ever.'

She shrugged.

'Don't you remember the hardships you endured coming to this place?' he asked urgently. 'Don't you remember the stove you bought and sold at such a high profit? You made that boarding-house what it is today. Surely you'll want to move on, start another business?'

Now there was helplessness in her expression. She was right; starting another business would be difficult, if not impossible. She had her young son to care for now so she couldn't afford to take risks, and Sam doubted if George Dickinson paid her a decent wage. Knowing George, he'd have her grateful to him for offering her employment at all.

'Don't give in, Mrs Carter,' he said.

She looked at him for a long moment.

'We need to get back,' she told him. 'Nice to see you, Mr Hunter.'

'And you, Mrs Carter. I hope to see you again while I'm in Dawson.'

She nodded, lifted her son into her arms and walked off. There was no spring in her step as there had once been. The sight of her was enough to break a man's heart.

October 1901, Liverpool

Liverpool was experiencing yet another dreary, damp evening, but it cheered James to round the corner and see the light burning brightly in his home. He quickened his pace, eager to be there.

As soon as he walked through the door, Ivy ran to him, wrapped her arms tight around his waist and buried her face against his jacket.

'What's wrong, love?'

'Nothing,' she murmured, her voice muffled by his jacket. 'I just need you to hold me.'

James held her close for several minutes and wondered what was bothering her. Something was wrong, of that he was certain, but he knew Ivy would tell him all in good time.

When he had left for work that morning, she'd been bright and cheerful enough. She'd been planning to invite Matron for tea next week to help them celebrate her namesake's first birthday.

He could still remember how he'd laughed when Ivy had suggested the name for their daughter.

'Let's call her Elizabeth after Matron,' she had said.

Dear Matron. She would always be

'Matron', never 'Elizabeth'.

And now their daughter was one week away from her first birthday. Where did the time go?

'Is a man to get any food in this place?' he asked with a chuckle.

Ivy lifted her head and smiled.

'In a minute,' she replied. 'It's all ready – won't take long to dish up. I need you to hold me close for another minute.'

As he held her, James thought he could possibly guess at the reason for the sadness in her eyes.

As they ate – a nourishing stew that only Ivy could make so tasty – the twins, Martha and Albert, had them laughing with their chatter.

Four years old now, they were happy, confident children. Some might say they should learn to be quiet at the table and speak only when spoken to, but James and Ivy didn't hold with that.

Perhaps it was only natural that, after their own orphanage upbringing, their children would be showered with love. He and Ivy might not be able to give them material things, but they gave the children anything that would make them confident and secure, give them a sense of belonging, of being an essential part of a close family.

Later, when the twins were in bed and baby Lizzie was sleeping soundly, James and

Ivy sat at the kitchen table enjoying a quiet few minutes together.

'Out with it, love,' James prompted gently. 'What's bothering you?'

'Nothing really,' she answered with a smile. Her hands were wrapped around her cup. 'I've everything I ever dreamed of – you, three beautiful children, good friends, enough money.'

How he loved her. In all the years he'd known her, she had never asked for anything, never longed for things he couldn't give her.

'Yes, we're very lucky,' he agreed.

'We are.' She took a sip of tea.

'But?' he asked knowingly.

She thought for a few moments.

'I know it's impossible,' she told him at last, 'but I really wish I could be with Mel right now. I always miss her, you know that, but she sounds so sad at the moment, Jimmy. It's not like her.'

'Ah.' Yes, he'd guessed.

Like Ivy, he'd been worrying about his sister. He had read Amelia's letters, too. Those letters were infrequent, brief and flat. Usually, Amelia wrote as she talked, like an excited butterfly flying from one subject to the next.

He saw Ivy's bottom lip tremble.

'Come here.' He reached for her and pulled her to sit on his knee.

'Oh, Jimmy.' She sobbed. 'What will become of her?'

She buried her face against his neck and he could feel her tears wet against his skin.

'She'll be fine, love,' he murmured, gently stroking her back. 'It's taking her a while to bounce back, that's all.'

'But it's been eighteen months now!'

James thought of his bright, ambitious, energetic sister.

'With Miles dying so suddenly,' he said carefully, 'and so young ... and dying when he'd only just returned to her, come home to meet his son – well, that was a hard blow. But knowing Amelia, discovering that he'd gambled away the business will have hit her even harder.'

'Jimmy! That's a terrible thing to say!'

'I don't mean it like that,' he said quickly. 'It's not the money as such, it's–' He broke off to gather his thoughts.

'Amelia and I were left at the orphanage gates with nothing,' he explained, adding with a smile, 'except that confounded trunk. And I suspect my sister still drags that thing along the street with her when she shops.'

Ivy laughed at that.

'I'll never forget the look on Miles's face when he realised Mel intended to take it to America,' she said. 'And how they got the thing all the way to Dawson, I shall never know!'

James chuckled.

'Only death will make Amelia give up that trunk.'

Serious, he went on.

'And that's the point, love. That trunk represents security to Amelia, just as the boarding-house did. It was hers. So long as she had that, she knew she'd survive, and she knew that Jack was assured of a good fortune. Losing it will have hit her hard. Poor Jack's lost a father and a future – that's all Amelia will known.'

'I suppose so,' Ivy agreed, her arms tight around his neck, 'but it's as if she feels she has nothing left to live for, and that's nonsense. She has Jack. That boy means the world to her.'

James, too, would love to be with his sister right now. But, as Ivy had said, it was impossible.

Even if they could afford it – and they most certainly couldn't – they couldn't go to see Amelia in Dawson. They had the twins and a baby; they couldn't take those children across that vast ocean. Nor could they leave them behind for so long. And James couldn't be away from his work.

So even if they had a fortune, they would still be in the same position. There was nothing they could do for Amelia. And that, perhaps, was what hurt the most.

'What would you say if Amelia walked in

the room right now?' he asked Ivy.

'I'd tell her to pull herself together,' she answered immediately. 'I'd remind her that she has Jack, and her health, and I'd tell her that life's too short to waste a single minute. I'd remind her that she arrived in Dawson with nothing but that trunk. She started that boarding-house with nothing. What she's done once, she can do again.'

'We'll put all that in a letter,' he announced.

'It's not that simple, Jimmy,' she said, shaking her head. 'You have to be more tactful in a letter. You can't smile to take away the sting of your words.'

She was right, of course.

Before James could think of something else, they heard Lizzie's cries.

'She'll be hungry.' Ivy gave him a quick kiss, jumped off his knee and went to check.

James finished his tea and then took Amelia's last letter from the drawer. It had arrived a week ago and although Ivy hadn't said much at the time, he'd known it had upset her. He took the single sheet of paper from the envelope and read it again.

Nothing's happened here, so I've no news. Jack and I are well.

Jack might be, he thought sadly, but Amelia wasn't.

Tell me your news. How are the twins? They must be growing quickly now. Do they still love baby Lizzie?

I'll write more when I have something to tell you. Meanwhile, all my love as always...

James put the letter away and stepped outside. Liverpool was quiet in the darkness. How the city had changed, he thought. With all the building work in progress, especially by the docks, Amelia wouldn't recognise her old home.

It wasn't only the streets of Liverpool that were different, though. The whole country was changing. After Queen Victoria's death in January, the people had seemed lost for a while. Now, everyone seemed eager for change, and James wasn't sure he liked change.

Amelia would like it, but – that was it!

He went back in the house and when Ivy joined him, he took her in his arms.

'Amelia,' he said, 'is the most stubborn person I know. What's keeping her in Dawson now? Hm? Nothing!'

'What do you mean?' Ivy asked curiously.

'She set sail for America with her new husband and a head full of dreams,' he reminded his wife. 'Now, that husband is gone. Her business is gone, too. There's nothing to keep her there. Why, she could just as easily work in Liverpool as she could over there.'

Ivy's eyes suddenly lit with hope.

'Amelia would rather die than come home

thinking she had to admit defeat,' he said, 'but if we said we needed her–'

'Oh, Jimmy!'

'Why, she's probably even hoping we'll ask. I bet she's waiting for an excuse to come home.'

James hugged her tight.

'Only last week, Arthur Whaley was talking to me about their new hotel, and he said he wished Amelia was here to help out. Think of it, Ivy! She could come home and work for the Whaleys, just as she used to,' he said. 'In the morning, we'll write to her.'

'Oh, if only she would come home.'

'She'll be back before Christmas, love. You mark my words!'

November 1901, Dawson

It was early morning in Dawson and Amelia dressed quickly, ready for the day ahead. In the next room, she could hear that Bella was already awake and on the move.

Amelia smiled to herself as Bella's voice drifted through from the next room. She was singing 'The Arkansas Traveller'. My, she was a wonderful singer! Her voice could lift the heaviest of hearts.

'Doesn't Auntie Bella have a beautiful voice, Jack?' she murmured to her son.

'Bella,' he gurgled.

Smiling, Amelia reached for his boots and put them on. Hugging him to her, she was about to take him downstairs when she caught sight of James and Ivy's letter. A week had passed since its arrival, and she still hadn't replied. Tonight, she would do just that. She had no idea what she would say to them, but she must say something.

Meanwhile, as always, there was work to be done. George Dickinson had taken to calling unannounced, and it wouldn't do if their boss thought they were shirking their duties.

Bella joined her and, as soon as they'd fed the children and eaten a hasty breakfast themselves, they began work.

The work helped Amelia to cope. It stopped her thinking. The harder she worked, the less she thought. And the harder she worked, the more tired she was. She would fall asleep quickly instead of lying awake and longing for Miles and what might have been.

As she put clean cloths on the dining tables, she was still humming 'The Arkansas Traveller' to herself. She chuckled out loud. Unlike Bella's beautiful voice, her own would send the customers scurrying for cover if she dared to sing.

Just then, Bella came into the dining-room.

'Bella, that song you were singing this morning – "The Arkansas Traveller". Sing it again. Here.'

'What?' Bella hooted with laugher. 'What's got into you?'

'Indulge me,' Amelia pleaded.

Bella began to sing, hesitantly and self-consciously at first, but her naturally exuberant nature couldn't be stilled for too long. A few bars in, Bella was giving it her all. She moved among the empty tables, her hands resting on the back of each one for a moment. When she finished, Amelia clapped loudly.

'Where did you learn to sing like that?' she asked curiously.

'Learn? Lord, I never learned. My grandmother used to sing, though. I suppose I picked it up from her. She always used to say "Better to sing than cry", and I suppose she's right.' Bella shrugged. 'It cheers me up.'

'Me, too,' Amelia said thoughtfully, remembering the way Bella's voice had lifted her spirits that morning.

'So,' Bella said meaningfully, 'have you given any thought to the letter?'

'I've thought of nothing else.'

'And?' Bella pressed.

'And I'm still not sure,' she admitted. 'I'm going to answer it this evening – assuming I get time.'

The letter had come as a shock. Written by James – rare in itself – it had told of Mr and Mrs Whaley's plans for their new hotel.

Amelia had gone to work for the Whaleys at their boarding-house as soon as she had left the orphanage. She'd been working for them when Miles entered her life. She liked the couple immensely, and still had fond memories of the food and drink they'd arranged for her and Miles's wedding day.

But the idea of employing her as manageress of their new hotel was not appealing.

At first, the thought of running home to Liverpool to lick her wounds had filled her with joy. That feeling, however, had only lasted a few minutes.

She missed her brother and Ivy, of course she did, and there were days when she would do anything to spend an hour or so with them, but she wasn't ready to return to Liverpool. A holiday there would be wonderful. She wasn't, however, willing to return. Not yet.

The door burst open and their employer walked in. Typical, Amelia thought crossly. They had been working until their hands were raw all morning and now, just when they'd stopped for a brief moment, he had to catch them out.

'Good morning, Mr Dickinson,' they greeted him dutifully.

'Morning,' he replied, looking around him. He didn't miss a thing.

Fortunately, he strode straight through to

the office. His office now, Amelia thought wistfully.

She pushed the thought aside, as she always did, and tried to be grateful.

He had won this boarding-house – *her* boarding-house – from Miles fair and square. He could easily have thrown her and Bella and the children on to the streets. But no, he was giving them board and lodging. Working them hard, admittedly, but at least he was keeping a roof over their heads.

But for some reason, Amelia was finding it difficult to be grateful this morning. That letter from James had unsettled her. She hadn't felt right since it had arrived. It had forced her to a crossroads, made her realise that she must act. She must either return to Liverpool and face a future managing the Whaleys' hotels, or she must stay in Dawson.

'We'd better get back to the kitchen,' Bella whispered.

'You carry on,' Amelia told her. 'I'll join you in a minute.'

She hesitated, then walked to the office and knocked on the door.

'Come in!'

She stepped inside the small room.

'Ah, Mrs Carter.'

His smile was pleasant enough, but you never knew what George Dickinson was thinking. At least, Amelia never knew. She couldn't fathom the man at all.

With her, he had always behaved like the perfect gentleman. Yet, rumours still flew around Dawson about him. Some even hinted that he'd cheated at the poker game, but Amelia refused even to consider that. If she ever believed he had cheated, she would want to kill him with her bare hands.

He was her employer, that was all. It wasn't her place to know how he thought.

'I wondered if I might have a word with you?' she said.

'Of course. Is something wrong?'

'No, not at all.' She took a deep breath, knowing it wasn't her place to speak, yet unable to keep her idea to herself. 'I don't know if you're aware of this, Mr Dickinson, but Bella – Mrs Jackson – has a beautiful singing voice.'

He gazed back at her, puzzled.

'I originally employed Mrs Jackson because of the way she has with the customers,' she explained. 'Of course, she has many other qualities. She's honest and hardworking. But she is also charming with the customers.'

Amelia felt herself blush at that, and it wasn't helped by his dry response.

'I'd noticed.'

Of course, he had known Bella for many years.

'Yes, well – the thing is, before you owned

the boarding-house, I was planning to arrange entertainment.' How it galled her to share her plans with this man. 'I think that if Bella sang in the evenings, business would be even better than it is now.'

She gave him a moment to mull it all over. 'I appreciate that it's no longer my concern,' she went on lamely, 'but I still believe it's a good idea. I think it's worth a try, at any rate.'

He leaned back in his chair – the new chair. On the day he'd taken over owner-ship, he had brought his own chair into this office. Some days, she wished she could burn the thing.

'When the customers have finished eat-ing,' she rushed on, 'we can only offer liquor. Some stay and drink here, but most go elsewhere. They're only here for the food. But if Bella sang, I think people would stay. More than that, I think people would come in especially to hear her.'

'Then we'll give it a try,' he said at last, taking Amelia completely by surprise.

Belatedly, she realised she hadn't even mentioned it to Bella. For all she knew, her friend would refuse.

'She'll need to be paid, of course,' she pointed out. Over her dead body would he get something for nothing.

'Of course,' he agreed in that same dry tone. He suddenly sat forward.

'As you know, Mrs Carter, I was extremely impressed with the way you ran this establishment. I still am. I was thinking of selling it, but now I'm not so sure.'

Selling? His words brought a cold shiver. What would happen to them if he sold up?

'I'll leave it to you,' he told her. 'If the customers approve of your entertainment, we'll make the necessary arrangements as regards extra payment.'

Amelia was about to argue. By the time they knew that, Bella could have been singing for nothing for weeks.

On the other hand, when they knew how successful the venture was, Amelia would know how strong a bargaining tool she had.

'Mel, have you lost all reason?' Bella demanded when, somewhat belatedly, Amelia voiced her idea.

'No. It's a wonderful idea, Bella. You love singing and it cheers people up. It will be a huge success, I'm sure of it.'

'But I can't do it!'

'Nonsense. There's no such word as can't.'

Bella rolled her eyes.

'And what do you suppose I could sing?'

'Anything that takes your fancy.'

'I'd have to learn the words to lots of songs.'

'You would,' Amelia agreed. 'I can help you with that. Think of the extra money, Bella. Think of the children.'

Bella sighed.

'We'll give it a try on Friday night,' Amelia said firmly.

'This coming Friday?' Bella paled at the thought.

'Yes. And then we'll decide how much it's going to cost Mr Dickinson!'

On Friday evening, the building was full. Amelia tried not to raise her hopes too high. This was a new venture and many of the customers would be there out of curiosity. Customers might be thin on the ground when that curiosity had been satisfied.

Bella was nervous. In fact, she looked ill with nerves. Amelia had to confess that, in the same position, she would be terrified.

Amelia had done all she could to notify the city of Dawson that entertainment would be provided, but she'd had no idea that so many people would turn up.

'You'll be fine, Bella,' she said firmly. 'Just think of the extra money. Think of the children. Think of the future. Oh, and just be yourself.' She gazed at the crowd and then pointed. 'Look, Sam Hunter's come to hear you sing.'

Bella looked across the room to where Sam Hunter was standing.

Amelia spotted the blush that reddened her friend's cheeks. She could sympathise. Sam Hunter had a strange effect on her, too.

He had had since the first time they'd met.

Encouraged by shouts and cheers from some of the men, Bella started to sing. She began with 'The Arkansas Traveller', and followed that with 'The Sidewalks of New York'. People were clapping and cheering, and by the time Bella launched into 'The Band Played On', Amelia wondered if they'd ever be able to stop her singing.

Bella was enjoying herself and the customers were having a night to remember.

When Bella took a short break, Sam Hunter approached Amelia.

'I gather this was your idea, Mrs Carter,' he said.

'It was. Bella has a beautiful voice. I thought it might be good for business.'

'For George Dickinson's business?'

'Yes,' she admitted. 'But as you said, Mr Hunter, I won't be content to work for Mr Dickinson for ever.'

He smiled at that. It was a smile that would have had Bella blushing.

'I'm delighted to hear it.'

Bella returned and, laughing happily, agreed to a man's request to sing 'The Band Played On' again.

Amelia noticed that several men threw coins for Bella. Her mind raced. If they saved hard, she and Bella could rent another property. Together, they could open another boarding-house.

Amelia had arrived in Dawson with little more than the clothes on her back. Then, just when she managed to put something aside, Miles had managed to lose it. But until the day Miles lost everything, she had been successful. What's more, she could be successful again.

George Dickinson appeared at her side, startling her. She had expected him to come to see if trade was good, but she hadn't spotted him arrive.

'Well, well, Mrs Carter,' he murmured, gazing around him. 'I congratulate you.'

'Thank you.' At least he wasn't taking the credit.

'You have a surprisingly sharp business mind,' he went on.

'Thank you,' she said again, glowing at the compliment.

He gazed at her for a moment.

'You and I could go far,' he murmured eventually.

She didn't know how to respond to that. Fortunately, she didn't have to as he seemed to gather himself.

'In a few days, we'll discuss future arrangements,' he said briskly. 'I don't intend to let Mrs Jackson sing for nothing, and I certainly intend to reward you as well, Mrs Carter.'

She would look forward to that chat. Meanwhile, she intended to have a good, long think about the future.

When Bella finished singing, her eyes were alight with excitement. Laughing, she took Amelia aside.

'Thank goodness I wore a dress with a pocket,' she said urgently. 'We need to count our reward, Mel. A couple of men handed me pieces of gold. Gold, Mel! And I lost count of the dollar coins...'

Laughing, they hugged each other tight. Oh, yes, Amelia would have a long, hard think about the future before her chat with George Dickinson.

April 1902, Dawson

'You look beautiful tonight,' Bella remarked. Amelia laughed.

'After a day like today? I'm worn out!'

'Nothing wears you out. You have more energy than the rest of us put together.' Bella paused. 'Seriously, Mel, it's wonderful to see you looking so good. Looking as you used to before–'

She broke off, but Amelia knew what she'd been going to say. Before Miles had died. Before she had lost the boarding-house.

'I feel good,' she answered quietly.

George Dickinson was paying her fairly well, and she was managing to put money aside for the future – her and Jack's future. She was now managing the business and, as George would be the first to admit, making a success of it.

There was the money that the men gave to Bella when she sang, too. She and Bella split it between them, and some nights it was a sizeable amount. Mr Dickinson had made no claim on that. Mainly, Amelia suspected, because he had no idea of the sum involved.

She didn't think badly of him, though. In fact, the longer she worked for him, the more she came to admire him. He was a good businessman who was always willing to listen to her ideas, he was well-respected for the most part, and he'd treated them fairly. Even Bella, suspicious of him from the start, was warming to him.

Just as she was thinking of him, he walked in through the door.

Amelia thought how very smart he looked this evening. He was every inch the wealthy, respectable businessman. His clothes were always immaculate.

'Mrs Carter, I wonder if you could spare me a few minutes?' he said.

'Yes, of course.'

He stood back to allow her to walk into the office. While he sat at the desk, Amelia sat on the other chair, facing him.

'Mrs Carter,' he began, 'as you know, I've admired you for a long time now.'

Panic gripped her. Surely he wasn't going to sell up now that the business was doing so well?

'Thank you,' she said, uneasy.

'From the moment I walked over the threshold for the first time, I've been highly impressed. You have a quick mind, you're a hard worker, you know exactly what will bring customers through the door...'

Was he softening her up before telling her that he'd decided to sell up? What would become of them?

'As you know,' he went on, 'I've been happy to leave this business in your capable hands.' He paused. 'We get along very well, too, wouldn't you say?'

'I would, yes,' she replied truthfully.

'So I've been thinking—'

'Yes?'

'How would you feel about entering into a partnership with me?'

Shock had Amelia's mind racing, yet she couldn't think straight. She was so relieved that he wasn't selling the boarding-house that nothing else seemed to register.

'There's no need to give me an answer now. You'll need time to think about it.'

'What sort of partnership?' she asked curiously. 'I'm not wealthy, Mr Dickinson, as you know, and—'

He leaned back in his chair.

'I have four businesses in Dawson,' he reminded her, 'and, of those, this is the most successful. I'm not saying it's the most lucrative, of course, but business here is increasing on an almost daily basis. What I want, Mrs Carter, is your business expertise.'

George Dickinson was saying this to her? Amelia could hardly believe it.

'You know what people want, what they expect,' he went on. 'You possess an understanding of people that I don't have. It's that understanding I want. If my other businesses are to do as well as this one, I need you working alongside me, Mrs Carter.'

'There's River View for a start,' he went on, naming the hotel that Amelia had always admired. 'It should be far busier than it is. Working alongside each other, I think we could make it the finest hotel in Dawson.'

Amelia thought he was probably right.

'Will you think it over?' he asked.

'I will,' she promised him. 'I most certainly will!'

Chapter Seven

May 1903, Dawson

Even as a teenager, George Dickinson hadn't been nervous when in female company. Long before he had made his money, he'd had a presence about him and, these days, women were usually flattered simply to be with him. This evening, however, he was very nervous.

As he ate, he went over and over the words he'd planned to use. For the last few days, those words, mentally uttered a dozen times an hour, had sounded plausible. Now, they seemed so foolish that he doubted he would ever be able to say them.

He could see that Amelia, sitting opposite him, had no idea how he was feeling. She was completely at ease as she watched the other diners.

Why should she guess at his inner turmoil? He had invited her to dinner here so that they could discuss this very hotel. It was business; there was no reason for her to think he had other things on his mind.

He had always lived by the principle that if you didn't ask, you didn't get. Now, he was uncertain. He didn't want to make a fool of himself. The thought of Amelia laughing at him was unbearable.

He was forty-three years old, and fairly attractive to members of the opposite sex, so far as he knew. At least, the evidence had always suggested that. He was also successful and wealthy.

If it were anyone other than Amelia, he would be confident that these qualities were enough. Amelia was different, though. She was as bright, intelligent and ambitious as any man he'd ever met.

True, she had fallen in love and married a fool, but George couldn't condemn her for that. Love was a powerful, unpredictable emotion, as he'd found out for himself.

She was also a very striking woman. Her auburn hair gleamed in the light and her green eyes sparkled with vitality. Here he was, in love with the woman sitting opposite him, and he was as tongue-tied as an errant five-year-old.

Their meal was eaten, their business discussed and, any minute now, Amelia would insist on returning home.

'It's a lovely evening,' he remarked, his throat dry. 'Would you care to walk with me before going back to the boarding-house?'

If she found the question unusual, she didn't show it.

'Yes, I'd like some fresh air.'

They collected their coats and set off, talking about the city in general as they walked along Dawson's still-busy streets.

She took long, confident steps and George merely had to keep pace with her. He wasn't surprised when she headed for the water's edge. He had often seen her there, and he knew she liked to go there to be alone and think.

The wind coming from the water was chilly, but she didn't seem to notice.

'Mrs – Amelia–' They were on first name

terms, yet he often forgot and referred to her as Mrs Carter. How he longed to make her Mrs Dickinson. 'Oh, it's nothing.'

She looked surprised, but didn't comment.

He wished he could rid himself of this feeling of unworthiness. Of course, he knew exactly what it stemmed from – that confounded poker game with her late husband.

Miles Carter, in George's opinion, had been a weak-willed, foolish, rash man. He'd also been gullible and conceited. George had seen the potential of the boarding-house immediately, and he'd wanted to own it.

Convincing Miles Carter that he enjoyed his company had been child's play. In fact, winning the boarding-house had been one of the easiest things George had ever done.

Yet, from the moment it had been his, he'd regretted it. Every time he looked at Amelia, he had to acknowledge that he had cheated her out of everything.

Of course, if he hadn't, he wouldn't have come to know her so well. He wouldn't be on the brink of asking for her hand in marriage, and it hadn't been cheating as such. It might not have been totally honest, though, and if ever she found out...

But he was being ridiculous. No-one knew. She couldn't possibly find out.

171

George was the only person who knew, and Peter Tavener, of course. But Peter was as loyal as the day was long. He had been with George for almost fifteen years now.

'Amelia,' he began again, shivering slightly as a gust of wind blew off the water.

She looked questioningly at him.

'It's a year now since we went into partnership,' he reminded her.

Again, he felt guilty. Financially, their partnership was too one-sided. But he'd worried that if he were more generous, she would walk out on him as soon as she could afford to.

'It is,' she agreed. 'What are you getting at, George?'

'We work well together, don't we? We have the same dreams and ambitions.'

She nodded.

'I believe we do, yes.'

'I've been thinking – oh, the blazes to it, Amelia. I'm trying to propose to you. I'd like to marry you.'

She stumbled as she took an involuntary step back from him.

'That was a foolish way to come out with it,' he apologised, 'but I've been trying to find the right words all evening.'

'Marry you? Oh, my!' She put a hand to her throat and took a huge breath.

'Yes.' He could feel the heat in his face, despite the chill from the water. 'I'm not asking you to love me,' he stumbled on. 'I realise that your heart still belongs to your late husband, but perhaps, in time, you might grow fond of me.'

His face was so tense that it hurt when he attempted a smile.

'Young Jack seems to like me,' he rushed on, hitting what he knew was her weak spot, 'and I know I'd be a good father to him. He's the son I never had, Amelia. Why, he spends hours with me in the office. I've had him counting money.'

She smiled at that.

'I know, and he loves to think he's helping.' The smile quickly faded. 'I don't know what to say,' she confessed. 'This has come as a shock, George.'

She hadn't told him to stop being ridiculous, nor had she given him a straight 'no'. His spirits rose and his heart raced. He could see that she was considering his proposal.

'I'm flattered,' she said, looking straight at him, 'of course I am.'

He waited for the 'but'.

'My main concern is Jack,' she said. 'You're right, he's very fond of you. And he does need a father,' she added vaguely.

'Then let me—'

She waved a finger to silence him.

'As you know, George, I grew up in an orphanage. I had nothing other than a trunk

173

– well, I had my brother and my best friend, of course – but before I was old enough to understand such things, I vowed that I would have security in my life.'

'I can give you that, Amelia.'

'But it's Jack.' She paused as if searching for the right words. 'All I want in the world is to know that his future is secure.'

His racing heartbeat was growing painful.

'Marry me,' he said, struggling to breathe, let alone talk, 'and you and Jack will have that security. I'm a wealthy man, Amelia,' he reminded her. 'I'll change my will,' he blurted out, 'so that, when I die, Jack will inherit everything I have. Everything, Amelia!'

She frowned, playing around with a stone with her foot, and then turned her open gaze on him.

'Why, George? Why would you do that?'

'Because I want to marry you.' He let out his breath. 'Because I want to give you everything. Because I love you, Amelia.'

He reached for her hand and was surprised to realise that it was cold. She was trembling, too.

'I have grown fond of you,' she said, and he was touched to see that she was blushing.

She threw back her head to look at him.

'Yes!' She took a deep breath. 'Yes, I'll marry you, George!'

April 1904, Dawson

There was a spring in Amelia's step as she walked along the street towards the boarding-house.

The streets were busy. A group of noisy children almost knocked her over before running on their way, laughing all the time. She smiled to herself. The sun was shining and it put everyone in a good mood.

She was still smiling when she rounded the corner and collided head-on with Sam Hunter. His hands went out to grip her arms to steady her.

'Mrs Dickinson,' he acknowledged.

'Mr Hunter.'

As always when she saw this man, the years fell away and she was once again on his boat as he brought her and Miles safely to this place.

They had met as strangers, and they'd almost been business partners. Amelia liked to think they had become friends, too.

'You're looking well,' he told her, finally releasing his grip on her arms.

'Thank you. I am well. And you?'

'Yes, yes.'

They stood in the street, people having to walk either side of them.

'I should apologise,' he said, 'for our last meeting. I didn't congratulate you as I should have.'

Amelia had tried to forget their last meeting.

Last December, just days before Christmas, he had walked into the River View Hotel, the hotel that she and George had made into the finest in Dawson, with a face like thunder.

When he had seen her, he'd strode over to her.

'Bella tells me you've married George Dickinson,' he'd said. 'Surely it can't be true?'

'It is,' she had said, taken aback by the expression on his face. He'd seemed almost … well, angry.

For a minute he had simply stared at her. He hadn't said a word. Then he'd shaken his head as if words failed him and strode off.

Amelia hadn't seen him since.

'I'm sorry about that,' he said now. 'Will you accept my belated congratulations?'

'Of course.' She pulled herself up to her full height. 'If you think I married George solely for his money, you'd be very wrong, Mr Hunter.'

Not that it was any business of his. It was just that Amelia valued his friendship. She couldn't bear him to think ill of her.

'Then your husband is a very lucky man,' he said, causing her to blush for some reason. 'But that's George – he always gets what he wants.'

176

What the devil did he mean by that? The words were spoken lightly enough, but Amelia was convinced there was some hidden meaning to them.

She couldn't respond to that.

'Young Jack?' he asked. 'He's well?'

'He is, thank you,' she replied, grateful for the change of subject. 'He's at school at the moment.'

'Excellent.' He shuffled his feet. 'Well, my congratulations to you,' he said gruffly. 'I hope you'll be – I hope you are very happy, Mrs Dickinson.'

'Thank you. I am. We are.'

He always had this effect on her, she thought crossly. It seemed he only had to look at her to render her incoherent.

'It's good to see you again, Mr Hunter.' She gave him a nod and a smile, and carried on her way.

The spring had gone from her step. She wished now that she had said something to him, something to remind him that her husband was a good man. Of course, he'd never said so, not in so many words, but she had the distinct impression that he disapproved of her choice of husband.

He'd had no respect whatsoever for Miles and he seemed to have little more for George. As if it was any of his business, she thought crossly.

By the time she reached the boarding-house, she was completely out of sorts. She found Bella in the office, singing to herself, and her mood immediately lifted.

'I've just bumped into a friend of yours,' she told her. 'Sam Hunter.'

'Sam's in town?' Bella's face lit up, as it always did at the mention of the handsome river boat pilot.

'He is.'

'Did he say he'd be coming here this evening?'

Amelia had to smile to herself.

'He didn't mention it, no.'

She sat down opposite Bella and cast an eye down the ledger that was now completed in Bella's neat hand. Since Amelia had married George and moved to the River View Hotel, Bella had taken full responsibility for the running of the boarding-house.

'I don't think he – Sam Hunter, that is – I don't think he has a very high opinion of George.'

'You know what it's like, Mel,' Bella said with a shrug. 'People are jealous of George and his money. Rumours have always flown around about him.'

'Hm.' Amelia frowned.

'Hey, come on, Amelia, you know they're false. Good heavens, you've been married to the man for almost a year. He's a good man.'

'At least you've changed your opinion of him,' Amelia said with a smile.

Bella had known George for years and never had a good word to say about him, but Amelia had never discovered the reason for it.

'I have,' Bella said seriously. 'When I first knew him, he was young.' She gave a rueful smile. 'George was ambitious, ruthless, even. He stopped at nothing to get what he wanted. But that was a long time ago. He's changed, Mel.'

'He is a good man, isn't he?'

'He is. He's been good to us, all of us, ever since he took over this place.' She chuckled. 'And he's as proud as can be of you and Jack.'

Amelia was pleased with Bella's verdict. She trusted her friend's judgement, and it made it easier to dismiss the rumours she had heard lately.

Marriage to George had come as something of a shock. Their wedding day had been like something from a fairy tale. George had spared no expense in giving Amelia, and the residents of Dawson, a day to remember.

Amelia still didn't know exactly how wealthy George was, but his extravagance on their wedding day had surprised her. She hadn't complained, though.

The only dark cloud in her life was

George's gambling, and perhaps she was being silly about that. She hated risk of any sort, and she especially hated gambling.

She had seen it all before with Miles. She'd grown used to his moods, the good days when he had won and he'd showered her with cash, and the bad days when she'd had to pay off his debts. She had grown used to it, but never liked it.

Perhaps she still hadn't recovered from realising that Miles had gambled away their boarding-house.

But George, she felt sure, was far more careful than Miles. All the same, it had come as a shock to realise just how much time he spent sitting around a card table with his friends.

'You are happy, aren't you, Mel?'

Amelia replaced her concerned frown with a bright smile.

'Happy? Of course I am. What girl could want for more?'

She should be happy. What she'd said was true; she had everything a person could dream of. She had the most wonderful son in the world, she had a good, kind, generous husband and she wanted for nothing.

Twenty-four years ago, when she and Ivy had been eight years old, Amelia had vowed that, one day, she would fill her beloved trunk with the finest clothes imaginable. Now, she had all the clothes she wanted.

It was just as well, she thought with amusement, as her trunk was full of all sorts of things – like the sheets and pillow-cases that Matron had given her and Miles on their wedding day. They had been mended often over the years and, even though she had new ones, she would always treasure them.

She was happy. Just because George was fond of his gambling didn't mean anything. He was a successful businessman, not a fool.

'Do you think Sam Hunter will come in this evening?' Bella asked.

'I've no idea,' Amelia replied with a smile.

She looked forward to these afternoon chats with Bella, and she pulled up a chair and made herself comfortable.

'I know it's none of my business,' she began, 'but I've been curious for – oh, years now. Just how far do you and Mr Hunter go back?'

Bella smiled fondly.

'A long time.' She sat back in her own chair, a gentle smile on her face. 'He and Ben – that's my husband – were great pals.'

'Do you still miss him? Your Ben?'

'I do,' Bella said softly. 'He was a right devil at times, and he had a temper, but yes, I miss him. I miss him for the children's sake, too. It doesn't seem right.'

'It doesn't.'

'Sam helped me through,' Bella confided. 'As soon as he heard that Ben had died on the Chilkoot Pass, he looked out for me. He gave me money, and he brought me here. He said I should come to Dawson because there would always be work to be found, but I think it was because he wanted to keep an eye on me and the young ones. He felt he owed it to Ben.'

'Are you in love with him?' Amelia asked curiously.

'No!' Bella spluttered with laughter at the idea. 'He's a good man, though. A handsome man, too,' she added with a twinkle.

Amelia couldn't deny that.

They talked of other things and Amelia relaxed – until Bella asked where George was.

'He's away,' Amelia murmured. 'Some of his friends are meeting up and–' She didn't know for sure that they were gambling, so she kept her doubts to herself. 'Just catching up on each other's news. He'll be back after the weekend.' She rose to her feet.

'It's time I collected Jack from school,' she said with a bright smile.

January 1905, Liverpool

'Mam!'

'Well, hold still, for goodness sake.' Ivy was running out of patience. 'You'll not have your photograph taken looking like that,

182

young lad!'

Ivy despaired of her son, she really did. Martha was as gentle and biddable as it was possible to be – she took after her father. But Albert was as headstrong and stubborn as his aunt Amelia.

The twins were nine years old now, and although they were well behaved in company, Albert especially could be a trial. He was full of mischief.

Ivy had been thrilled when Matron had told them of her Christmas gift to them. She had arranged – and paid – for them to go to a studio and have a family photograph taken.

'You'll be able to send one to Amelia,' she'd said.

Ivy had been delighted!

Amelia had sent them a photograph taken on her wedding day, and Ivy had rejoiced at the smile on her face. They had all studied the photograph, trying to guess at the man behind the broad smile. George was just as handsome as Amelia had written in her letters. He wasn't as tall as Miles, but handsome nevertheless.

'You're not too old to have your ears boxed,' Ivy told Albert sternly. 'Now, stand still while I comb your hair.'

James came downstairs looking smart but uncomfortable.

Why was it, Ivy wondered, that it was such

a task getting her family dressed up?

Lizzie was easy enough, thank goodness. Four years old now, she had beautiful thick curls falling down her back and was happy enough to let her mother or her big sister brush them until they gleamed.

'Are we all ready?' James asked hopefully, tugging at his collar.

Ivy shook her head in despair.

'These three are, just about. You'll need to keep an eye on them while I change into my dress, Jimmy.' She rushed off for the stairs. 'And don't let them touch anything!' she called out.

What his response to that was, Ivy didn't know, but she heard the children giggling. The sound brought a smile to her own face.

Finally, they were ready.

They had decided to walk to the studio, calling at the orphanage to collect Matron on the way. Ivy had insisted that she be in the photographs, too.

'Mel will want a photograph of you!' she'd insisted.

Matron, reluctantly, had agreed.

It always felt odd to Ivy to walk up the front path to the orphanage. Memories rushed at her – Amelia racing up the path laughing, the two of them with their heads bent as they planned their futures.

The building hadn't changed. Ivy thanked the Lord that she no longer lived there, but she still had a certain fondness for St Joseph's. She knew James did, too.

'Matron's not been well these past couple of days,' Doris told them in a whisper.

'Not well?' Ivy looked at James. She couldn't ever remember Matron being unwell.

'What's wrong with her?' James asked.

Doris shrugged.

'The doctor's given her a tonic, but it don't seem to have done much good. She's out of bed, ready to have her photograph took, but she looks bad.'

The sun was shining, casting a beam of light through the window, but Ivy shuddered.

For the first time, Ivy realised just how quickly the years were passing. They had thought Matron was old when they'd been children, but children always thought someone over thirty was ancient!

The truth hit Ivy with a jolt. Matron had passed her seventieth birthday. When she came into the front hall, Ivy saw just how ill she looked.

'Are you feeling all right, Matron? I mean, well enough to come with us?' she asked.

'Of course I am. The walk will do me good. We'll walk slowly, mind,' she warned them.

James exchanged a look with Ivy and she knew just what he was thinking. Matron had aged. She looked frail.

They talked of Amelia and the children as they walked, and Ivy managed to convince herself that Matron would soon be her old self again. Once the damp, cold winter months were behind them, she would be feeling fit and well.

It was only a short walk and it didn't take too long for the photographer, a young man bursting with confidence, to arrange them to his satisfaction. Ivy only hoped the children weren't pulling silly faces at the crucial moment.

As they walked away from the studio, they laughed at themselves and speculated on how they would look when the photographs were printed. Ivy wondered if she was the only one to notice that Matron didn't laugh quite so loudly.

When they left the orphanage to walk home, Ivy tried to remember another time when the children hadn't been given milk and biscuits. She couldn't.

'She's a bit under the weather, love, that's all,' James said, guessing at her thoughts. 'She'll be right again soon enough.'

'Yes.' Ivy gave him a bright smile. 'Yes, of course she will.'

But she wasn't convinced.

April 1905, Dawson
Amelia watched George pack his suitcase.

She wished she could ask him not to go, but she couldn't.

He hadn't told her where he was going exactly but, despite his saying it was 'business', she knew a game of poker was involved. Several games, she suspected. She knew because she had overheard him talking to Bill Constantine about it.

She was used to George's comings and goings, and she didn't usually mind, but today was different.

Today, she had raced back from the doctor's, ready to share her exciting news with him, but the sight of that suitcase took the joy from the day. It wasn't the right time to tell him.

If it had been Miles – but it wasn't Miles so it was foolish to think along those lines. Besides, Miles, too, would probably be heading off for a game of poker.

George would be back next week, and she would make sure they had a quiet evening together. Her news would wait.

She couldn't even begin to imagine how he would feel when she told him she was carrying his child. True, he couldn't have loved Jack more, but did he want a child of his own? They had never spoken of it so she didn't know.

'Why the frown?' he asked suddenly.

'Nothing.' She replaced the frown with a quick smile. 'It's just that I thought you were leaving in the morning.'

'I am, my dear, but I'll be leaving early and I have an appointment this evening. I'll be back late from that and won't have time to pack in the morning.'

It wasn't her place to ask where that meeting was or what it was about. Neither was it her place to suggest what he did with his money or his time. He was a good husband and a good father to Jack. She should be grateful for that.

The clock struck the hour.

'I'll have to rush, Amelia. You know I hate being late.' He came forward and took her in his arms. 'Don't wait up for me tonight.'

'All right.'

She wouldn't have the chance to talk to him tonight, so she'd leave it for a week. As soon as he was home, she would tell him he was about to become a father.

Her spirits lifted immediately. He would be thrilled, she knew it.

'I've been thinking,' he murmured, 'about us taking a trip.'

'A trip? But we can't, George. There's so much to be done here.'

He shrugged at that, and there was a teasing light in his eyes.

'I thought we could go to England – maybe next year.' He nodded at the photograph of James, Ivy, Matron and the children that sat on the dresser. 'It's high time I met your family, my dear.'

'England? Oh, my!' Her heart raced at the possibility. 'England,' she said again.

Already she was walking the familiar streets of Liverpool.

'Could we, George? Could we really?'

'Of course we could.' He kissed her soundly on the lips. 'And now I must go.'

He walked out of their bedroom, leaving Amelia alone with her excitement. Her mind was racing, her imagination knew no limits. England! Jack would be able to meet his cousins.

Laughing, she reached for her coat and ran out of the hotel and into the street. If she didn't talk to someone, she would burst.

She raced the length of the street to the boarding-house, where she found Bella in the kitchen.

Annie, the new girl they had employed, was working alongside her. She looked startled and embarrassed to see Amelia. Amelia had no idea why. According to Bella, the girl was hardworking and conscientious.

Annie nodded and smiled, and then carried on washing pots.

'What brings you here at this time of the day?' Bella asked.

'News.' She looked at Annie and then back at Bella.

'Let's go to the office,' Bella said. 'I won't be long, Annie,' she added for the young girl's benefit.

'Annie looked embarrassed about something,' Amelia murmured as they walked along to the office.

'I should think she did. Don't you remember how flustered we used to be when the boss walked in unannounced?'

'Well, yes, but–'

'You married the boss,' Bella reminded her, 'so now you're the boss.'

Amelia hadn't thought of it like that.

'So what's this news?' Bella asked with amusement. 'You look fit to burst, Mel.'

'I am.' Amelia closed the office door behind them. 'I'm pregnant!'

'No!' Bella clapped her hands and then hugged Amelia tight.

'Oh, Mel, I'm so pleased for you! What does George reckon to it?'

'I haven't told him yet,' Amelia explained, 'so you're not to utter a word. He's got a meeting lined up tonight and then he's leaving for a week. I'm going to tell him when he gets home.'

Bella smiled.

'He'll be thrilled, Mel,' she said softly.

'Yes. Yes, I think so.'

'Well, well, well. How exciting. A brother or sister for Jack.'

'Yes.' Amelia's smile was huge. 'And

there's something else. It's typical of George to drop this on me just as he's walking out of the door, but he says we can go to England to visit James and Ivy–' Amelia burst into tears.

'Whatever is it, Mel?'

Laughing and crying, Amelia shook her head.

'I'm so happy, I can hardly believe it all,' she said, wiping the tears from her face.

It was a few minutes before she composed herself.

'Marrying George was the best thing I could have done,' she said softly. 'I didn't think I'd ever be able to love him, but–' She gazed at her friend. 'I do, Bella. Not in the way that I loved Miles perhaps, but I do love him.'

'I know you do,' Bella said, smiling. 'Aw, I'm so happy for you.'

They talked of England, and of James, Ivy and the children before Amelia took her leave.

That evening, although she had planned an early night, Amelia was far too excited to settle. Besides, she wanted to have a few minutes with George before he left for the week. She needed to tell him how grateful she was to him, and how much she appreciated all that he did for her and Jack.

Her son was sleeping soundly and she stood for a while, gazing down at him. How

191

she loved him!

Five years old now, he seemed to grow more like his father every day. He was tall for his age, and his light hair was sometimes a painful reminder of Miles.

She quietly crept out of his room, and then left the hotel to take a walk along the deserted street.

She thought of calling at the boarding-house again, but she didn't want company. She was more than happy walking alone in the chilly evening air with her thoughts.

Mostly, her thoughts centred around the child she was carrying – hers and George's. She also thought of taking that trip to England to see James and Ivy and the nephew and nieces she had never seen. And Matron. How good it would be to see Matron again!

It was too dark to walk far and, besides, George would be home soon. She walked slowly back to the hotel, admiring its size and its fine lines as soon as it came into view.

The noise, a loud bang, startled her. It sounded as if it had come from the hotel. She quickened her pace, her heart racing. Whatever had made such a noise?

There was another identical bang, like the sound of a gun being fired.

She broke into a run, her feet clattering on the quiet street. The noise would have woken Jack and he'd be frightened – especially when he realised she wasn't there.

She was a few yards from the hotel's entrance when she saw that her way into the building was blocked. Something was lying half in and half out of the doorway.

Not something, she realised with a sick feeling – someone.

'Oh, no!'

Her feet were leaden as she tried to coax them forward. There was enough light coming from the hotel for her to recognise George's fine jacket.

She felt paralysed with fear as she stood over her husband's motionless form.

'Help!' she screamed, finally galvanised into movement.

'Help! Quickly! Oh, please, someone help! My husband's been shot!'

Chapter Eight

April 1905, Dawson

There was a scream locked inside Amelia's throat, and it was taking all she had to keep it there. She longed to scream, shout and rail against the injustice of life. Instead, she stared blankly ahead.

She was sitting in the lounge of the hotel – George's hotel, George's and hers – surrounded by people she had known for years, yet she felt as if she was watching and listening to everything from a great distance.

She had no real idea of the time. About nine or ten o'clock in the morning, she supposed.

The children – her beloved Jack, and Bella's Jane and Isaac – were talking quietly. Their heads were bent and they looked subdued. They were as confused as everyone else, poor things.

Jack sidled up to her, put his arms around her waist and buried his head against her.

'It'll be all right, my darling boy,' she whispered, hugging him tight.

That's what Bella had said to her – 'It'll be all right.' It's what people said when they had no idea what else to say and when they couldn't take anything in.

News of the shooting had travelled fast and Bella had been the first to arrive. She had stayed with Amelia all night.

My husband is dead – Amelia mentally repeated those words, but still they made no sense at all.

People were still milling around outside the hotel. A constable from the Royal Northwest Mounted Police was talking to them.

'I'll stay with you again tonight, Mel,'

Bella said, giving her hand a squeeze. 'Shall I take the children off for their breakfast? Yes, I'll do that. I'll cook something for you later. You have to eat.'

Without waiting for an answer, Bella took Jack by the hand, gathered her own children to her, and took them off to the kitchen.

That scream was still locked inside Amelia's throat. She couldn't grasp what had happened.

Minutes later, she looked up to find the constable from the Royal North-west Mounted Police gazing down at her.

'Constable Dover,' he told her grimly. 'I need to talk to you, Mrs Dickinson,' he added.

Mrs Dickinson. She had barely got used to her new name and now the man who had given her that name was gone. Gone without even knowing of the child she was carrying.

'Of course,' she said, rising to her feet.

'Somewhere private,' the constable added.

Amelia took him to George's office. The room looked as it always did. It was full of George. His handwriting was in the ledger that lay open on his desk.

The constable, standing tall and proud in his red serge jacket, looked around him.

Amelia had always had a great deal of respect for the Royal North-west Mounted Police. She had cheered madly when, last

195

year, King Edward VII, in recognition of their men's distinguished service in the South African war, had granted the prefix Royal.

It was these policemen who had insisted that everyone coming to the Yukon had enough supplies. Amelia might have cursed their rules on the journey over the Chilkoot Pass, but she knew it was largely thanks to them that a lot more people hadn't perished. It was this same police force that had forbidden the use of handguns and kept the area safe. More importantly, perhaps, they had turned a blind eye to the pettier crimes so that life trickled along in relative safety. She had always respected them, yet she couldn't warm to the constable standing before her. He seemed an unsympathetic, cold man.

'Who did this to my husband?' she asked him, her voice shaky.

'That's what I intend to find out.' He turned the pages in the ledger on George's desk.

'Perhaps you would like to tell me all you know.'

Amelia didn't know how to answer that. The truth was, she knew nothing. 'My husband was out for the evening,' she said.

'Where?'

No, she couldn't take to this man at all.

'I don't know,' she admitted. 'He told me

it was a business meeting.'

Even to her own ears, that sounded lame. Few people conducted business so late in the evening.

'Did your husband gamble, Mrs Dickinson?'

This constable was annoying her now.

'He occasionally gambled, yes,' she said, 'but I can't see what that has to do with anything. My husband has been shot, constable. Your job, surely, is to keep guns out of Dawson.'

'It is,' he agreed. 'Your first husband was a gambler, too, I believe.'

'Miles? What does Miles have to do with anything?'

'Possibly nothing,' the constable allowed. 'He died from typhoid fever, am I right?'

'Yes.'

'Perhaps you would care to tell me where you were last night,' he went on. 'I gather you were away from the hotel at the time of the shooting.'

'I was. I'd been for a walk.'

'Do you often take walks at that time of night?'

'Not often, no. I was waiting for George to come home – I was happy–' She broke off. The reason for her happiness was none of this man's business. 'I simply wanted some fresh air,' she said.

'I see. And where did you go?'

'I just walked along the street,' she told him.

She was a breath away from bursting into tears and finally letting go of that scream, but she wouldn't give this man the satisfaction of seeing her lose control. She kept her shaking hands in her lap.

'Did you see anyone? Talk to anyone?'

'No.'

'Did you hear the sound of a gun being fired?'

'I did, yes.' She shuddered as she recalled the sound. 'As I was walking back to the hotel, I heard two shots. I didn't know where they had come from. I only knew that I must get back to the hotel quickly as I thought the noise would wake my son.'

'He's five years old, yes?'

'Yes.'

'So you hurry back to the hotel,' the constable mused, 'and although you hear the gunshots, you don't see anything.'

'I didn't see anyone, no. I was too far away.'

'Did your husband have enemies?'

'Not that I know of. No, of course he didn't. Why should he?'

The constable shrugged.

'People may have been jealous of his success,' she said, 'but that's been the case for many years. No-one would want him dead.'

'Someone did,' the constable pointed out mildly.

He was right, of course. Someone *had* wanted George dead.

'You do realise,' he went on, 'that it's against the law to own a gun?'

She frowned at him.

'Of course I realise that.'

He rubbed his thick moustache thoughtfully.

'The thing is, Mrs Dickinson, we've been looking into your husband's affairs recently. There are things we don't like – handguns and marked cards.'

Amelia gasped at that.

'Did your husband own a gun?' Constable Dover asked.

'No.' Amelia felt the colour rush to her face at the lie.

George had owned a gun. She had seen it once. When she'd asked about it, he'd been abrupt, told her it was none of her business.

'Are you sure?' the constable asked.

'My husband may have owned a gun,' she said at last. 'I don't know.'

'And if he did have a gun, where might he have kept it?' She could hear his sarcasm. He didn't believe her.

'I've no idea. I do seem to recall seeing him cleaning a gun once, but I have no idea where it was kept.' She rose to her feet. 'Constable–'

'Dover,' he reminded her.

'Whoever killed my husband is out there somewhere.' The spread of her arms took in the whole of Dawson. 'If you were as interested in knowing who that person is as I am, you would be out there now. I'm sorry, but I can't help you.'

He looked at her for a long moment.

'I'll need to speak to you again.' He touched his hat. 'Good morning, ma'am.'

When he walked out of the room, leaving her alone, Amelia dropped to the chair at George's desk and buried her face in her hands. Her whole body had started to shake and there was nothing she could do to stop it.

What had he meant when he'd said they had been looking into George's affairs recently? And why all those questions about gambling? The gun – how had he known that George kept a gun?

April 1905, Liverpool
Ivy was having to keep a very tight grip on her tongue. It was Easter.

It was also St George's Day. The city of Liverpool was swathed in bunting. So what was wrong with her husband? He looked as if he had lost a pound and found a farthing.

They had been to church and had lunch, and now, having collected Matron from the orphanage, they were enjoying the Easter parade. Or supposed to be enjoying it. With James scowling, it was proving difficult. He'd been sharp with the children, too.

The whole of Liverpool was in a party mood. Everyone was happy and enjoying the day to the full. Everyone except the Penrose family, she thought grimly.

'I soon won't recognise my own city,' Matron mused as James pushed her through the park.

It was sad to see Matron in a wheelchair. In fact, the first time she'd seen her, Ivy had been quite upset. It was a sign that they were growing older, that one day, Matron wouldn't be with them.

That was another reason James ought to be thankful for this day. He had his family – the twins and his lovely Lizzie – with him, and Matron, despite being confined to her chair, was happy and enjoyed the day.

'It all brings work to the city,' James replied, gazing around them at the signs of building work.

'It does that, young James. Oh, yes, it's a good thing. The city's thriving.' She laughed at the twins, hanging on to their sister by one hand each, raced off ahead. 'That's not the only thing that's thriving. What do you feed those young ones on, Ivy?'

Ivy smiled fondly.

'Not enough, they tell me. They're always hungry. Always.'

201

Young Lizzie was the worst of the three children. Four years old now, she ate almost as much as her father. Martha and Albert, seven years old, could eat them out of house and home, too.

Ivy was still working for Rose Hodge, though, so they had no money worries. Rose had become a friend, a good friend, and James was quite happy with the arrangement.

She looked across at him. He was frowning as he pushed Matron's chair. His thoughts were miles away, she realised.

He caught her watching him and gave her a smile. It was a tight, forced smile and Ivy was alarmed. Whatever was wrong with him?

Whatever it was, it had quite ruined Ivy's day. She had been looking forward to this so much. She loved it when they all dressed in their Sunday best and had nothing to do other than enjoy the day. How was she supposed to enjoy it, though, when James clearly had things on his mind?

They left Matron at St Joseph's and walked slowly from the orphanage back home.

Fortunately, the children had worn themselves out and there weren't too many arguments before they were in bed and asleep.

'Right,' Ivy said grimly, finally having James to herself, 'whatever's wrong with you? It had better be good, too,' she warned him, 'because you've ruined everyone's day!'

He looked amazed at that.

'You've certainly ruined mine,' she scolded.

Thinking about it, she didn't suppose Matron or the children had noticed his strange mood. They had been lucky enough to take pleasure from the day. But Ivy knew her husband well, and that faraway look in his eyes had worried her.

'Sorry, love,' he murmured.

He was gazing at the fire, watching the sparks fly up the chimney. It was chilly this evening, and the warmth from the fire was welcome.

'I had–' He thought for a moment, frowning. 'I don't know if you'd call it a dream or what,' he admitted, 'but I've had this horrible feeling that Amelia's in some sort of trouble.' He gave her a weak smile. 'It sounds daft, love, I know, but I haven't been able to shake it off all day.'

It didn't sound daft at all. James and Amelia were twins; they had always shared a special bond. Martha and Albert were the same; when they weren't fighting with each other, they had an uncanny knack of knowing what the other was thinking.

'What sort of trouble?' she asked, worried herself now.

'I don't know.' He reached for her hand and pulled her on to his lap. 'I expect I'm being daft.'

'Oh, I hope so, Jimmy.' Ivy slipped her arm around his neck, glad of his familiar warmth. 'In her last letter – and it's only three days since that arrived – she sounded fine. No, she sounded better than fine; she sounded truly happy.'

'She did,' James agreed, and he seemed slightly reassured.

'Young Jack's doing well,' she went on, 'and George sounds perfect for her. Better than Miles,' she added, although she immediately felt guilty for voicing that particular thought.

'He does,' James agreed, having no such qualms.

'I wish we could meet him,' Ivy said wistfully. 'He must be a special sort of man. Amelia has a great deal of respect for him.'

Ivy shivered, despite the warmth from the fire. Was Amelia in trouble?

'I'll make us a cup of tea.'

She had wanted something to do with her hands, but it wasn't helping. Letters from Canada took ages to reach Liverpool. Just because Amelia had sounded happy in her last letter, it didn't follow that she was still happy, or safe.

She carried the tea back into the sitting-room, and retook her place on James's knee.

'Tell me about this dream or whatever it was,' she said.

'There's not much to tell,' he said

thoughtfully. 'I woke up with a start. It was probably around midnight. I've no idea what woke me. It was as if Amelia was calling out, asking for help.'

The bond between twins was strong and Ivy trusted James's instincts. Now, she, too, was convinced that Amelia was in some sort of trouble.

'Do you know what I wish?' she asked, and he smiled.

'I do, love. You wish she had never laid eyes on Miles Carter and never gone across that ocean.'

Ivy chuckled. Of course he knew; she'd told him often enough over the years. But it wasn't funny. The worst thing of all, of course, was that if Amelia was in trouble, there was nothing they could do.

'She's got George to look after her now,' Ivy pointed out. 'If she is in trouble, George will take care of things.'

'Yes. Yes, he will,' James agreed.

They sat quietly for a few minutes, drinking their tea, but Ivy knew that they were both imagining all sorts of horrors.

'I hope she's all right,' Ivy whispered.

James hugged her tight, but he said nothing. There were no words.

Ivy would write to her first thing in the morning and pray that soon they had a letter from Amelia – one that made them laugh at their fears.

April 1905, Dawson

Bella was at her wits' end. None of this was fair. They had buried George that very morning, yet, because the whole of Dawson was agog, Amelia wasn't being allowed to grieve as a young woman should. She was trying far too hard to be brave and strong, and it was taking its toll.

Bella was also worried about the police. Constable Dover and his colleagues had been asking far too many questions for her liking. They seemed to know a lot more about George than they were willing to tell. Those questions weren't aimed at those closest to George, either. Everyone in Dawson, it seemed, had been questioned.

Of course they would want to find George's killer, Bella accepted that. They all wanted that.

If George had been killed in a bar brawl, that would have been different. Bar brawls were common enough. But this shooting was a serious matter as far as the police were concerned. No handguns were allowed, by law, and the police did a good job enforcing that law. The fact that someone was keeping a gun in Dawson, or had perhaps visited Dawson with a gun, was very serious indeed.

Her thoughts returned to her friend.

Amelia, tired to her bones, had gone for a

lie down, and Bella hoped the rest would do her some good.

Bella needing answers, was on her way to see Sam Hunter. She was glad he was in town; he might know why the police were questioning everyone. If they had learned anything and were close to catching George's killer, he would probably know about that, too. How he came by this information, Bella had no idea, but Sam always seemed to know what was going on.

She spotted him when she reached the water's edge. He was about to climb down from his boat.

'Sam!' She called his name and waved.

He waved back, left his boat and began striding towards her.

'How's Mrs Dickinson?' he asked immediately.

'Oh, Sam!' It was so good to see a friend. 'I don't know,' she admitted. 'At the moment, she's taking a rest. That's rare in itself as she's not the type to rest, normally. She likes to keep pushing herself until she drops.'

'The shock will have exhausted her,' he said.

'Yes.'

They walked along the water's edge, both wrapped up in thick coats.

'Have you heard anything, Sam? The police seemed to be talking to everyone in Dawson about it. Why? What's going on?'

'I don't know,' he answered. 'I had Constable Dover looking around my boat for almost an hour this morning. He seemed interested in whether or not I knew that George Dickinson owned a gun–'

'They asked Mel the same thing!' she broke in. 'In the end, she had to tell him that he did.'

'I told them the same thing,' Sam said, nodding. 'As his one-time business partner, I suppose they assumed that I would know. They also wanted to know about his gambling habits.'

'Oh, for–'

'So would I,' Sam put in grimly, 'if I were them. George Dickinson was a cheat, Bella.'

'No, Sam, you're wrong. I always thought so, too, and when Amelia first met him, I told her not to trust him. But he changed.'

Sam pulled a face at that.

'If he was dishonest,' Bella pointed out, 'you wouldn't have gone into business with him.'

'He fooled me,' Sam said simply. 'I trusted him because I needed him,' he added. 'The capital he offered to bring to the business was too good to turn down. But he was a cheat, Bella. It cost me – oh, yes, it cost me dearly to buy out his share in the business, but it was the best thing I ever did. I never trusted the man.'

He gave her a questioning look.

'Didn't you ever find it odd that he be-friended someone like Miles Carter?' he asked her.

'No,' she replied, frowning. 'They both had a mutual friend. I remember George coming to the boarding-house one day and telling Miles that their friend was staying at the hotel. Their friendship started from there.'

'How coincidental,' Sam said dryly.

Bella decided to dismiss his distrust of George.

'Have the police found out anything?' she wanted to know.

'I've no idea,' he told her. 'If I hear any-thing, I'll let you know. Judging by the way the place is still swarming with constables, I very much doubt it.'

They fell into step and walked away from the water and towards the town.

'How are the children?' Sam asked.

'They're fine,' Bella told him, smiling fondly. 'Poor Jack's a bit lost at the moment, and they're watching over him. It's good to see. They're good kids.'

'They are.'

'Mind you,' she added, 'Isaac can be a little devil at times. You'll never guess what he–'

'Bella! Oh, Bella!'

Bella's heart leapt into her throat at the sight of Annie running towards her. She had left Annie at the hotel with instructions to make sure Amelia had everything she needed. Bella had also told the girl to try to persuade Amelia to eat something nourishing if she should leave her bed.

She and Sam both broke into a run to meet up with Annie.

'I've been for Doctor Lewis,' Annie gasped, out of breath. 'It's Mrs Dickinson. She's taken poorly!'

Bella didn't waste time with words. Besides, none sprang to mind that told her how she felt. All she wanted was to get back to her friend, her very best friend.

The three of them ran back to the hotel.

They arrived at the same time as Dr Lewis, and it was he who went to Amelia's room, leaving the three of them to wait downstairs.

When he finally joined them, his expression gave nothing away. He was a good doctor, young and thorough.

'She's all right?' Bella asked, fear raising her voice.

He nodded.

'And the baby?' she persisted.

She realised, belatedly, that as neither Sam or Annie knew about the baby, she should have kept quiet. It was too late now, though.

'Yes. For the moment, everything is fine,' Dr Lewis told her, 'but Mrs Dickinson needs to rest for a while. Perhaps more importantly, she needs to eat.'

Bella knew that. Amelia could go for days without remembering to eat a meal.

'I'll see to it,' Bella promised.

She would, too. Amelia could protest all she liked, but she would eat and rest.

'I'll call tomorrow morning,' the doctor promised.

'Thank you.'

Bella offered up a silent prayer of thanks. Amelia was all right, and the baby was all right. At the moment, nothing else mattered.

Bella knew that she couldn't take much more, never mind Amelia. Amelia was the most honest, kind, thoughtful person she had ever known – it was so unfair.

'I must go to her,' she told the others. 'And coax her to eat something.' No, not coax. She would order her to eat. In fact, she would cook a nourishing meal and stand over her friend until every mouthful had been swallowed.

'Bella.' Sam touched her arm. 'You know where I am if you need me.'

'Yes.' And, as ever, she was grateful to him.

'I'll let you know if I hear anything,' he promised, and he walked out of the hotel.

May 1905, Dawson

Amelia stood for a moment outside the door of the hotel and tried to take stock.

211

She was a strong, independent woman. Everyone said so. In which case, she could cope with all this.

Where she had been going wrong, she had decided, was by trying to blot everything from her mind. She'd withdrawn into herself, too. She hadn't eaten, she hadn't even left the hotel. No wonder she had started feeling so ill; ill enough to throw poor Annie into a panic.

But she was fine. What's more, she knew it was high time she put her life in order.

With a determined spring in her step, she set off for Mr Manilow's office. Mr Manilow had been George's lawyer and, although Amelia had written to the man twice, she had received nothing from him.

She knew – at least, she was fairly confident – that, on their marriage, George had amended his will so that his property would fall to her. She had asked that he make provision for Jack, but he'd told her that everything he owned would be left to her.

'What if I die first?' she had wanted to know.

'Amelia,' he'd said, laughing, 'you'll outlive us all. But,' he'd added seriously, 'in that case, everything we have will go to Jack.'

If only he'd known about the child she was carrying, she thought sadly.

But, by rights, the hotel – everything – belonged to her now. She needed to know where she stood so that she and Jack could pick up the pieces of their lives. With or without George, she had to provide for Jack and their unborn child. Her own feelings must be put aside.

As luck would have it, she reached the office at the same time as Mr Manilow. He frowned when he saw her, as she knew that he had been trying to avoid her. Indeed, if he'd seen her coming, she was sure he would have avoided her again.

'Mr Manilow,' she greeted him. 'I thought I'd better call in person. I've written two letters that, as yet, haven't prompted so much as an acknowledgement from you.'

He looked up and down the street. Something was wrong, she thought curiously.

'You'd better come inside, Mrs Dickinson,' he said with some reluctance.

Once inside his office, he offered Amelia a seat. She took it and waited for him to speak.

'This is very difficult,' he said at last, 'but I've had instructions – from the police – that the matter of your husband's last will and testament cannot be dealt with until...'

'Until?' she prompted.

'Until the police have caught your husband's – killer,' he said quietly.

'What? But that could take months,' she pointed out.

'Yes, indeed.' He shuffled some papers on

his desk. 'Although I'm sure the police will reassess the situation if that is the case.'

'But what about the hotel?' she asked. 'What about my husband's other businesses? What's to happen to those in the meantime?'

'As much as is possible,' he said, 'they are to carry on as normal.'

'But that's preposterous!'

'It is very – awkward,' he agreed.

'My husband's will,' she began, but he cut her off.

'I'm sorry, Mrs Dickinson, but I'm not allowed to discuss the matter at the present time.'

He wouldn't meet her gaze, she noticed. Why, oh, why, had George dealt with this man?

'I'm sorry,' he said again. 'Really, I am. At the moment, however, there is nothing I can do. I ask for your patience, Mrs Dickinson.'

Patience? Amelia knew exactly what her friends would say, that she had been absent when that particular quality had been handed out.

She rose to her feet.

'Then, for the moment, there's nothing I can do, is there?' she said. 'However, I'm far from happy with the situation.'

He made a few more apologetic noises as Amelia swept out of his office.

There was something she could do, she

214

thought angrily. She could have a word with that Constable Dover. He had no right to do this. None whatsoever.

Her opportunity came sooner than she could have hoped.

The constable was at the hotel, waiting for her, when she arrived.

His questions could keep, she thought crossly. First, he could answer a few of *her* questions.

'Constable Dover,' she said, 'the very man. I've been to see my lawyer – my husband's lawyer – and he informs me that he's had instructions from you–' To be fair, he hadn't mentioned this man's name, but that was by the by. 'From you,' she continued, 'to leave my husband's last will and testament unread.'

'That's right, ma'am,' he answered, his hat in his hand for once.

'That's madness!' she declared. 'My husband was a successful businessman. His businesses won't run themselves, will they? What is supposed to happen in the meantime?'

'I'm sure the matter will soon be resolved,' he said, and there was something in his voice – in his expression, too – that sent a chill down her spine.

'Have you found out who killed my husband?' she said shakily.

'Mrs Dickinson,' he said slowly, 'I can tell

215

you that we've found the gun we believe was used to kill your husband.'

'Then that's something, I suppose.' Why was she suddenly so frightened? Confound the man.

'You would recognise your husband's gun, I assume?'

'Yes,' she said, frowning. What did he mean by that? Yet, she had a sneaking idea. She had searched high and low for George's gun. She'd looked in all the places he would have been likely to keep it, but hadn't found it.

'Then perhaps you would come along with me and take a look at the gun in question.'

'When I have a moment–'

'Mrs Dickinson,' he said patiently, 'that wasn't a request. Please, now. Come along with me.'

By the time she reached the police station, she felt like a criminal. She was shown the gun, and she had no doubt that it had belonged to George.

Then three officers fired questions at her. The questions didn't make sense. They flitted from one subject to the next. Where had George kept his gun? Why did she disapprove of gambling when she had married two men who were known poker players?

'People in Dawson say you disapprove strongly of gambling,' one officer said. 'Why is that? Because your first husband gambled everything away? Because you thought of that boarding-house as yours and he lost it in a poker game?'

'I did, yes,' she said, teeth gritted, 'but I can't see what this has to do with my husband's murder.'

'He lost it to your late husband, I believe? To George Dickinson?'

'He did, yes.'

'Some people say you resented your husband, Mrs Dickinson. Some say you only married him to get your revenge.'

Amelia was furious. How dare he say such things?

'That's complete nonsense, and I'd advise you not to listen to tittle-tattle,' she said, speaking as calmly as she could. 'At first, I did. I didn't like having to work for Mr Dickinson in what I considered my own business, but, he was a fair man. Once I got to know him—'

'On your marriage to Mr Dickinson, I believe he wrote his will in your favour. Did you know that?'

'I did, yes. I asked him to do that – well, to be honest, I asked him to provide for my son.'

'So there were conditions regarding your acceptance of Mr Dickinson's proposal?'

'My son, Jack, isn't – wasn't – my husband's son. I wanted to make sure that Jack would be provided for as he would have

217

been if my first husband hadn't died.'

'So there were conditions?'

'If you like, yes,' she retorted.

The three men exchanged glances.

Amelia got to her feet, but one of the officers pushed her back into her seat.

'I would like to go home,' she said hotly. 'My son will be waiting for me.'

'I'm afraid you won't be going anywhere,' the constable told her quietly.

Amelia felt the room spin. The constable's voice seemed to be coming from far away.

'What?' she cried, trying to grasp his words through the blackness that threatened to engulf her. 'Are you telling me–?'

It couldn't be right. There must be some mistake! But she knew it was true. She could see the truth of it on the constable's grim face.

'You're arresting me for my husband's murder? Oh, no! You've made a mistake. Listen to me, you've made a terrible mistake!'

Chapter Nine

May 1905, Liverpool

Ivy's boots clattered on the pavement as she hurried home. She would make herself a cup of tea and read Amelia's letter.

She smiled to herself – James and his daft notions. Thanks to him and his silly dreams, they had both been worried to death about Amelia. They hadn't slept a wink.

A letter was waiting at home for them, though. She knew that because, after she had left Martha and Albert at the school, she and Lizzie had been coming out of the baker's when she'd bumped into Victor, their postman.

'There's no need to ask,' he had told her cheerfully, 'because it's there waiting for you.'

'A letter from Canada?'

But, of course, it was a letter from Canada! What else did she ever ask him about?

Ivy could have hugged him. At long last they had news and Ivy could laugh at their silly fears.

She was only a few yards from the house when the first spots of rain fell.

'Would you believe it?' she murmured. 'Come on, Lizzie,' she said, tugging on her daughter's hand, 'we need to get the washing in. Aunt Amelia's letter will have to wait a few more minutes.'

The sky, bright and blue when she had pegged out her washing earlier, was now a heavy grey. A whole line full of washing would be soaked if she didn't get to it quickly.

Ivy ran through the house, stopping only to put Amelia's letter on the table, and out into the yard.

She was taking sheets off the line, handing pegs to Lizzie, when she heard the commotion out in the street. Glass was broken, a horse's hooves – and then she heard her neighbour scream.

'What the–?'

Her washing forgotten, Ivy grabbed Lizzie's hand and ran back through the house and into the street where a small crowd was already gathering.

Maggie, her friend and neighbour, was lifting up her four-year-old son, who was limp in her arms.

'Whatever's happened?' Ivy asked in amazement. 'Oh, my!' She spotted the blood pouring from Henry's leg.

'The horse ran out of control,' Maggie sobbed, 'and Henry was knocked into the wall.'

Mr Dobbs must have been on his way to the shop to deliver his potatoes. Now, he had just managed to bring his horse under control, but he was as pale as poor Henry.

'It wasn't my fault, missus. The horse were frightened by–'

'Never mind that,' Maggie said. 'I'll have to get him to the infirmary.'

'I'll take you,' Mr Dobbs offered, still keeping a tight rein on his horse.

'The children–'

'Just go, Maggie,' Ivy said immediately. 'I'll stay with the children. They'll be fine with me. Go on!'

Mr Dobbs lifted Maggie and Henry on to the back of his cart, along with sacks of potatoes, and they set off.

'Don't worry,' Ivy called to her. 'It probably looks a lot worse than it is.'

She hoped so. Henry had been breathing, but it was clear he knew nothing of what was happening around him.

'Where are they taking Henry, Mam?' Lizzie asked.

'To the infirmary,' Ivy said, lifting Lizzie to her and hugging her tight. 'He's hurt his leg and they'll make it better for him. He'll be home soon.'

Ivy prayed that she was telling the truth.

Ivy let herself into Maggie's house where two-year-old Eli and five-year-old Catherine, oblivious to the commotion outside, were playing at the kitchen table.

Fortunately, they were good children and, soon, the three of them, with Lizzie taking charge, were settled quietly while Ivy washed a few dishes and tidied Maggie's kitchen.

It was only when the children were watching the raindrops chasing themselves down the window that she remembered her washing. What wasn't still on the line was sitting in the basket in the yard. It would be soaked right through. Not that it worried her. There were far more important things in life to worry about.

'Henry will be back soon,' she told the children over and over again, and each time she said it, she prayed that it was true.

She gave them lunch, then, as the rain had passed, and as they were full of energy, she wrote a quick note for Maggie, just in case the poor woman arrived home to an empty house, and then took the three of them up the street and along to the park.

On the way back, they met Martha and Albert from school. Maggie's house was still empty, but Ivy made the children toast and kept them occupied.

James would be home and wanting his dinner soon. She had planned to make a fish pie and decided that she still would. She'd just make sure there was enough for her neighbours, too.

They were on their way out of Maggie's house when young Catherine spotted her mother and Henry. With a shriek of joy, Catherine raced off to meet them.

Smiling, Ivy waited on the doorstep. She felt almost faint with relief as she watched Henry limping gingerly along the street, a huge grin on his young face.

'Oh, Ivy!' Maggie said, her voice still shaky. 'I thought he was gone when I picked him up off the road this morning. I really did.'

Ivy had thought the same thing.

'The doctor says I'm to keep a close eye on him for the next couple of days, but he's all right. They've stitched his leg and bandaged him up.'

Smiling, Ivy ruffled the young lad's hair.

'You gave us a fright, Master Henry,' she told him.

'Thanks for looking after these two,' Maggie said softly. 'I don't know what I'd have done if–'

'It was nothing,' Ivy told her, 'and I know you would have done the same for me.'

'Let's hope I never have to,' Maggie said gently.

Oh, Ivy hoped not. It would be a long time before she rid herself of the picture of Maggie scooping her seemingly lifeless son into her arms.

'I was about to make a fish pie,' Ivy

explained. 'You're all more than welcome to share it.'

'Aw, thanks, love, but I'll get something. My Alan will be home soon and he'll be hungry. You get along home, Ivy, and take care of your own. And thanks. Thanks again.'

It was bedlam in Ivy's kitchen as she busied herself with the dinner. She liked it that way, though.

When James came home, the twins climbed all over him, telling him everything.

'And Henry's all right?' he asked, looking at Ivy.

'Fine,' she said. 'He was wearing a grin from ear to ear. It's put years on Maggie mind, and–' She clapped a hand to her forehead.

'Oh, James, in all the excitement, I forgot. There's a letter from Amelia in the hall.' She smiled at him. 'You and your daft ideas. Go and get it, love.'

She was dishing up the food and getting the children to the table as he read.

'Does she have any news?' Ivy asked.

He was silent, and she looked up. At the expression on his face, she knew that something was very wrong.

'Jimmy?'

He glanced at the children, and gave a slight shake of his head.

'Read it later,' he said quietly.

Ivy had been as hungry as the children, but her appetite vanished. She watched James pushing the food around his plate and felt sick with worry.

It was difficult acting normally, but they managed it until the children were finally in bed.

'Where's that letter?' Ivy said. She had managed to convince herself that James was reading between the lines, that he was worrying about nothing.

He handed it over silently.

She sat down, and was glad she had. The words leapt off the page at her, making her giddy and nauseous.

'Oh, Jimmy!' she whispered, and she clutched at the hand he put on her shoulder.

Ivy couldn't take it in. How could George be dead? How could Amelia be in prison accused of his murder? How could she be locked in a cell?

Tears were flowing freely down her face as she read Amelia's last words.

Please don't worry about me. I am innocent and I'm confident that the truth will come out. I'll write again soon. In the meantime, I'm sending all my love. Say a prayer for me.

Ivy put the letter aside, turned for the reassuring arms of her husband, and cried.

'What will happen to her?' she asked, rubbing the tears from her face.

'I don't know, love,' James said, his voice gruff with emotion. 'It's a misunderstanding, that's all. They'll find the truth, the real killer.'

'And George – gone.' No, Ivy simply couldn't take it in. 'It's so unfair. She was happy with George and now–'

She couldn't go on. She buried her face and clung to her husband.

May 1905, Dawson

'Try to think, Bella,' Sam said urgently.

'I'm trying!'

Bella was running the hotel until Amelia was back with them.

It was late and she and Sam were sitting in the kitchen trying with very little success, to come up with names of George's acquaintances.

'He must have mentioned names,' Sam persisted.

'But he didn't, Sam,' Bella said with a groan. 'He was such a private person. I always thought he was devious, but no, he was just private. He was happy that way. And Amelia never knew where he was half the time. She always believed he was at a business meeting when anyone with half a brain knew he was out gambling.'

She flushed. That had sounded disloyal. It was true, though. Amelia had believed every word George had said. And why not?

Having been married to one gambler and put up with the problems he caused, it wouldn't have been easy to worry about another one.

Sam got to his feet, stared out of the window into the darkness and sighed loudly. 'I can't understand why she married the man!' he exploded.

Bella wished that Sam would calm down. Getting worked up about the rights and wrongs of Amelia's marriage to George would help nothing. Usually, he was a calm, logical man. Nothing upset him. Or if it did, he never showed it.

'Because she loved him,' Bella said calmly.

'Did she?'

Bella thought for a moment before answering.

'In her own way, yes. Not as she loved Miles, of course. But yes, she loved George. She only told me that the night – the night he was shot. He was good to her, Sam.'

'Ha!' He turned away from the window and banged his fist down on the table in frustration. 'So good to her that she's locked up on a murder charge!'

'It's hardly George's fault,' Bella pointed out dryly.

'I wouldn't count on that, Bella. George wasn't shot for being good to his wife. Nor was he shot because he was an honest, respectable businessman.'

He was right, of course. Someone had hated George enough to kill him. Someone had risked everything to see him dead. George must have wronged that person.

Bella was as keen to know the truth as Sam, but she could think of no-one. She had no idea of the men George mixed with and meanwhile, her very best friend was accused of murder. Bella hadn't cried. She daren't. She knew that once she allowed the first tear to fall, she would never stop crying.

'Someone must know something,' Sam said on a long sigh.

'If they do, they're keeping it to themselves.'

'They are.' Sam nodded at the truth of that. 'I've spoken to practically everyone in Dawson – nothing.'

It showed. Sam looked as if he'd had as much sleep as the rest of them. She knew he wouldn't rest until he had the truth.

'There was that Bill Constantine,' she murmured. 'He seemed a decent enough chap, but I know that both George and Miles knew him. It was because of him that Miles got involved with George in the first place.'

Sam shook his head.

'He's been living in Montana for more than a year now.'

Bella's head hurt. The lack of sleep, the worry – it was taking its toll.

On top of that, she had young Jack asking every ten minutes when his mother would be home, and it was breaking her heart.

There were times when Bella wondered what madness had possessed them to come to this hostile land. Money, she supposed, was the answer to that particular question. She and her Ben had dreamed of finding gold and, when he died, Bella hadn't much cared where she and the children had ended up. At the time, it had been easier to come here than make a decision. Besides, Sam had urged her to come so that he could look out for them all.

The promise of gold had brought Amelia and Miles here. Or, in Amelia's case, it was more the promise of security.

Money had brought George here, too. Like Amelia, he had known that someone with a good head for business could make their fortune in Dawson.

Sam, too, had spotted the potential. An experienced river boat pilot, he had known that people would pay him handsomely to ferry them safely across those treacherous rapids.

Riches? Pah! Bella would throw every last cent in the river if it would bring Amelia back to them.

'You know Edward Letterman?' Sam asked, and she nodded. 'Did you ever hear George mention him? A game of poker with him, perhaps?'

'No. Why?'

'His name keeps coming up, and when I start asking questions, people clam up.' He sighed again. 'I don't suppose he's of any interest to us.'

Bella thought hard, but she had never known George to have dealings with the man, or even mention him.

'George's killer – well, it might be someone from his past,' Bella said thoughtfully. 'When I knew George – before we came here – believe me, he upset a lot of people.'

'I'm sure he did,' Sam said dryly.

'He was no-one then,' Bella went on, 'but he was determined to make a success of his life. And although I know you shouldn't speak ill of the dead, it has to be said that he didn't much care how he did that.'

Sam walked over to her and gave her shoulder a squeeze.

'Try to rest,' he said, 'and take care of the young ones. Don't worry, we'll soon find out what happened.'

Don't worry? How was she supposed to do that?

'The Mounties don't seem to be doing much,' she muttered.

'That's because they're convinced they have their man – or woman,' he corrected himself. 'But they're wrong. You know that and I know that. Before long,' he added grimly, 'they'll know it, too.'

Bella clutched at his hand.

'Oh, Sam, I hope you're right. I can't bear to think–'

'I know,' he said gently.

After giving her shoulder another squeeze, he strode to the door.

'I'll let you know if I find out anything,' he promised.

'Thanks.' Another thought struck Bella. 'I thought you were leaving Dawson in the morning?'

'I was. But it can wait.'

By the time Sam finally managed to see Amelia Dickinson, his temper was in shreds. No visitors, they had said. How dare they? Sam had had to threaten them with the biggest, most important names he could think of – and pretend those big names were personal friends. No visitors, indeed.

'Even murderers have rights,' he'd told the constable. 'And Mrs Dickinson certainly isn't that. You're all going to look extremely foolish when the truth comes out. And come out it will!'

But eventually, he was taken to Amelia.

He supposed he should have been shocked by the sight of her, but he wasn't. He had prepared himself for the worst. He'd known she wasn't the type to get hysterical. She looked as if she had lost weight – well, that wasn't surprising given all that had happened – and she looked as if she'd had no sleep or food since being brought to this dull place. Yet her eyes, although dark with shadows, were dry.

Although she had been told she had a visitor, she clearly didn't know who that visitor was. Sam noticed the way she looked at him, looked behind him, and then tried to hide her disappointment.

'Mrs Dickinson,' he greeted her. He had to consciously remember that she was no longer Amelia Carter.

'Mr Hunter.' As she said his name, he noticed a tell-tale tremble from her bottom lip. 'I was told I wasn't allowed visitors.'

'I was told the same thing,' he replied dryly and, amazingly, there was the ghost of a smile on her lips as he said this.

She was sitting at a table and made no attempt to rise. Perhaps the effort was too much for her.

Sam sat opposite her.

They could be overheard because one of the constables was keeping watch, but Sam had nothing to hide.

'Mrs Dickinson,' he began, 'I've been asking around – about acquaintances of your husband–' Belatedly, he realised that, apart from a brief word at her husband's funeral, he hadn't offered his condolences. 'Your late husband,' he said, and he had to clear his throat. 'I'm sorry about–'

'Thank you,' she cut him off.

'As I said, I've been asking around, and I wondered if you'd heard your late husband mention Mr Edward Letterman?'

'Why?'

'Well – it seems he and your husband were friends.'

'I think you'll find, Mr Hunter, that Mr Letterman and my husband were business acquaintances.'

'So you do know of him? Your husband spoke of him?'

A small spot of colour came into her face.

'My husband didn't speak of him, no. However, I did see his name on some – paperwork in my husband's office.'

'I see.' He waited for more, but nothing was forthcoming. 'Mr Letterman doesn't own a business,' he said.

He waited for her to argue, but she was silent, thoughtful.

'Perhaps they were friends,' Sam pressed on. 'Perhaps they enjoyed the occasional game of poker.'

'Mr Hunter, I really can't see that my husband's–'

'Mrs Dickinson,' he interrupted, 'you may be content to take the blame, and the consequences, for your husband's murder, but I'll not rest until justice is done. I'm trying to help you, woman, not pry into your affairs.'

Again, there was that tell-tale trembling of the bottom lip. Her voice, however, was as strong as ever.'

'I'm sorry. And I thank you for your help.'

'It may be,' Sam went on, 'that your husband was planning to meet Edward Letterman the night that–' He broke off, finding it difficult to say, 'the night your husband was murdered.' Did he mention that to you?'

She thought for a moment.

'My husband only told me that he had a business meeting.' She gave a slight shrug. 'I knew it was a strange time to conduct a business meeting, but I didn't question it. It wasn't my place.'

Despite having the worries of the world on her shoulders, Amelia sat still and erect. She was very proud – or stubborn – and Sam had always found it attractive in her.

Every time he looked at her, even in these circumstances, he was reminded of the way she had dressed as a man so that he would take her across the rapids. And he had brought her to this place. He wished he never had.

'Did he ever mention playing poker with Peter Tavener?'

'No.' She looked at him for a few moments. 'I know he and Mr Tavener played together, though, because Miles told me. Usually, when Miles played poker with George, Peter Tavener and Bill Constantine played with them.'

'I see.'

When he had spoken to Peter Tavener, he hadn't mentioned playing poker with George Dickinson. He had, however, said, 'His missus has done us all a big favour – got her own back. Yup, and the world's well rid of him.'

It was unusual for Peter Tavener to be so outspoken. Although Sam knew he hadn't killed George, he was convinced that Peter Tavener knew something about this whole sorry affair. He was keeping that something quiet, though.

'About Mr Letterman,' she said, eyes downcast. 'The item I saw on my husband's desk – it was a mining stake for some place I haven't heard of before. I didn't question it, obviously, but I did think it odd that George would buy a mining stake.'

Buy it? Sam very much doubted that.

'That's enough!' The constable, sitting at a nearby table, rose to his feet and indicated that Sam should leave.

Sam wasn't going to argue. Amelia had been more help than she would know.

'Your son,' he said gently, 'is fine. Bella is taking good care of him.'

If he'd wanted a reaction from her, he got one. Her eyes swam with tears. They would never fall, he guessed that, but she gazed back at him with eyes filled with heartbreak.

'Thank you.' Her voice now was little more than a whisper. 'Tell Bella to hug him for me.'

With that, she turned and was gone, led away by the silent constable.

Sam's heart was heavy as he watched her go. What if they didn't discover the truth? What if Amelia ended her days labelled as a killer? What if her son–

He refused to think that way. Someone out there knew the truth. Someone would talk.

While the police arranged Amelia Dickinson's trial, Sam would do whatever it took to make those people talk. He refused to admit defeat.

As Amelia walked back to her tiny cell, tears rolled down her cheeks. She wished now that she had written to Jack. She could have given the letter to Sam Hunter.

She brushed the tears away with an impatient hand. Crying had never solved anything, and it never would. She needed to think, not cry.

But she had thought. She'd tried to think of anyone who had shown any disrespect towards George since she had known him. She'd tried to think of any strangers she had seen in Dawson – but there had been plenty of those. She tried to recall every detail of the walk she had taken on the night George was shot. She had been close to the hotel when she'd heard the shots. The killer, whoever he was, had been close to her.

It was impossible to think clearly. Indeed, at times, she was convinced she was losing her sanity.

Her mind insisted on flitting to Liverpool. She held the dream close, the dream she so often had of holding Jack's hand in hers as they walked off a huge ship and straight into the arms of James and Ivy. She would give all she had to see them both right now.

She should write to them, too. Her last letter would have had them out of their minds with worry. She must let them know that she was all right.

Except she wasn't all right. She was far from that. Again, she brushed her tears away.

She had good friends, and she must be grateful. Bella would be making sure that Jack as all right, and Sam Hunter was doing his best to help discover the truth. But what could he do?

Somewhere, George's killer would be laughing at them. He had known that he'd got away with his crime. He would be happy in the knowledge that she had taken his place.

Amelia lay on her narrow, hard bed and stared at the ceiling. She must think.

Instead of worrying about Jack, longing for James and Ivy, dwelling on all the things she had never said to George, she must think of a means of proving her innocence.

Yet, how could she not worry about Jack? How would he cope with no mother to care for him? And what would become of her unborn child?

June 1905, Dawson

As Sam made his way to the saloon in Whitehorse, he could feel his heart racing. He thanked the Lord his grandmother had taught him how to play poker.

The thought of his grandmother made him smile. She had been as tough and as wily as any man he'd ever met, yet there had been an inner softness to her that he'd loved.

She'd been a good poker player, too. While threatening him with all sorts of punishments if she ever caught him gambling, she had taught him the finer points of the game.

'A fool's game, Sam,' she had told him as she'd dealt the cards.

His thoughts switched to Constable Dover. Amelia and Bella couldn't find a good word to say about the man, which was understandable, but Sam liked him. He'd been the only member of the Royal Northwest Mounted Police to accept that maybe, just maybe, Amelia Dickinson was innocent of her husband's murder.

Dover was a very correct man, and liked to do everything by the rules, but at least he was willing to listen. Yes, Sam liked him.

He pushed open the door to the saloon and looked around him. His visits to Whitehorse were rare, but he usually saw someone he knew. This evening, he found himself surrounded by strangers.

While he was looking around him he saw his old friend approaching.

'Seymour!'

They shook hands.

'Good to see you,' Sam said.

'You're looking well, Sam. Business good?'

'Very.' But Sam's mind wasn't on business.

'I've set up the back room for you,' Seymour said in a whisper. 'It should suit your purpose. Come and have a look.'

'Thanks, I appreciate it.'

Sam followed him through a crowd of customers and into a small, dusty room where busy spiders had made themselves at home.

In the centre of the room was a card table and four chairs. Opposite the door was another door that led to the storeroom. Sam opened that door. It was used to store liquor, and would suit his purpose.

'Will you have a drink?' Seymour asked.

'No thanks.' He needed a clear head.

'So tell me what this is all about,' Seymour suggested.

Sam owed him the truth, but he didn't want to talk about it. Not yet.

'Later,' he promised.

It was a little after six o'clock. In another hour, Edward Letterman should be arriving for a poker game.

Sam had found Letterman via another old friend, Charles Brady.

'He'll be keen to make big money,' Charles had told him. 'Rumour has it he lost everything at a poker game in Dawson.'

Yes, Sam had heard the same rumour. Some people believed he had lost it to George Dickinson.

As soon as he'd the word that Letterman would play, Sam had contacted Seymour and asked to loan him a room in his saloon.

Seymour, to his credit, had agreed immediately, even before Sam had assured him that it was legal.

As luck would have it, Letterman was first to arrive.

'I haven't seen you in Dawson for a while,' Sam remarked.

'No, I've had – things to do here,' he said, adding, 'I didn't you know played poker.'

'Badly,' Sam said, smiling broadly. 'I've only taken it up recently. George Dickinson got me into it.'

Letterman darted a suspicious glance at him.

'I went into business with him a few years back,' Sam went on genially. Before Letterman could comment, he added, 'I never

trusted the man, but we were partners so–'
he shrugged '–I played the odd game with
him.'

'Yes, I heard you went into business with
him,' Letterman said. 'It didn't last long,
though, did it?'

'No. We both had different ideas and,
thankfully, I was able to buy out his share. It
suited us – we both made money on it.'

'I'll bet you didn't make money playing
poker with him,' Letterman remarked.

'What makes you say that?'

'You said you were a poor player.'

'Ah.' Sam had put that story out to entice
Letterman. 'I'm learning, and I feel lucky
tonight.'

Just then, they were joined by Charles
Brady and his son Charles Junior, who,
despite being head and shoulders taller than
his father, was affectionately known as
'Tiny'.

For three hours they played poker and
Sam decided that, despite his grandmother's
teaching, he simply didn't have what it took
to be a good player. His mind insisted on
wandering to more important matters.

He took a small sip of his drink and
watched Letterman. The man was winning
despite the vast quantities of liquor he was
drinking.

He was relaxing, too, Sam noticed. The
haunted look was leaving his eyes and he

was smiling now and again.

Finally, Charles and his son decided to call it a night.

'One more game?' Sam asked Letterman.

'You want to lose more?' Letterman said with a laugh.

'No, I want to win some back.'

Delighted to be on a winning streak, Letterman was more than happy to play another game.

When he'd won, he rose unsteadily to his feet. 'We'll have to fix something up for when you're back in Dawson,' Sam told him. 'You should at least give me a chance to win my money back.'

'Sure.'

'It won't be at the River View Hotel, though. I've no idea what will happen to that now that George Dickinson's dead and his wife's locked up for it.'

Letterman shrugged.

'A pity she's locked up, really,' Sam mused. 'She should have made a fortune from her marriage to him. That's only fair, I say. Rumour has it that George Dickinson cheated her first husband out of their boarding-house.'

'That's no rumour,' Letterman said, so unsteady on his feet that he dropped back into his chair. 'It's fact. I was at that game,' he said proudly.

'And George Dickinson cheated?'

'Marked cards,' Letterman said, nodding.

'Well! I always knew he was a cheat, but–'

'Yeah, he was born a cheat and he died a cheat.'

Sam frowned, puzzled.

'If you knew that, why did you play with him?'

'I made sure we didn't use his cards. I insisted on it.'

'Ah, I see.' Sam took a breath. 'Any idea who killed him?'

Letterman's eyebrows shot up.

'What do you mean? His wife's in prison, ain't she?'

'Yes, but she didn't murder him. A woman couldn't take a gun to any man, let alone her own husband.'

If Sam had been in a better frame of mind, he would have had a small smile at that. If any woman was capable of shooting a man it was Amelia Dickinson.

'Didn't kill him?' Letterman licked his lips. 'Who says that?'

'I do,' Sam told him.

'Who did, then?' he blustered.

'I think you did, Edward.'

'Me?' He lurched to his feet. 'What makes you say that?'

'Just a hunch.'

'I heard that his own gun was used,' Letterman said.

'So did I.' Sam's heart was pounding.

243

'Why did you use that?'

'Me?' Letterman laughed. 'You've got the wrong man. I didn't kill him.'

'I think you did,' Sam insisted. 'I think he cheated you just as he cheated Miles Carter. Marked cards, you say? You wouldn't let him get away with that. No-one would. If Miles Carter hadn't died of typhoid fever, I expect he would have done something similar and, if we're honest, he wasn't half the man you are.' A bit of flattery wouldn't go amiss.

'Like you, he lost everything,' Sam went on. 'George Dickinson didn't deserve to get away with it. He had enough money – he didn't need to cheat everyone out of what was rightfully theirs.'

Letterman laughed again, a desperate almost hysterical sound.

'You're right, Sam. A cheat like Dickinson deserved all he got.'

'Hear, hear,' Sam agreed. 'Good riddance, I say.'

'The thing is, I've got witnesses who swear I was twenty miles away at the time,' Letterman said.

'Good for you,' Sam said affably. 'I hope they're friends. I hope they didn't cost you.'

Letterman pulled a face.

'No, they're not friends. Acquaintances would be a better term. And yes, I paid them handsomely, but they know better than to cross me.'

Sam felt the room spin. He was dizzy with relief.

'Clever work,' he said, trying to clear his head. 'Kill Dickinson and then make sure everyone says you were twenty miles away.'

'And no-one will ever prove otherwise,' Letterman said.

'And you sleep at night?' Sam still kept that pleasant smile on his face. 'Knowing that the man's wife is in jail for a murder she didn't commit?'

'That's not my business,' Letterman snapped.

He picked up his hat and took his coat from the peg on the back of the door.

'Tell me,' Sam murmured. 'If you never used his cards, how did he manage to cheat a man like you?'

Letterman swayed dangerously.

'I used my own deck – a fair game, I thought – but no, he managed to mark them somehow.'

'And you killed him for that?'

'He took everything I had. Everything!' He shrugged himself into his coat. 'You can talk all you like, Sam Hunter,' Letterman said, his hand on the door, 'but no-one will believe you. Like I said, I've got witnesses who will swear I was miles away!'

Chapter Ten

June 1905, Dawson

Sam was as eager to leave the dingy, smoke-filled room as Edward Letterman. The other man had his hand on the door handle. He was even smiling.

Why shouldn't he smile, though. He'd relieved himself of a burden. In admitting to Sam that he had murdered George Dickinson, he must have rid himself of a huge weight. Didn't it help to talk? Wasn't the guilt lessened after his confession? As far as Letterman was concerned, only Sam knew the truth. And what did it matter if Sam talked? As Letterman had been quick to point out, he'd paid people to swear that he had been twenty miles away at the time of the shooting.

He wasn't as tall as Sam, and he had a gaunt look about him. His hair was thin and lank. In other circumstances, Sam might have felt sorry for him.

'When you say George Dickinson took everything you had,' Sam said, his voice tight, 'what exactly was that?'

'Every cent I had,' Letterman told him

gruffly. 'Everything I had in the world, including a mining stake. A couple of miners had struck gold nearby and I knew I'd get a good price for that stake.'

'And you lost it?'

'I was cheated out of it.' Letterman clearly didn't like the word 'lost'. I was cheated out of everything. I wasn't going to stand for that. Would you?'

'No,' Sam answered slowly, 'but you've still lost it, haven't you? Killing George Dawson has achieved nothing.'

'It means he'll never cheat anyone else!' Letterman's eyes glittered dangerously. 'And if I were you, Sam Hunter, I'd keep this conversation to myself.'

'You would?'

'I would!'

Sam feigned regret.

'That's a pity, Edward. You see, the thing is–' With an apologetic shrug, Sam moved to the back door that opened into the storeroom. He pushed it open.

'No!' The shock of seeing Constable Dover in his distinctive red serge tunic rendered Letterman speechless. 'But–'

In a desperate bid for freedom, he yanked open the door, but it was too late. Far too late.

Letterman was a lot stronger than he looked, but Constable Dover and Sam soon managed to overpower him and force him back to a seat at the table.

Sam knew nothing but relief. He had known in his heart that Letterman was guilty, and he'd managed to convince Constable Dover of the man's guilt, but he hadn't dared to believe that getting Letterman to admit the truth would be so easy.

June 1905, Dawson

Amelia stood at the water's edge, with Jack's hand tightly clasped in hers. She closed her eyes and inhaled deeply. The crisp wind felt deliciously cool on her face.

The sky was a deep, unbroken blue and the surface of the river, reflecting that blue, sparkled like diamonds in the weak sunshine.

This was her third day of freedom and, still, Amelia couldn't quite believe it. She found it impossible to stay indoors for long. Her nerves were in shreds and she couldn't relax for a moment.

Even now, standing in the fresh air with her beloved Jack beside her, she was on edge.

In that jail, she had protested her innocence every time she'd drawn breath. She had vowed to everyone who would listen that justice would prevail. Yet she hadn't dared to believe it herself.

Even now, when justice had prevailed, she couldn't quite believe it. She had walked free with her head held high, but inside she'd been quivering.

Unable to relax, she was constantly guarding against any disaster. She felt that if she dared to relax for even a second, Jack would be snatched away from her and she would be back in jail.

'Let's walk, sweetheart,' she said, forcing a bright smile to her face for Jack's benefit.

It was all she could do – walk. The moment she was still, her mind filled with all sorts of terrors. Yet her nightmare was over. She must accept that and start living again.

Her freedom had come courtesy of Sam Hunter, Amelia knew that. If it hadn't been for him, she would still be locked up as a murderer.

'Sam must have spoken to everyone in Canada,' Bella had told her. 'He wouldn't rest, Mel, until he had the truth. Until you were free.'

Amelia owed him her thanks, but she hadn't seen him. According to Bella, he had delayed a trip he had to make until he'd found George's murderer and then, with that solved, he'd headed off.

Amelia had never known anyone like him before. From the time of their very first meeting, when she had tried to persuade him to take her and Miles on his boat, she had been impressed and a little envious of the way he was so at ease with the world.

A half-smile touched her lips as she recalled the way she had taken such care to dress as a man so that he would allow her on his boat. He hadn't been fooled for a second. Yet he had brought them here and she was grateful for that.

It seemed she would be for ever in the man's debt.

The police – that Constable Dover – had merely told her she was free to go. If she hadn't demanded a few answers, she wouldn't have known that Edward Letterman had killed George out of revenge.

Her breath caught in her throat as she realised she wouldn't have known that George had cheated Miles out of their boarding-house, either. She could have done without knowing that particular detail. George had betrayed her.

'He didn't know you then,' Bella had pointed out earnestly. 'He'd done bad things in his time, but he changed, Mel. He loved you and Jack so much.'

'He betrayed me,' Amelia said sadly, and she found that a hard truth to swallow.

It didn't matter that he hadn't known her. It didn't matter that it was Miles he had cheated. The truth was, he had cheated. For all she knew, the hotel – everything he owned – had been obtained by cheating.

The way she felt right now, Amelia could

raze River View Hotel to the ground.

That evening, when Jack was sleeping soundly and Bella's two children had been persuaded to go to bed, Amelia paced around George's small office. Her mind was in turmoil.

After a while she sat at his desk and pulled open the drawers. Most of them were empty because the police had taken what they thought to be important paperwork. She was sifting through the remainder when Bella came in.

'I'm surprised George didn't keep a copy of his will here,' Amelia murmured.

'Perhaps he did. Perhaps the police took it.'

'It doesn't matter now,' Bella pointed out. 'You'll know everything tomorrow.'

'I know,' Amelia told her with a sigh. 'But–' She broke off. It was pointless voicing her fears to Bella.

Besides, Bella was right. Amelia had an appointment with George's lawyer at nine o'clock in the morning and she would know more when she had seen him.

'We're probably penniless,' she said with a lightness she didn't feel.

'No, love,' Bella said urgently. 'George told you himself that he'd provided for you and Jack.'

But how much was George's word worth? The thought came unbidden, causing her

251

bottom lip to tremble.

'I know what you're thinking,' Bella said gently, giving her shoulder a squeeze, 'but he loved you, Mel. You know he did. He was ruthless in business, yes, but – well, wasn't that one of the things you admired about him?'

'There's a difference between being ruthless and cheating people out of what is rightfully theirs,' Amelia muttered.

Bella didn't have an answer to that one.

'Wait and see what tomorrow brings,' she said instead.

'And what will we do if we have nothing?' Amelia asked. 'For all we know, Bella, George could have left everything he owned – this place, the boarding-house, everything – to someone who's a complete stranger to us. We could all be homeless.'

Bella visibly paled at the thought, but she was a born optimist.

'If that's the case,' she said briskly, 'we'll get by. We've got a little money,' she reminded Amelia, 'and that trunk of yours must be full to the brim with gold sweepings.'

'Not quite,' Amelia said, but the thought made her smile.

From the moment she had first taken out the lease on the boarding-house, she had made sure the floors had been swept meticulously. It was amazing how the tiny amounts of gold that had fallen from the men's pockets mounted up. Yes, her trusty trunk might just save them if it had to.

'You're right,' Amelia told her. 'We'll get by.'

She only wished she felt as confident as she sounded. But she had never wanted to 'get by'. She hadn't battled the elements and made that awful journey across the Chilkoot Pass to 'get by'. She hadn't worked her fingers to the bone in the boarding-house to 'get by'.

It wasn't just her and Bella, either. Bella had young Isaac and Jane to care for, and Amelia had her darling Jack and her unborn child to think about. They had a lot of mouths to feed.

That, she realised suddenly, was if Bella stayed with her. Amelia had taken it for granted that they would stay together, but maybe Bella had other ideas.

'Bella – if George has – what I mean is, if I don't get anything from George's estate, and we can't stay here, what will you do? Will you want to take Isaac and Jane and go – somewhere else?'

'What?' Bella stared at her open-mouthed.

'If I'm left penniless,' Amelia reminded her, 'life will be a real struggle.'

'Mel, I'm not here because of–' Bella shook her head in amazement. 'What are you thinking of? We've been friends from the moment Miles brought me to the boarding-house and you looked at him as if he'd taken leave of his senses.'

Amelia laughed at the memory, and Bella hugged her fiercely.

'You're my best friend, Mel,' she said gruffly. 'Yes, it'll be a struggle, but we work well together. We're survivors, me and you. Don't worry, we'll be fine. All of us.'

'Yes. Yes, of course we will.'

George must have provided for her in his will. One of the reasons she had been arrested for his murder was because Constable Dover had known she stood to inherit on George's death. The police must have checked that with George's lawyer.

There was no need to worry, she told herself. No need at all.

Amelia hadn't slept a wink. She'd spent the night tossing and turning and mentally going over every eventuality. She wanted to be prepared for whatever Mr Manilow had to tell her.

She was at his office early and he was shaking her hand at nine o'clock prompt.

'Please, sit down, Mrs Dickinson.'

She was grateful to sit. Her legs, like the rest of her, were trembling.

He looked more at ease than the last time she had seen him, she noticed, and she wasn't sure if that was a good sign or not.

'Please accept my sincere condolences, Mrs Dickinson,' he said solemnly.

'Thank you.'

He hadn't bothered to offer his condolences the last time she saw him, Amelia thought crossly.

'Now then, to business,' he said, shuffling a vast amount of papers on his desk. 'Your husband's will is very straightforward. He was a very organised man.'

'Indeed,' Amelia agreed.

As he read George's will, Amelia had to concentrate hard. It didn't sound very straightforward to her. Several times, she had to interrupt Mr Manilow and ask him to explain it more clearly.

However, as each sentence was read out, she began to relax. George had been true to his word. Almost everything he owned had been left to her with the proviso that, if she predeceased him, everything passed to Jack.

'A sum of one thousand dollars is bequeathed to Mrs Lucinda Dickinson,' Mr Manilow explained.

'Lucinda Dickinson?'

The name meant nothing to Amelia. George had told her his mother was dead. He'd never mentioned any other family.

'His brother's widow,' Mr Manilow explained.

Her sister-in-law. Amelia hadn't even known the woman existed. How was it possible, she wondered, to know so little about one's husband? Whenever George's name was mentioned, she felt as if she was discussing a complete stranger.

Amelia had known nothing of his business dealings, or his gambling habits. She certainly hadn't known that he played with a marked deck of cards. Now, it appeared she'd known nothing of his family, either. Her marriage had been a sham.

There was very little capital, which surprised Amelia. Perhaps it shouldn't have. Heaven knows, George had been a gambler and even he couldn't have cheated all the time.

'You've inherited a great deal of very valuable property, Mrs Dickinson,' Mr Manilow told her, smiling.

As well as the hotel, the boarding-house and a large house that George had thought they might live in at some point, it seemed she owned a mining stake. The mining stake that was Edward Letterman's, by rights.

'Thank you,' she said, gathering her thoughts. 'I would like the mining stake to be passed on to Mr Edward Letterman's family.'

She sat upright, glad now that she'd sacrificed a night's sleep to give the matter so much thought.

'I would like River View Hotel to be sold and the proceeds to be split between the hospital and the school. I would like the same thing to happen to the house.'

'Mrs Dickinson,' he spluttered, wide-eyed. 'Perhaps you need more time—'

'I need no more time,' she assured him. 'The boarding-house I will keep.'

The boarding-house was rightfully hers. It always had been.

'Will you deal with these matters for me?'

'Well—'

'Or perhaps I should ask someone else?'

'Oh, no, no. There's no need for that. However,' he said, 'I feel I must advise you to think very carefully indeed, Mrs Dickinson. These are considerable properties we're discussing.'

She could see from the expression on his face that he was attributing such stupidity to her gender.

'I'm well aware of that, Mr Manilow. However, I would like you to dispose of them. All except the boarding-house.' She rose to her feet. 'And I'd be grateful if you could attend to this as quickly as possible.'

'Well, yes, certainly,' he agreed, flustered.

'Thank you. I'll look forward to hearing from you.'

She swept out of his office and into the street, and she walked straight past the hotel.

Bella, she knew, would be anxiously waiting for news, but Amelia needed a few minutes to herself. She needed to take stock.

She headed for the water, as she always did when she needed to be alone with her thoughts.

'Forgive me, Jack,' she whispered.

Had it been foolish to give away so much? She brushed some hair back from her face, but the wind was strong and soon whipped it back, making her eyes smart.

Foolish or not, she wouldn't have been happy if she had found herself the owner of so much property. She would never have known if George had acquired it by fair means or foul.

Besides, she might not be as wealthy as she could have been, but she was wealthier than she had ever been. The boarding-house – thanks in part to George's capital – was a thriving success.

If she decided to sell ... she would give that matter some thought. At the moment, she longed to get away from Dawson, but she wasn't sure if that was simply because she was still shaken by life.

So lost was she in her own thoughts, that she didn't notice the rainbow straightaway. When she did, its brilliance took her breath away.

Usually, a rainbow filled her with hope for the future, but this one was different. Every colour in the bright arc was trying to out-shine its neighbour. Yet, around it, menacing clouds were gathering. Despite its beauty, this rainbow chilled her.

She was being fanciful, she scolded herself. Yet, she watched until the rainbow had faded from view and still she couldn't shake off her strange feelings.

Pulling herself together, she headed back to the hotel to tell Bella her news.

June 1905, Liverpool

Matron Elizabeth Johnson couldn't sleep. There was nothing new about that, but for some reason, she felt more restless and unsettled than usual.

That wasn't surprising, she decided as she moved awkwardly out of bed and into her wheelchair. Given the worry about Amelia, it was a miracle any of them had slept at all.

But that was over. This afternoon, James had raced to the orphanage waving Amelia's letter in his hands. The girl was free!

If she wasn't mistaken, there had been the telltale tracks of dried tears on James's face. Matron wasn't surprised. The relief had been immense and she had shed a few tears herself.

To think of a girl – a woman, now, she reminded herself – like Amelia locked up, condemned as a murderer, had been more than any of them could bear.

How she hated this wheelchair, and how she hated having to sleep on the ground floor. She missed her old bedroom with its view of the city.

She managed to get herself along the hallway and to the kitchen, and she put milk on the stove to boil.

Then she gave herself a strict talking to. The last time she had decided on a hot drink to help her sleep, she'd put the milk on to boil and promptly fallen asleep in her chair.

That, she told herself, was a sign of old age. Just lately, she'd been feeling every one of her seventy-one years. She was tired. Even on the rare occasions that she slept, she felt worn out.

Her mind flicked back to Amelia. How she would love to talk to her right now. She would give a lot to see the woman Amelia had become.

She could remember as clearly as if it were yesterday seeing the twins for the first time. Abandoned at the orphanage gates, they had been wrapped up and left in that huge trunk. Amelia's screams had been deafening, she recalled with a smile.

A rainbow, the brightest rainbow she had ever seen, had appeared and she'd chided herself for thinking of it as a sign from God. Maybe that hadn't been such a fanciful idea after all.

Amelia had always been a special child. Elizabeth remembered the day – how old would Amelia have been? Eight? – when she had demanded her trunk. It was all she had in the world and Amelia wanted it.

That trunk had followed her everywhere. Elizabeth wouldn't have been surprised to hear that it had even gone to jail with her!

Amelia's life hadn't been an easy one. Mind you, Elizabeth thought, that was partly due to the child's adventurous spirit. Not that Elizabeth could blame Amelia for falling in love with the handsome American, Miles Carter. He had breezed into her life, with tales of his family in Seattle and his life on board a ship, and swept Amelia off her feet.

Elizabeth could picture Amelia on her wedding day, the thought of sailing to America every bit as exciting as that of spending the rest of her life with her new husband.

Perhaps life in Seattle hadn't been as exciting as she had expected, but Amelia, never content to sit back and let life take its course, had set off on yet another adventure, this time to the Yukon.

Elizabeth poured her milk, and sat with her hands clasped around the cup.

It was difficult to imagine Amelia with a child of her own. She would be a good mother, of that Elizabeth had no doubt. Fiercely protective, of course.

As she swallowed her milk, the pain

returned. It was a dull, nagging pain in her chest that had been there, on and off, for days now. It wasn't a sharp pain, so there could be nothing to worry about. For all that, it was an unsettling pain, especially when the dizzy spells came with it.

With her milk finished, she was ready to wheel herself back to bed. The hot drink hadn't helped. Indeed, she felt quite unwell now. Her head felt as if it were filled with cotton-wool.

She was halfway along the hall when the pain increased to such an extent that she could feel the life being crushed from her.

September 1905, Dawson

Amelia was in George's old office with Ivy's letter in her hands, and tears blurring her vision when Bella found her.

'Mel! What's wrong?'

Amelia dropped the letter, threw her arms round Bella and burst into tears.

'There, now.' Bella looked to the letter on the desk with its familiar postmark. 'Oh, not bad news, Mel? Not James? Ivy?'

'No, no.' She clung to her friend. 'No, they're fine. It's Matron. She collapsed at the orphanage. She's dead, Bella.'

'Oh, Mel.' Bella held her close. 'I'm so sorry. I know how much she meant to you.'

Amelia nodded, took a deep breath and dried her tears.

'She was a special lady,' she told Bella with a watery smile, 'and she wouldn't have approved of anyone crying like this.'

'I'm so sorry.' Bella sighed. 'I came to tell you that Sam Hunter's here, but perhaps now isn't a good time.'

'In Dawson?'

'No, here, in the hotel. I thought you might want to see him.'

'I do. Just give me a couple of minutes, will you?'

Amelia spent those minutes taking deep, steadying breaths. She made sure her face was dry, patted her hair into place and walked out into the reception area.

All she wanted right now was to be alone, but she needed to talk to Mr Hunter, to thank him for all he had done for her. Without him – well, Amelia shuddered to think what would have become of her. Her thanks were long overdue.

'Mr Hunter,' she said, smiling. 'Thank you for calling. I was hoping to talk to you.'

She had forgotten quite how tall he was.

'Mrs Dickinson,' he acknowledged. He gave her a curious look – as if he could see the signs of tears in her eyes – but he didn't comment. Then he looked at her rapidly thickening waistline.

What would he make of that, she wondered. Everyone had been surprised to learn that she was carrying George's child.

'I'm very pleased to see you looking so well,' was all he said.

'Thank you.'

The reception area was busy and while Bella dealt with their guests, Amelia took Mr Hunter into the lounge and offered him a seat.

'I wanted to thank you for all that you did for me,' she said. 'I was sorry to hear you'd left Dawson so soon.'

'Yes, I had to make a trip. And it was nothing,' he added.

'It certainly wasn't nothing,' she retorted. 'Without your help–' She paused. 'Well, I strongly suspect that, at best, I would still be locked in that cell, accused of my husband's murder. I really am very grateful to you. More grateful than you'll ever know.'

'It was nothing,' he said again. 'I dislike injustice. Always have. I would have done the same for anyone.'

'All the same–' She broke off, seeing that she had embarrassed him, and they lapsed into what, to Amelia, was an uncomfortable silence.

It had to be said, however, that Amelia usually felt uncomfortable around this man. As ever, he looked completely relaxed. A stranger might not guess that behind those honest-looking brown eyes, was an incredibly quick mind.

'What do you plan to do now?' he asked

suddenly. 'I hear this hotel has been sold.'

'It has.' She nodded. 'I've been working here until the sale is complete. The boarding-house is mine – and I may sell that. I haven't decided yet.'

'Sell it?' He frowned.

'Yes. I feel it's time for change. I'd like to get away from here.'

'Ah.'

Yes, he had doubtless heard that many times before.

'Where will you go?'

'I don't know,' she admitted.

'Your old boarding-house will fetch a good price,' he said. 'The gold rush may be over, but people are still coming here. Having said that, it won't last for ever. It's probably a good time to get out.'

That pleased her. She felt sure he was right.

'I think so,' she agreed.

Again, that uncomfortable silence.

'Your son, Jack,' he asked at last, 'he's well?'

'He is.' She smiled; the first time she had felt able to smile since Ivy's letter had arrived. 'Yes, thank you.'

Again that silence, yet this time, he was looking at her curiously.

'You had bad news?' he asked.

What could she say? There was no point lying.

'Yes, I heard that a – friend had died.' It was strange to refer to Matron as a 'friend'. She was so much more than that. It was difficult to image how different her life might have been without Matron's influence.

'I'm sorry,' he said, and his genuine concern touched her.

'I grew up in an orphanage in England,' she explained, 'and Matron – Miss Johnson – took care of us all. She spent her life caring for so many of us, and it wasn't easy. Several times, the orphanage came very near to being closed. She was a very special person.'

'She sounds it,' he said softly.

'It's funny,' she said, 'but I never thought this day would come. Silly, really. When we were growing up, we always thought she was ancient.'

He smiled his understanding.

Amelia wondered why she had told him about Matron. Probably because the news had come as such a shock. And what she had told him was true; she hadn't expected this day to come.

In her dream, the one where she and Jack walked off the huge ship that had docked in Liverpool, she had run straight to James and Ivy and then walked to the orphanage to see Matron.

'I imagine everyone in England to look

just as they did when I left them,' she confided with a self-conscious smile. 'That's
ridiculous, isn't it? It's fifteen years since I
left Liverpool.'

'Are you homesick?' he asked.

'At times like this, yes,' she admitted.

Bella joined them then, and Amelia was
grateful. She was also surprised at how easy
Bella was with Mr Hunter. She treated him
as if he were a younger brother she must
scold.

'I'd better get back,' Amelia said at last,
rising to her feet. 'The new owners are moving in next week, Mr Hunter, and there are
things I need to do. It's been good to see you
and thank you. Thank you again.'

She strode back to George's study. Ivy's
letter was lying where she had left it and she
picked it up to read again. Not that reading
it again would change matters. Nothing
could bring Matron back.

The following morning, Amelia felt
exhausted. She hadn't slept, and that was
unusual. Usually, she was asleep as soon as
her head hit the pillow, but last night, she
had been unable to get comfortable.

'You need a rest,' Bella told her immediately. 'You look worn out and no wonder.
What with everything that's happened to
you, and now the news about Matron—'

Amelia nodded, but it was more than that.

She felt – aimless. Yes, aimless was the best way to describe it. She had no plans for the future. She assumed she would carry on running the boarding-house, but the idea filled her with no enthusiasm whatsoever.

In truth, she felt listless. She had no enthusiasm for anything. No energy, either. She had no wish to remain in Dawson. Equally, she had no enthusiasm for anywhere else.

Her conversation with Sam Hunter had made her consider returning to Liverpool, but, much as she longed to be with James and Ivy, she didn't even have any enthusiasm for returning home.

Last night, she had sat on her bed and taken the sheets and pillow-cases, those that Matron had given her on her wedding day, from her trunk. They had been used, but they were far too special to throw out.

In those days, Amelia had felt as if the world was hers, as if she could achieve anything she set out to. Now, she felt as if everything she touched brought disaster.

She rose to make herself and Bella a coffee, but she never made it to the sink. A sharp pain had her clutching the back of her chair and struggling for breath.

Panic ripped through her. The baby! She was going to lose the baby.

'Oh, no!' she wailed.

'It's all right, dear.' Bella was at her side

immediately, her face etched with concern. 'We'll get you back to bed and–'

Amelia cried out as another pain tore through her.

'I'm losing the baby, Bella! I know I am!'

'Nonsense.' She held on to Amelia as she shouted for one of the children.

'What is it, Mam?' Jane was the first to appear.

'Run to the doctor's,' Bella instructed her calmly. 'Be quick. Tell him Mrs Dickinson needs him now. He must come quickly.'

Jane was gone, doors crashing behind her.

'We'll get you upstairs and lying down,' Bella told Amelia.

Amelia tried to ride out the pain, but it wasn't easy. Every time she became convinced that she was about to lose her baby, she reminded herself that she had believed exactly that when Jack was born. This was different, though. This baby wasn't due for another couple of months.

With Bella's help, she was soon lying on her bed. The pain was increasing, and she wasn't sure how much longer she could stand it.

It hurt her to admit it, even to herself, but she had lost interest in this baby since George died. It had just been a child, almost an inconvenience. Now, frightened of losing it, her baby seemed more precious than life itself.

The pain went on, hour after hour.

Amelia's daughter was born late that evening.

'She breathing,' the doctor told Amelia gently, 'but – well, I'm sorry, but she won't survive. Premature babies are–'

'I beg your pardon!' Amelia was furious. Her heart raced, not from exertion, but from sheer, blind fury.

'Look, Mrs Dickinson, I'm sorry but the truth must be faced. This child is too–'

'Get out!' She waved her arms in the direction of the door.

The doctor left, but Amelia could hear him outside talking to Bella. Bella was asking him about getting Amelia to hospital, and the doctor was telling her that there was little point.

Amelia closed her mind to them. Let them say what they wanted.

When she and her brother had been found at the orphanage gates all those years ago, the doctor had been called. What would Matron have done if she had been told that the twins wouldn't survive? She wouldn't have listened. She would have made sure they survived.

'I'll call you Victoria,' she whispered, stroking her daughter's face, 'and one day, I'll tell you all about the woman who was Queen of England for so long. And I'll tell you all about Matron – her middle name was Victoria. I remember her telling me how much she disliked it.' She smiled at that.

'Yes, one day I'll tell you all about it,' she vowed to her daughter. 'Because I promise you this, my darling girl. You will survive!'

Chapter Eleven

October 1906, Fairbanks, Alaska

'Look where you're going!' Amelia cried. The workman put down his ladder.

'Sorry, ma'am.'

'And why aren't those doors on yet?' she demanded. 'You promised faithfully that they'd be fitted last week.'

'You'll need to talk to the boss, Mrs Dickinson.'

'Believe me, I intend to. The hotel is supposed to be opening for guests on the first of December, and I'll look extremely foolish if the doors aren't on.'

'With due respect, Mrs Dickinson–'

'I suggest,' she cut him off, her voice like ice, 'that instead of talking, you start working!'

He scuttled off and Amelia took a moment to look around her.

William Granger had been keen enough to win the contract for this refurbishment. There would be no problems, he had assured her. All work on her hotel – the Blue Ridge Hotel – would be completed easily by the first of December, he had said.

At the moment, it looked as if the work would never be finished and the grand opening was only six weeks away. Oh, yes, she would certainly be having words with the boss!

Taking a deep breath, she gave the wooden crate a shove. She managed to push it along the hallway and was about to steer it across the threshold and into the ballroom when a door, one of the many that were waiting to be hung, and that were still propped up against a wall, crashed down on top of it.

The crate gave under the weight, and the din had two workmen rushing to her side.

'Are you hurt?' one of the men asked worriedly.

'Hurt?' she repeated, her voice verging on hysterics. 'Have you any idea what you've done? This chandelier–' The sound of breaking glass had made her feel physically ill and she was shaking with rage. She was struggling to speak at all. 'This chandelier,' she began again, 'has been shipped from Italy! It's made of the finest crystal!'

The two men looked at each other, the taller man shuffling from one foot to the other in a nervous way.

'Apart from anything else,' she shouted, struggling to get the enormity of the situation through to them, 'there's no time to have a replacement brought here.'

'What would you like us to do?' the taller man asked, swallowing hard.

'I would like you to get my hotel finished!' she practically screamed at them.

The men were silent.

'Mr Granger will be here in the morning, yes?' she demanded.

'Yes, ma'am.'

'Tell him I want to see him. Eight o'clock sharp!'

With that, she abandoned her broken chandelier and strode off. If she didn't get out, those workmen would be shaking even more than they were now. She felt a breath away from committing murder.

She stepped out into the street, and took a few breaths to calm herself. Bella had said from the start that Amelia had taken on too much. Perhaps she was right. The Blue Ridge Hotel was her most ambitious project to date by far.

But no. She was dealing with incompetent workmen, that was all. Tomorrow, she would insist that Mr Granger supervise his workmen personally.

She strode off towards the café. At least that was thriving.

Fairbanks was thriving, too. Buildings sprang up like mushrooms and the residents were filled with optimism.

Gold had been discovered late here, and the newspaper claimed that, this year, output would reach between twelve and fifteen million dollars.

Just like Seattle, Fairbanks had suffered the effects of fire. Much of the town had been destroyed. She remembered Miles telling her about the fire in Seattle, and how the city had prospered with the consequent rebuilding. In exactly the same way, Fairbanks was prospering.

Bella had been doubtful at first, but they had said their goodbyes to Dawson and set off for a new life in Fairbanks.

The boarding-house had fetched an excellent price and, although she hadn't sold the gold sweepings that she'd been so careful to collect every day, Amelia knew they would save them if necessary.

A month after arriving, Amelia had opened the café. While the town was filled with builders as well as miners, she knew it made sense to aim straight for the men's stomachs. They offered a full, varied menu and served everything including cereals, fish, hot and cold meats, salads and sandwiches.

When she reached the café, she was pleased to see that only three tables were unoccupied. She smiled and murmured a quick 'Good afternoon' to three regular customers.

There was a dark-haired, stocky man sitting at a table in the corner, Amelia didn't know him, but she knew he dined at the café regularly and he always had the porterhouse steak. She must remember to ask Bella about him.

The table in the corner opposite his had been occupied and was still waiting to be cleared. Amelia was about to point this out when Hannah, the young waitress, rushed across to deal with it, giving Amelia a nervous smile as she passed.

Amelia walked around to the back of the counter. Eliza was putting cash in the till and Amelia, noting the contents, gave the girl an approving smile.

She walked into the kitchen. It was the busiest time of day as they prepared for the evening rush and the room was humming with noise and activity.

Bella was peeling potatoes. Her children, Jane and Isaac, were washing a huge pile of plates. Isaac, at fourteen, was a giant of a boy and his sister, two years younger, was dwarfed as she stood by his side. Jack was helping, too. He was putting everything away in its place.

Isaac and Jack were chattering away as they worked, and Amelia wondered how

Victoria could possibly sleep through the noise. Yet, sleep she did. A year old now, she was a gentle, placid baby. She was a small child, and the poor mite was constantly coughing and sneezing, yet she was happy.

Trudy, their cook, was stirring a thick vegetable soup. Amelia picked up a spoon and tasted it. She nodded at Trudy.

'It's good.'

'Of course it's good,' Trudy grumbled. 'Either you trust me to make a good broth or you don't!'

'If I didn't trust you,' Amelia responded quietly, 'you wouldn't be here.'

'Mummy!' Jack rushed over to her. 'Isaac says—'

'Later, Jack,' she told him, ruffling his blond hair. 'I need to talk to Bella first.'

'Oh?' Bella sounded wary.

'You'll never believe what's happened,' Amelia told her. 'One of the chandeliers has been smashed to pieces.'

'What?' Bella gasped.

'Completely ruined. Wait till I see Mr Granger tomorrow. Oh, and before I forget, and before he leaves, there's a man out front. He's dark-haired, stocky. Always sits at the table in the corner and always has the porterhouse steak. Go and look before he leaves.'

'I don't need to look,' Bella replied. 'That's John Talbot. He has a mining stake

276

nearby and is working it with his two sons. His wife died some years back. What makes you ask?'

'Just curious,' Amelia told her. 'I've seen him here several times.'

'Yes, we've a lot of regulars.'

'We have,' Amelia agreed, 'and we'll have a lot at the hotel too, if it's ever finished. I'll speak to William Granger first thing in the morning. After all of his promises–' She broke off, frowning impatiently at Hannah who had come into the kitchen and obviously wanted something.

'Bella, it's Mr Talbot. He said he'd like a quick word if you have a minute.'

'Of course.' Bella removed her apron and patted her hair. 'I won't be a minute, Mel.'

She was, in fact, ten minutes, but it didn't matter. As usual, there was a lot to be done and any conversation centred around the café.

It was late that evening when they finally locked up and, as ever, Amelia and Bella were exhausted. They sat in their tiny sitting-room, coffee in their hands, and slowly gathered their breath.

The children had been in bed for a couple of hours and Victoria, who often chose to wake and demand attention at this time of night, was sleeping soundly in the room next door.

Amelia, feeling calmer now, finally told

Bella about the disaster with the chandelier.

'I'm sure there won't be time now to get a replacement shipped out,' she muttered. 'If those stupid workmen had hung the doors when they were supposed to–'

'I'm sure they're doing their best,' Bella said mildly. 'It's not their fault that–'

'It's their fault the chandelier's broken,' Amelia retorted, 'and I'll make sure William Granger knows that! He'll pay for it. And he'll pay a lot more if the work's not finished in time for the opening.'

'If you hadn't taken on so much, Mel, you wouldn't be having all these problems.'

'What do you mean?' But Amelia knew. Bella hated change and she hated what she saw as risks.

'This project is too much,' Bella said urgently. 'Look at us. We're worn out. I'm managing the café and looking after four children, and you're running yourself into the ground with the hotel.'

'I'm not running myself into the ground,' Amelia scoffed. 'I have everything under control. These last twelve months have toughened me up so that I can cope with anything.'

'They've certainly toughened you up,' Bella said dryly. She took a breath. 'Mel, you're convinced that if you bring luxury to Fairbanks, money will follow and you'll be the richest woman in the land. Perhaps you will, but at what cost? You've gone too far this time. You're putting yourself and everyone else under too much pressure.'

'Pressure? Have you forgotten what I've been through since I left Liverpool. I've buried two husbands, I've started and lost businesses, I've been charged with murder and I've cared for two wonderful children who–'

'Who never see you!' Bella cut her off. 'Three times Jack has tried to speak to you today and three times you have fobbed him off. You'll pay a heavy price if you don't give them your time.'

'How dare you!' Amelia cried, jumping to her feet. 'Just when things are finally coming right for me–'

'For you?' Bella shouted in amazement. She shook her head. 'My, isn't that typical? That's the woman you've become. Completely selfish, heartless–'

She broke off, unable to compete with the noise coming from the room next door – they had woken Victoria.

Amelia, teeth gritted in fury, strode through to Victoria's room.

'There, there,' she soothed, stroking her baby's hot cheeks. 'Did we wake you?'

Bella had followed and, as soon as Victoria saw her, she lifted her arms.

'Mama!' she sobbed.

Amelia reached for her daughter, but

Victoria withdrew from her embrace. It was Bella she wanted. Amelia watched helplessly as her little girl coiled her arms around Bella's neck.

November 1906, Liverpool

Ivy wished she was anywhere but at this meeting.

Rose had persuaded her to come, and as usual, Ivy felt the odd one out. She had been working for Rose for almost eight years now. She was a lovely woman and they were good friends, but Rose was strong-willed.

It was Ivy's third meeting and she was no closer to having an opinion on the suffragette movement. She was frustrated by women who had no minds of their own, who simply existed to carry out their men's wishes, but she couldn't agree with all this talk of equality – it would only bring trouble.

She hadn't told James she was coming here. She hadn't lied to him, but she had led him to assume that she would be at Rose's house.

Looking at the ardent faces around her, she suspected many of the woman hadn't told their husbands where they were, either. A lot of them, like James, would be furious if they knew.

'We need deeds, not words!' one woman shouted.

This was the third time Ivy had heard that

same statement. Her third meeting, and her last, she decided. She had nothing to contribute. If women wanted the vote, there had to be better ways of getting it. Last year, several women had been imprisoned during protests.

Ivy couldn't even begin to imagine what would happen if she were to go on a protest march and find herself imprisoned. Whatever would James say? What would the children think?

It was as well, she thought suddenly, that Amelia wasn't here. The idea made her smile. Amelia would be the first to protest and the first to be thrown in jail, probably!'

She had never spoken to Amelia about it, but she guessed that, if she stopped to think about it at all, Amelia would be all for fighting for women's rights.

Rose was the same. Right from their first meeting, all those years ago, Ivy had seen a lot of Amelia in Rose. Ivy enjoyed working for her, if it could be called work, but Rose liked nothing better than a cause. If it wasn't better education for all the children in the country, it was votes for women.

Ivy wouldn't dare voice such an opinion here, but, if she had the vote, she wouldn't know what to do with it. She and James often discussed the state of the country, but she wouldn't know who was best suited to run it.

Politics didn't interest her. James, the twins and young Lizzie were her life. The twins were almost ten years old now, Lizzie was six, and it was their futures that concerned her.

Of course, Rose would merely say that, if she had the vote, she would be better able to secure them a good future.

It was only a small gathering this time. The meeting was being held at Georgina's, a friend of Rose's, and they were seated in her very impressive drawing-room.

Why was it, Ivy wondered, that women with money were most concerned about winning the vote? Was it because they were well educated and had a better understanding of politics? Or was it because they had more time on their hands?

Finally, the meeting drew to a close, Ivy was ready to go home, but Rose was chatting to Georgina, and she felt obliged to wait. All the same, Rose only lived a few houses away, whereas Ivy had quite a walk.

The other women were pleasant and friendly, but she knew that if she struck up too many conversations, they would be persuading her to make banners or join them on protests.

'Are you ready to leave, Ivy?' Rose asked, putting on her gloves.

'I am,' Ivy replied, relieved.

Rose laughed as half a dozen of the others

put on their coats and gathered up banners.
Ivy and Rose followed the noisy women
down the steps. They were almost on the
pavement when Ivy saw something that
made her stumble.

'Oh, my!'

James was walking toward them. It was
too much to hope that he wouldn't spot her.
Ivy saw him scowling at the women
walking on ahead with their banners. They
were only carrying them, not holding them
aloft, but he would know what they were.
Then, as if the world had slowed, she saw
him look up the steps towards the house. It
was the most casual of glances, but then he
looked again, his gaze colliding with Ivy's.

'Look who's here,' Rose said happily, un-
aware of Ivy's desire to vanish into the chilly
evening air.

'Oh, yes.' She pinned a smile to her face,
but she felt quite ill. 'James, what are you
doing here?'

'I could ask you the same question,' he
said, his expression grim.

'Have you come to meet Ivy?' Rose asked.
'My, what a gentleman you are, James!'

'Yes,' he said, and Ivy could see he was
struggling to keep a rein on his tongue.

'We'd better be off,' Ivy said, cringing inwardly. 'Goodnight, Rose.'

'Goodnight to both of you!' Rose said, and
she hurried off to catch up with the others.

Ivy fell into step with James, or tried to. He was striding off as if the devil was after him. She could feel his anger in every step he took.

She assumed the twins and Lizzie were still next door at Maggie's. It was young Henry's birthday, and the three children had been invited for tea and games.

'The children–' she burst out suddenly.

'At Maggie's,' he snapped back.

She breathed a sigh of relief. For one awful moment, she had thought something had happened to one of them.

The children were fine, that's what mattered. James was angry, rightly so, she supposed, but that wasn't the end of the world.

'I'll get the children,' she said, as they reached Maggie's door.

James didn't answer. Instead, he walked on ahead, let himself into their house and slammed the door shut behind him.

It was a relief to gather the children to her and listen as they told her all about Henry's party. They were far too excited to notice how quiet she was.

They were soon persuaded to go to bed. Mainly, Ivy suspected, because one glance at their father told them he would stand for no arguments.

He had listened to talk of the party, and he'd smiled in the right places, but even they could see he was in a stern mood.

'Perhaps you'd care to tell me where you've been,' he said at last.

'Oh, love, you know where I've been,' Ivy said gently. 'Rose thought I'd like to go to one of her meetings. She and her friends–'

'Suffragettes!'

'Yes,' she agreed lamely, 'but they're harmless enough.'

'Never mind giving them the vote,' he snapped, 'they should all be locked up.' He glared at her. 'You lied to me, Ivy!'

'Not really, love,' she answered. 'I did go to see Rose, but–'

'And you had no idea she was going to the meeting?'

She couldn't lie to him.

'Well, yes, I knew.'

'How long has this been going on?' he demanded.

'I've been three times,' she told him, 'and tonight was the last time.'

'Yes, it was!' he said hotly. 'No wife of mine will get involved with those … those…'

'They're decent people, Jimmy.'

'They're trouble!' he corrected her. 'Do you have any idea how many suffragettes have been arrested? They have no regard for the law and yet demand the vote.'

'They're–'

'I don't care what they are, Ivy,' he said, his voice low and angry, 'you won't be hav-

285

ing anything more to do with them. You'll tell Rose tomorrow that she'll have to find someone else to work for her!'

'What?' Ivy was horrified. He couldn't be serious. She couldn't lose her job. 'But that's ridiculous. I'll tell her I won't go to any more meetings, but I don't have to give up my job. Think of the money.'

'We don't need the money.'

'But–'

'My mind's made up,' he said firmly. 'You'll tell Rose tomorrow and we'll say no more about it.'

With that, he headed up the stairs to bed.

Ivy sat at the kitchen table for a few minutes. She would have to talk to him when he was in a better frame of mind. Tomorrow. She'd talk to him tomorrow.

She slowly climbed the stairs to bed.

James didn't say a word and she didn't know if he was awake or asleep. When she climbed in beside him, she strongly suspected he was awake. However, when she moved close to him, he rolled on to his side and put his back to her.

It was a long time before Ivy found sleep. She lay for hours, turning over, longing to reach out for warmth from James, yet afraid to.

She awoke early, but James was already out of bed. She dressed quickly and ran down the stairs. He was there, and the sight of him warmed her heart. She loved him in all his moods.

'Jimmy, I'm sorry, love,' she began slowly. 'I should have told you. It was just that – well, for one thing I knew you wouldn't like it, but for another, I needed to make up my own mind about it all. Last night, I finally did make up my mind. It's not for me, love. You know that.'

'You're right about that,' he retorted. 'It's not for you. I'll not stand for it.'

'James Penrose,' she said in despair. 'Will you stop being so angry and listen to me for a moment? For heaven's sake, I've said I'm sorry, and I've said I don't want anything more to do with any of it! What more do I have to do?'

He stared back at her, and it was difficult to tell if he was mellowing.

'One thing's certain,' she said, moving past him to put the kettle on to boil, 'your sister would be in the midst of it.' A smile touched her lips. 'At least you don't have to race off and get Mel out of jail.'

'She would be there,' he agreed, unsmiling. 'But you're not Amelia. You're my wife, Ivy.'

'So I am. But I may as well not be for all the shame I've given you. Is that it, James Penrose? Are you wishing you hadn't married me?'

'What?'

'It's a poor thing if a woman can get into bed without so much as a "goodnight" from her own husband. It was cold last night, and my feet were like two blocks of ice.'

'So I'm just a foot warmer to you?' he asked, and Ivy could see a smile struggling to get past his stern exterior.

'Why else do you think I married you?' she said lightly. 'It wasn't for your money.'

'Come here,' he said.

Keeping the smile from her face, Ivy walked into his arms.

He sighed as he held her close.

'I won't have you mixed up with those women,' he told her.

'And I have no wish to get involved,' she said, 'so we can forget all about it. Although I don't see why I should give up my job. I enjoy working for Rose and the money is useful.'

Ivy smiled as she hugged him tight. With any luck, it would be forgotten in a few days.

December 1906, Fairbanks

Sam Hunter had heard all about the Blue Ridge Hotel, but he'd had to see it for himself. Today's grand opening seemed the ideal opportunity.

He had assumed, people had been exaggerating, and he'd laughed, unable to believe such nonsense, when Bella had told him about the chandelier being brought all the way from Italy.

Yet now, standing in the hotel's reception area, surrounded by tall, elegant ferns, modern armchairs and small tables, he knew that no-one had exaggerated. The Blue Ridge Hotel was the finest for miles. Everything one touched whispered luxury.

Bella had let it slip that Amelia's original bank loan had been doubled. That was due mainly, according to Bella, to the cost of shipping everything to Fairbanks.

Interest rates were high, too, Sam thought. He respected Amelia as a businesswoman, but he couldn't help wondering if this was too ambitious, even for her.

She hadn't spotted him yet, and that surprised him given that she was watching the guests and staff closely. She had just moved on from the bank manager and was currently conversing with a mine director Sam knew by sight.

He was grateful for the opportunity to watch her unobserved, but he wasn't warmed by the sight of her as he usually was. There was something different about her, something distant. Her smile, the one that had always made his breath catch, was missing and in its place was a tight effort that couldn't quite reach her eyes.

Bella had said she'd changed, and that the woman with the heart of gold who had taken in Bella and the children was lost to them, but he hadn't believed it. He hadn't wanted to believe it.

He mingled with the growing crowd of guests. The restaurant was filled to capacity and people were sitting in the reception, chatting over drinks, as they waited for a free table.

Musicians were playing in the ballroom – a pianist, violinist and cellist – and although they played well, he would have preferred to hear Bella sing.

'She reckons I'm not posh enough for the hotel,' Bella had grumbled to him.

Sam glanced up and smiled inwardly as he saw the huge chandelier glittering above him.

Across the room, Amelia was complimenting a woman on her dress. A young girl, presumably the woman's daughter, was also complimented. And still Amelia's smile left Sam cold.

He watched her sweep across the room. She paused for a word with one of the waiters as she walked by. The party was in full swing, but Amelia still had a watchful eye on the staff.

Frowning, Sam left the ballroom and sought out the receptionist.

'I'd like to book a room, please,' he said, replacing the frown with a smile.

'When for?' she asked.

'Tonight, if possible. Maybe tomorrow night, too.'

The girl's efficiency would have won Amelia's approval and Sam soon had a room. He'd been tempted to book the best suite available but he neither wanted nor needed it.

'I hope you'll enjoy your stay with us, Mr Hunter.' At least the receptionist's smile was genuine.

He stood on the edges, watching the party for a while. It saddened him that Amelia's children – or Bella's – weren't around to join in the fun.

Young Jack was a fine boy and Sam would have enjoyed seeing what he made of all this.

Sam's room was the height of luxury – he'd expected nothing less – and the Blue Ridge Hotel was finally quiet, but he couldn't settle.

For years now, Amelia Dickinson had been on the fringes of his life. Every time he saw her, which wasn't often, and every time he thought about her, which was too often for his liking, his heart would begin its erratic beating to remind him of how she affected him.

Lately, he had even had thoughts of asking her to marry him.

He scoffed at his own thoughts. He had been determined to marry her. Somewhere along the line, Sam had fallen in love with her. It might even have happened the first time he saw her, when she had begged him to take her and her husband, Miles Carter, across the rapids. But now...

With a sigh, Sam climbed into his large, comfortable bed. Now, he didn't know how he felt.

Besides, what would she want with him? If this hotel, with all its luxury, meant so much to her, why would she bother with him? She had all she needed right here.

'Sam Hunter?' Amelia's finger hovered above the entry in the registration book. 'What does this mean?'

Juliet, the young receptionist, looked at Amelia as if she had lost her senses.

'Well, Mrs Dickinson, it means he's booked into–'

'Yes, yes,' Amelia cut her off impatiently. 'When did he book the room? When did he arrive? Is he here now?'

'Yes, Mrs Dickinson. He booked in last night, and said he'd let us know this morning whether he would be staying tonight as well.'

Amelia couldn't believe it. Sam Hunter was here – not only in Fairbanks but in her hotel – and no-one had told her.

'Ask him – oh, it doesn't matter.'

Amelia was halfway across reception when

she turned back.

'Ask him if he'll have breakfast with me in my rooms,' she said.

An hour later, Amelia was sitting at her breakfast table opposite Sam Hunter. As usual, now that she was with him, she felt awkward and tongue-tied. For all that, she felt good. She had come a long way since their first meeting.

'Were you here last night?' she asked curiously.

'For a while, yes.'

'I didn't know. I'm sorry.'

He shrugged.

'You were busy.'

She waited for him to compliment her on the hotel's opening celebrations, but he didn't.

'I'm never too busy for friends,' she replied.

His answering gaze was unfathomable and Amelia wondered if she had done something wrong, something that had upset him, but that was impossible.

She was always taken aback by the sight of him. It was a combination of the way he was so at ease, his height and good looks, the memories he brought to mind.

If it hadn't been for Sam Hunter, she might still be locked up in Dawson jail. If it hadn't been for him, she and Miles might never have made it across those treacherous rapids and into Dawson.

'Does Bella know you're here?' she asked.

'Yes, I saw her last night.'

Over the years, Bella had insisted that she and Sam Hunter were merely just friends, yet Amelia had never been convinced. Bella, she knew, wrote to him most weeks.

Amelia wished she didn't feel so self-conscious. He had always had this effect on her. It was as if he could read her mind, as if he understood her thoughts as well, if not better, than she did.

'You'll still keep the café?' he asked her.

'Oh, yes, it's doing well.'

'So Bella told me.'

'And I'm sure Bella's told you all sorts of stories about getting this hotel up and running.'

'She told me about the chandelier,' he said, smiling. 'You've come a long way since you bought and sold that stove,' he added quietly.

'Yes,' she agreed.

Then, she'd had Miles with her. His death, and the loss of the boarding-house, had flattened her. Then, just when she'd come to terms with that, she had married George and thought life was settled once more.

Looking on the bright side, she knew that losing George had made her more independent. She knew she could make it on her own.

'Jack is well?' he asked.

'He's very well, thank you. He's a bright boy and is doing well at his lessons. His tutor says–'

'He has his own tutor?'

'Yes. The pianist you saw last night is his tutor.'

'I see. And the children still live at the café?'

'Temporarily, yes. I've had so much to do here that it's been easier. They'll soon be joining me here, though.'

'You must miss them,' he remarked.

'Yes. Yes, I do.'

He was eyeing her with a look she couldn't analyse.

'Have you made up your mind about the length of your stay with us?' she asked briskly.

'Yes, I'll be checking out shortly,' he replied. 'I've seen all I need to see.'

Amelia wasn't sure what he meant by that. She was disappointed, too. She had the feeling that he wasn't impressed by the hotel. No, worse than that, she had the feeling that it was she who had been found wanting.

January 1908, Fairbanks

'When you have a minute, I'd like a word, Mel,' Bella said.

'Later, Bella,' Amelia replied, keeping her finger on the page so she didn't lose her place in the accounts.

'It won't keep until later. I've been trying to talk to you for the last couple of weeks – as you know.'

'You have,' Amelia agreed. 'Sorry. We'll talk this evening. I'll come along to the café.'

'Right.' Bella turned on her heels and left the office.

With a sigh, Amelia returned to her accounts.

It was late that evening when she finally made it to the café and most of the diners had left.

She checked the till, and was about to check the kitchen when Bella met her.

'I'll make us a coffee,' Bella said firmly, 'and then we'll talk in the sitting-room.'

Amelia wasn't given a chance to argue. She sat in an armchair and closed her eyes. She was tired, and it was good to sit and relax.

'Here we are,' Bella said, putting coffee on the table at Amelia's side.

'What's so urgent, then?' Amelia asked lightly.

'I'm getting married on Saturday.'

For a moment, Amelia thought she must have misheard. Then she thought Bella must be joking.

'You're what?'

'I'm getting married on Saturday,' Bella repeated.

296

'Married?' Amelia simply couldn't grasp it. 'But I didn't know – I mean, how long have you been–'

'John – Mr Talbot – and I have been courting for six months now,' Bella explained, 'and–'

'Mr Talbot?' The name sounded familiar. 'Oh! The porterhouse steak man.'

'Yes.'

'You're marrying Mr Talbot?'

'I am.'

'Well, I don't know what to say. It's all a bit sudden.'

'It's nothing of the sort,' Bella argued. 'I expect you're the only person in Fairbanks who doesn't know we're getting married. You're so wrapped up in the hotel you don't notice what's going on around you. Life isn't all business, you know.'

It was true that Amelia had been busy with the hotel, yet she'd had no idea about Bella and Mr Talbot.

'Congratulations,' Amelia said, somewhat belatedly, she realised. 'I'm happy for you.'

'Thank you.'

'You do love him, don't you?'

'Of course I do.' Bella laughed, an exasperated sound. 'The whole of Fairbanks knows that!'

Was Amelia really so out of touch?

'It's just that I've always thought you had your eye on Sam Hunter,' she explained.

Bella laughed at that.

'Oh, Mel, how many times do I have to tell you? Sam and I have been friends – just friends – for years.' She shook her head in despair. 'You really are blind, aren't you?'

'What do you mean?'

'Sam only has eyes for one woman,' Bella confided.

'Really?' Amelia didn't like to gossip, but she was curious. 'Who's that?'

Bella tutted.

'The woman who dressed as a man to try to persuade him to take her on his boat. The woman who robbed him of sleep as he travelled the whole of the Yukon trying to find out who had killed her husband and, therefore, prove her innocence. The woman who–'

'No!' Amelia's heart was racing. 'Oh, Bella, you are wrong!'

'No, I'm right. It's plain to see. Haven't you noticed the way he looks at you?'

Amelia shook her head.

'And haven't you noticed how, whenever he's within shouting distance, you struggle to string two words together?'

Yes, she had noticed that. From the first moment they had met, she had noticed the effect he had on her. Could Bella be right?

Right or wrong, Amelia decided, mentally telling her heart to slow its pace, it didn't matter. She was independent. A woman of

298

means. The last thing she needed was a man in her life.

'Now then,' she said, swiftly changing the subject, 'we need to decide who will cover for you on Saturday.'

'I shall be away for a month,' Bella said calmly. 'John and I, and Jane and Isaac, are going away. His sons will stay here and work the claim, but the rest of us are having a honeymoon.'

Amelia's head was reeling. Had she been told he had sons? If she had, she'd forgotten. That wasn't important, though. What was important was that Bella was going away for a whole month.

'A month?' she said shakily. 'But how shall I manage? What about the café?'

'The café?' Bella shook her head in a bemused fashion. 'I imagine your first concern will be for Jack and Victoria.'

'Yes, of course, but I still need to think of the café.'

'I'm sure you'll come up with something.'

On Saturday, standing in the watery sunshine with her children by her side, Amelia was still trying to 'come up with something'.

She had people who could manage the hotel and the café if she were absent for a few hours, but there was no-one she could leave in charge for a whole month. How would she cope?

The carriage pulled up, ready to take the newlyweds and Jane and Isaac away.

Bella came over and gave Amelia a quick hug.

'Have a wonderful time, Mrs Talbot,' Amelia said weakly.

'We will,' Bella promised. 'You have fun, too.'

'Fun? I've no idea how I'll cope with you leaving at such short notice. I mean–'

'You'll cope,' Bella cut her off.

'You don't care, do you? You're leaving me in the lurch, and you don't care!'

Bella laughed softly.

'Oh, Mel–' She didn't have time to complete the sentence as her new husband called to her to hurry.

Seconds later, the carriage pulled away, leaving Amelia and the children to wave until it was lost from view.

Chapter Twelve

February 1908, Fairbanks

'You're back!' Amelia cried in amazement, hugging Isaac tight. 'Thank heaven for that!'

He was as tall as Amelia now, but she was so pleased to see him she could have hugged the breath from his body. No-one had any idea how difficult it had been without Bella, and it was wonderful to see Isaac and know that Bella was back from her honeymoon almost two weeks early.

What a relief! Amelia should have known that Bella wouldn't leave her to cope on her own for too long.

'We're back,' Isaac told her, 'because Mam's poorly. She sent me to tell you. She can't come to work.'

'What? Your mother is ill?' Amelia had never known Bella to be ill. Never. But still, as Amelia hadn't been expecting her back for another fortnight, it wasn't the end of the world. Bella could have a few days to recover.

'All right, Isaac, and thank you for coming to tell me. Tell your mother that I hope she's better soon.'

Isaac nodded.

'So did you all have a nice time?' she asked him.

'Not really. Mam wasn't well so—' He left the sentence unfinished.

The boy looked quite concerned, Amelia noticed.

'She'll soon be better,' she told him with a smile. Bella had an excellent constitution. 'Tell her I'll be along to visit her when I have a moment...'

When that moment would be, Amelia had

no idea. She was still cross with Bella for leaving her in the lurch with no warning. It was all well and good Bella telling her that the whole of Fairbanks had known she was getting married, but the whole of Fairbanks didn't have successful businesses to run. People had no idea of the work involved. It was never-ending.

On top of that, Amelia had two children to care for. Bella was fond of telling her that she couldn't have wished for two more biddable children and, yes, Jack and Victoria did manage to entertain themselves. They still demanded time, though. Time that Amelia couldn't spare.

It was two days later, with no further word from Bella, when Amelia decided to pay her friend a visit. This was too much.

Bella wasn't a sickly person. She was as fit and strong as anyone and Amelia strongly suspected that – she dismissed that thought before it formed. If Bella said she was ill, then she was ill. All the same, Amelia suspected that, if she hadn't been so wrapped up in her new marriage, she would have been back at work sooner than this.

However, Amelia could spare a few minutes – ten at the most – and at least she might leave with some idea of when Bella was expected to return.

Bella's door was opened by her exhausted-looking husband.

'The doctor's with her now,' he explained as he showed Amelia inside. 'He may let you see her for a few minutes.'

'The doctor? She's in bed?' The shock hit her with a jolt. She hadn't imagined there might be a need for a doctor. Bella had no time whatsoever for doctors. 'But whatever's wrong with her?'

'We don't know,' he replied, and Amelia could see the worry etched in every line of his face. 'Perhaps we'll know more when the doctor's seen her.'

The doctor, however, couldn't enlighten them.

'I'm afraid you can't see her today,' he told Amelia. 'Mrs Talbot has a high fever and she must have complete rest. She's sleeping now.'

He looked to John Talbot.

'I'll call again first thing in the morning. If her condition worsens, then call me immediately.'

As soon as the doctor had gone, John Talbot sank into the nearest chair and buried his face in his hands.

'What brought it on?' Amelia wanted to know. She was so shaken that she was trembling. 'She was fine two weeks ago so what happened?'

'We don't know, Mrs Dickinson,' he said wearily. 'One moment she was her usual self, the next she said she felt tired and needed to rest. She was shivering and then she complained of being too hot.' He shook his head in despair. 'If the doctor doesn't know what ails her, how can I be expected to?'

Tired? Hot and cold? With a sick feeling in her stomach, Amelia dropped into a chair beside John Talbot. Her head was filled with visions of her last days with Miles. Like Bella, he had complained of being tired, and of being hot one minute and chilled the next.

'How are you managing?' she asked at last, determined to concentrate on practical issues. 'Do you need help? I can send someone–'

'Bless you,' John Talbot said softly, 'but we're managing. Isaac and Jane are good children. They're a great help. And my sons–' He broke off. 'Thank you, but we can manage.'

Amelia felt helpless.

'I can at least bring food,' she said. 'I'll speak to my chef and call again this evening. I'll make sure he prepares enough for the five of you plus something nourishing for Bella.'

'She's not eating, Mrs Dickinson.'

'Then I'll have to make sure he prepares something nourishing and tempting for her.' Amelia rose to her feet. 'I'll see you this evening when I bring your meals.'

As Amelia walked back to the hotel, she was still trembling. Her legs were refusing to co-operate and she was a breath away from bursting into tears.

When she reached the hotel, she knew she couldn't go inside. She needed to pull herself together before she faced people. She walked straight past, and kept on walking, eventually coming to a halt on the edge of the town where she was alone. And then she did burst into tears.

It was two days since young Isaac had called to tell her that Bella was ill. Two days! All Amelia had done in that time was worry about the business. Instead of rushing to her friend's side to see what she could do to help, she had fretted about the hotel and the café.

What did it matter if Bella couldn't work alongside her? It didn't. What mattered was – she stopped short. What had Bella said to her?

'My, isn't that typical? That's the woman you've become. Completely selfish, heartless–'

Amelia shuddered. When was the last time she had spared a thought for Bella's welfare? She had been cross with her for leaving her to cope with the business alone, then she'd doubted that she was ill enough to warrant staying at home.

Selfish? Yes, Bella was right. If only Bella

was with her now to tell her so.

March 1908, Liverpool
Ivy sighed, tore a sheet of paper into tiny squares and threw them on the fire.

'What is it, love?' James asked, peering at her over his newspaper.

'This letter to Amelia,' she said with another sigh. 'I've decided to start again. It's too depressing.'

'Oh?'

'I started by telling her that the orphanage is threatened with closure again,' she explained, 'and the Lord knows what she'll think of that. With Matron only just gone—'

'It's been more than two years,' James reminded her.

As always, Ivy was taken aback by the passing of the years. He was right; more than two years had passed since Matron had died. It would be a long time before Ivy forgot her funeral, and the way the huge crowd had gathered around the grave, oblivious to the torrential rain, rumbles of thunder and flashes of lightning.

All the same, it doesn't seem right that, after all her hard work, the place is probably going to close anyway. It makes me so angry! It's children's lives they should be thinking about, not money.'

'True.'

'Anyway, then I told her that Rose was

306

getting married again and moving back to London.'

Ivy still hadn't quite got used to that idea. It was nine years since she had first started working for Rose Hodge and she was going to miss her dreadfully.

Not that anyone would call it working, Ivy thought with a small smile. When she had first been told about the job, Rose had insisted she needed someone reliable and trustworthy to clean and run errands for her. In truth, she had wanted company. Over the years, Ivy had spent many a happy hour chatting to her.

With another sigh, Ivy laid down her pen and leaned back in her chair. Perhaps she would write to Amelia tomorrow, when she was feeling in a more positive frame of mind.

For a few moments, she watched the sparks dancing their way up the chimney. She had everything she could ask for. Her husband and children were happy and healthy, and they had no financial worries.

All the same, she couldn't help wishing. She wished she could see Amelia, she wished Rose wasn't returning to London and she wished Matron was still with them, still fighting to keep the orphanage open.

'Jimmy,' she said suddenly, 'I've just had a thought.'

'Oh?' Again the newspaper was lowered.

'Now that Rose is leaving, I've got more time on my hands.'

'And?'

'I could help out at the orphanage. There must be dozens of things I could do. Organise some fundraising for one thing.'

James laid his newspaper aside and leaned forward to poke some life into the fire. This evening, after a bright, sunny day, it had turned chilly and they were both sitting as close to the fire as they could.

'Well, I suppose–'

'I'll go along tomorrow and see about it,' she said, excited at the prospect. It would be good to have some purpose in life. 'The new matron seems like a nice woman.'

Emily Appleby was young and energetic and, although it felt odd without Matron at the orphanage, Ivy had taken a liking to the woman. Like Matron, Emily made time for everyone.

'Nice or not,' James pointed out, 'it's money the place needs.'

Ivy was all too aware of that, which was why she would have a think about fundraising. If she had learned anything from the nine years she'd known Rose, it was that people – even people like Ivy – could make a difference in the world.

'I wonder if Amelia ever thinks about home,' she murmured. 'Or about us, come to that.'

'Of course she does!' James frowned. 'What makes you say a strange thing like that?'

'Oh, I don't know.' The truth was that, for some time now, Ivy had had the feeling that they'd been forgotten. Amelia's letters, when they came, were full of facts and figures – how busy her hotel was, how many diners visited her café. In her last letter, she hadn't even mentioned Jack or Victoria.

'I suppose she's a businesswoman,' Ivy said with a wistful smile, 'and forgets that some of us are far more interested in the children than how many guests are staying in her hotel.'

Ivy wondered what Amelia thought of her own letters. Those were usually filled with news of James and the children. But why not? Albert and Martha, eleven years old now, were growing up quickly, and young Lizzie, at seven, thought she knew it all. They were Ivy's life and if she didn't fill her letters with news of them, she would have nothing to say.

'I expect she tries to reassure us that she's well and happy,' James said, 'but I know what you mean.' He smiled. 'My sister will soon be the richest woman in Canada.'

Ivy chuckled.

'She might, at that.'

'But you'd rather hear how the children are getting on,' James guessed, 'and you're curious as to whether there's a new man in her life.'

'I am. That's far more interesting than the hotel and café. When her last letter arrived and I saw that she'd enclosed a photograph, I was so excited. I could have cried when I saw it was a photograph of the hotel!'

Admittedly it was a grand-looking place and Ivy supposed that, if she owned it, she would be proud of it. All the same, it was only a building.

'When I write tomorrow,' she said, 'I'll ask if she has a more recent one of the children.'

With that settled, Ivy felt better. Tomorrow, she would pay the orphanage a visit and offer her services. Then she would write to Amelia and tell her just what she thought of the letters she had been writing lately.

May 1908, Fairbanks

'Bella, what do you think you're doing?' Amelia cried. 'Come down at once!'

'It's all right, Mel, I'm just–'

'It isn't all right,' Amelia said firmly. 'Come down. Now!'

Shaking her head, Bella left the chandelier she had been cleaning and climbed down the steps.

'Stop fussing, Mel,' she said. 'Your concern is touching, and surprising, but I'm perfectly well. Really.'

'It's only three weeks since the doctor said

you could return to work,' Amelia pointed out firmly, 'and you still need to put some weight back on.' She eyed her friend critically. 'You are eating properly, aren't you?'

Bella hooted with laughter.

'Yes. Now stop fussing.' She nodded at the chandelier above them. 'That's covered in dust. I spotted it earlier. When it catches the sun, it looks bad.'

'Then let me do it.' Amelia grabbed the cloth from Bella's hand and climbed the steps. 'Gosh, you're right. I'll make sure it's cleaned more often in future.'

As she came down the steps, Bella was adjusting her shoe and Amelia made the most of the opportunity to look at her friend without being observed. She was pleased to see that, although she was still far too thin, Bella did appear to have gained a little weight. There was more colour in her face, too, and her hair was shining.

'I could easily have managed that,' Bella tutted, looking up.

'Perhaps.' Amelia smiled at her. 'Do you know, you really are looking better, Bella.'

Bella spluttered with laughter.

'Isn't that what I've been trying to tell you for weeks? Now, what did you want to see me about?'

'Nothing, really. I thought we'd sit and have a cup of tea together.'

'Again?' Bella couldn't hide her surprise.

'This is getting to be a habit.'

'A jolly nice habit.' Amelia nodded. 'Life's too short, Bella, and we need to relax now and again. That reminds me,' she added, 'would Isaac and Jane like to spend the day with us tomorrow? Or are they getting too old these days?' Isaac was fifteen now and Amelia often thought he must get tired of Jack hanging around him. 'The thing is, Jack's new pony is arriving.'

'Well, yes, I'm sure they'd both love to.'

'Good.' Amelia smiled ruefully. 'Victoria wants one, of course, so we'll probably have tantrums.'

'A pony? But she's only two!'

'I know, but what Jack has, she has to have.'

Bella said very little as they sat in Amelia's office, having a leisurely tea-break, and Amelia began to worry.

'You're very quiet, Bella. Are you sure you're feeling all right?'

'Yes. I'm just curious about this change in you. Not that I'm complaining but–' Bella suddenly clapped her hands together. 'It's Rory Adams, isn't it? He's responsible for the new you. Well, I never!'

'Rory Adams?' Amelia echoed in amazement. 'What are you talking about?'

'You know exactly what I'm talking about.'

She was wrong; Amelia didn't have the faintest idea.

'Don't tell me he comes here to admire the chandeliers,' Bella scoffed.

Rory Adams was a lawyer from Seattle whose two brothers had settled in Fairbanks. He was about fifty, Amelia supposed, which put him at fifteen years her senior. A pleasant man, she decided, thinking of the chats they had enjoyed about various things. He was polite and charming.

'He certainly doesn't come here to see me if that's what you're implying,' Amelia said, but even as she spoke, she felt the colour fly to her face.

It had to be said that he was becoming a very frequent guest at the hotel. And now she came to think of it, she had wondered what brought him to Fairbanks so often. He was here now and, only that very morning, had asked Amelia if she would dine with him this evening.

Amelia had gladly accepted. Now, she had doubts. If Bella was right, the last thing she wanted was to encourage him. She didn't want or need a man in her life and, if he thought she did, he was very much mistaken.

'No,' she said. 'You must be wrong, Bella. He has no interest in me. Why would he?'

'I can think of a dozen reasons. Firstly, you're a very attractive woman. Secondly, you're an intelligent woman. Thirdly, you're a successful businesswoman.'

'Stop!' Amelia was forced to laugh. 'You're my dearest friend so you're sure to look at me differently. A stranger would see nothing of the sort.'

'Pah!'

'You do get some insane notions in your head, Bella.'

'In that case,' Bella said, unperturbed, 'it must be the chandeliers. It's lucky we gave that one a good clean.'

They both erupted into gales of laugher.

'Stop it.' Amelia wiped the tears from her face. 'I'm having dinner with him this evening and—'

'Now she tells me!'

'He only asked me this morning. But there's nothing in it. Really. All he wants is some company when he dines. A lot of people do. Most people do.'

'So if Rory Adams isn't responsible for the new you, who is?' Bella asked.

'Is there a new me?' Amelia asked lightly, but she knew exactly what Bella meant.

'Believe me, there is. I have my old friend back and it's wonderful. What happened?'

'You became ill,' Amelia said softly. 'I was really cross with you for leaving me in the lurch and I couldn't believe it when Isaac told me you were ill. When I realised the doctor was with you, and that you were complaining of—' She shuddered.

'I remembered how Miles had died,' she

confessed, 'and I was frightened you were going to leave me, too. I thought of all the fun we'd had over the years, and what great friends we had become. I suppose I realised, a little belatedly, that we hadn't had much fun lately, and that I'd been too wrapped up in this place.' She waved her arms to encompass the hotel. 'All of this seemed so meaningless.'

Bella smiled at that.

'Poor John thought he was going to be burying me, too,' she murmured. 'But,' she went on briskly, rising to her feet, 'I'm fully recovered and I can't sit around here all day. Thanks for inviting Isaac and Jane tomorrow, they'll be thrilled.'

She hugged Amelia.

'You silly thing, Mel. Even at your worst, you've always been my best friend. Right from the moment we met, when you looked at me as if I was something Miles had dragged in off the streets.'

'He had dragged you in off the streets,' Amelia replied, deadpan, and again, they burst into laughter.

'You look like a princess, Mummy,' Victoria whispered, her eyes wide.

'I do?' Amelia scooped her daughter into her arms and laughed.

'Yes.'

In that case, Amelia decided, she would

change her dress. She didn't want Rory Adams thinking she was making a special effort for him. Confound Bella! If she had kept her ridiculous notions to herself, Amelia would be looking forward to dining with the man. As it was, she was a bundle of nerves. She didn't know how to handle the situation at all, and until Bella had spoken, she hadn't imagined there *was* a situation.

When she finally walked into the dining-room, wearing a plain blue dress, Rory Adams rose to his feet, a huge smile on his face.

'I'm delighted you can join me, Mrs Dickinson,' he said, pulling out her chair for her.

'I like to pretend I'm a guest now and again.'

They both chose soup to start and while eating, Rory Adams gave Amelia his life story. He had grown up in Tacoma and now lived in Seattle with his three grown-up sons. His wife had died when the youngest child was only two – the same age as Victoria now.

'I know Seattle well,' Amelia told him. 'My first husband's family run a business there – a general store and livery stables. The Carters, do you know of them?'

His eyes widened at that.

'Yes. Yes, I know the family.' He frowned briefly. 'Then you must have married Miles Carter?'

'I did, yes.'

The idea of Miles and Amelia as a couple seemed to surprise him, but he didn't comment.

'I keep in touch with Constance, Theo's wife,' Amelia went on, 'so I still hear news.' Their letters were few and far between these days, though. In fact, thinking about it, it was probably a year since she'd heard from Constance. She made a mental note to drop her a few lines.

'There was talk of expanding the business,' Rory said lightly. 'I gather that was the oldest son's idea. Is he Theo?'

'Yes, that's him.' She shook her head in amazement. 'And Jacob, his father, will have been against it. Jacob will go to his grave resisting change.'

They chatted about Seattle and, when they were mid-way through their main course, Amelia realised that she was quite relaxed with him.

At forty-five, he was younger than she had imagined. He was an interesting companion and had a knack of laughing at himself that was endearing.

'So what brings you to Fairbanks so often?' she asked.

'I told you that my brothers had both settled here, yes?'

She nodded.

'I'm doing some legal work for them,' he

explained, 'but, really, I like to see them. We're a close family. Besides,' he added, eyes twinkling, 'I enjoy visiting my favourite hotel.'

Amelia, not sure if he was flirting with her or not, quickly averted her gaze. The reception area was just visible from their table and she was in time to spot a man walking out. She had only seen his back but she could have sworn it was Sam Hunter.

Her heart began racing uncomfortably and she wasn't sure if Rory Adams comment was responsible or if it was the thought that Sam Hunter might be in Fairbanks.

Knowing her face was flushed, and knowing there was nothing she could do about it, she returned her attention to her companion.

'Why, thank you, Mr Adams. I'm glad you enjoy staying with us.'

Conversation turned to other things – Fairbanks, the weather, England, Amelia's family – but Amelia was no longer relaxed. She wanted to race over to the reception and see if Sam Hunter had checked in.

Finally, their meal was over.

'Thank you so much, Mr Adams, I've had a delightful evening,' she said. 'I hope everything was to your satisfaction.'

'It was perfect, Mrs Dickinson.' He rose to his feet and reached for her hand. 'The food, the company – perfect.'

Amelia wondered if he could feel her hand shaking in his.

'I'm glad,' she said briskly, 'and now, if you'll excuse me, I have things to attend to.'

'Of course.' With a slight bow, he released her hand.

Amelia left the dining-room without a backward glance and headed to the reception desk.

'Was that Sam Hunter I saw?' she asked the young desk clerk.

'It was. He's booked in for three nights.'

'I see,' Amelia murmured, and she headed to her rooms.

Amelia hadn't slept at all well and, naturally, Jack and Victoria were awake far earlier than usual. Jack was almost incoherent with excitement and could talk of nothing other than the imminent arrival of his pony.

Isaac and Jane arrived as they were finishing breakfast and they were equally excited.

Amelia was grateful they were there. While Jack and Victoria chatted to them, Amelia had time for another coffee.

She had spent the whole night tossing and turning, alternating between worrying that Bella might be correct and that Rory Adams might have romance on his mind, and wondering what Sam Hunter was doing in

Fairbanks and whether she would see him. This morning, she was none the wiser on either subject and was exhausted before the day had even started.

It was soon time to set off and, as the five of them stepped out of the hotel and on to the main street, there, only a couple of yards from them, was Sam Hunter.

Amelia hadn't seen him since the day of the hotel's opening and, although nothing had been said, she'd had the feeling they had parted on uneasy terms. She could still remember asking him how long he was staying at the hotel and his telling her, 'I've seen all I need to see.'

Given that, she had no idea how to greet him and she was immensely grateful that Jack was busy telling him about the new pony. Jack's words were tumbling out so fast that it was a wonder Sam grasped any of it. Yet, he did.

'You can come with us,' Jack offered before Amelia had a chance to get a word in.

'Oh, I'm sure Mr Hunter is very busy, Jack,' she said.

'Not at all,' he replied, much to Amelia's surprise. 'I would love to accompany you. I'm eager to see this new pony. I hear your mother owns a fine animal, Jack. By all accounts, she's an excellent judge.'

Amelia felt herself blush at the compliment.

'I haven't ridden for a long time,' she told him, 'but any knowledge I have is all thanks to Miles and his family. I'd never even sat on a horse until I went to live in Seattle.'

She did have a fine animal, though. Smoke was a gentle, beautiful, five-year-old grey gelding and she had fallen in love with him on sight. She was determined to find more time for riding.

'I have excellent staff taking care of the guests' horses,' she said, 'and it seemed silly not to take advantage of that.'

'Indeed,' he agreed.

They continued on their way and Amelia found herself walking with Sam Hunter while the children went on ahead.

It touched her heart to see that the children were such good friends. Jane, thirteen now, had matured enormously since Victoria was born and had endless patience. Isaac was fifteen, yet he treated Jack, eight now, as if they were the same age.

As she watched, Victoria demanded to be carried. Jane laughed and swung her into her arms.

'They all know that if they don't do as she wants, Victoria will throw a tantrum,' Amelia explained to Sam with a smile. 'She's developing quite a temper for one so small.'

'Yes, Bella told me that she was spirited,' he explained. 'That she takes after her mother.'

Amelia felt herself blush. This was ridiculous; the man had seen her widowed twice, he had seen her dressed in a man's clothing, and he had seen her in a jail cell accused of murder. If he hadn't formed an opinion of her by now, he never would, and it was far too late for Amelia to try to change that opinion.

Bella had once said that Sam had feelings for her, but Amelia quickly dismissed that thought. Bella could be a romantic fool at times.

'She's strong-willed,' Amelia admitted, dragging her thoughts back to her daughter.

'She's adorable,' he said softly. 'You should be very proud of your children.'

'I am,' she told him. 'For a while – well, getting the hotel off the ground took up a lot of my time and I suppose–' She broke off, finding it difficult to put her thoughts into words. 'They had to do without a mother for a while,' she admitted at last. 'That was wrong. I should have made more time for them. The business wasn't that important.'

'They don't appear to have suffered,' he pointed out.

They didn't, but Amelia felt guilty whenever she recalled the days they had spent with Bella, the times Jack had wanted to talk to her and she hadn't had the time.

'But I, of all people, should have known better,' she insisted. 'As you know, I grew up in an orphanage, and we had the most wonderful matron taking care of us all. She always had time for every one of us. Always.'

She thought for a moment.

'Yet, it was that same orphanage – well, the growing up with nothing that made me yearn for security for my own children. I wanted them to have everything.'

'That's understandable,' he said.

'Not really,' she argued softly. 'Given the choice of riches or love as a child, I would have chosen the latter every time. Every child would.'

There was no more time to talk as they were at the stables in time to see Alan Busby, the young groom, leading Jack's pony around the yard.

'He arrived an hour ago, Mrs Dickinson,' the groom told her, 'and I'm just settling him in.' He ran an experienced hand down the animal's shoulder. 'He's in good condition.'

Amelia could see that. Merlin was a young chestnut gelding with four white socks. He stood at fourteen hands, and the way he danced around the yard made Amelia wish she'd chosen a smaller, more placid animal.

'Jack will be fine,' Sam said, as if he could read her thoughts.

'He's had plenty of lessons,' she said, nodding, 'and he has no fear. All the same, the animal does look a little – spirited.'

Her worries dissolved a little when, later, Jack was up on Merlin's back. He had been told he wouldn't be riding the pony until it had been given a chance to settle in its new home, but no-one on earth could have stopped him sitting on Merlin for a quick walk around the yard.

The groom led him and Jack's smile stretched from ear to ear.

Amelia wished Miles could have seen him. How proud he would have been of his son.

When it was time to settle Merlin in his stable, the children went along to help.

'I'll look after Victoria,' Jane promised, holding the child's hand.

Amelia smiled at that. Jane always looked out for the child. One day, she would make a wonderful mother.

Left alone with Sam Hunter, Amelia showed him the other stables. She wanted to show him her own horse, but Smoke was still out being exercised.

'I'm glad to see you looking so much better,' Sam remarked suddenly.

What on earth did he mean by that? As ever, she felt awkward and tongue-tied with him.

She was reminded of the day they had first met. Ten years had passed since she had found herself looking into his face when he had sought her out in Dawson.

She had been sitting outside her tent, she

recalled, and he had quite taken her breath away. In Dawson, everyone had been living on their nerves for a long time, yet he had looked as if he had no cares in the world.

Then years on, he looked exactly the same – very tall, strong and completely at ease with himself and those around him.

'What are you thinking?' he asked curiously.

'Oh, I was remembering–' Her throat felt tight and she had to swallow. 'I was trying to think how long ago it was that we first met.'

'Ten years,' he said without hesitation, and she was surprised he remembered. He smiled suddenly. 'I was very curious about the woman who bought a stove for twelve dollars and sold it an hour later for twenty-two. I knew then that you would go far.'

Amelia smiled at the memory.

He touched her face and Amelia jumped back as if she had been burned.

'Are you happy?' he asked, not seeming to notice the way his gesture had startled her.

'Happy? Why, yes, of course. I have two wonderful children, many dear friends, two successful businesses–'

She was smiling, yet she felt that smile falter. Something was missing from her life. She had known that for some time but, until this moment, she'd had no idea what it was. Now, she knew exactly what that something was, and the knowledge had her heart racing unbearably.

Sam leaned forward slightly, and for one startling moment, Amelia thought he was about to kiss her.

'I'm glad,' was all he said as the sound of the children approaching reached them.

She shook her head to clear her thoughts. Of course, he hadn't intended to kiss her.

Amelia turned to smile at the children, and to lift a laughing Victoria into her arms, yet her head was spinning.

In that moment, above all else, she had longed for Sam Hunter's kiss.

Chapter Thirteen

April 1909, Fairbanks

'What do you think?' Amelia demanded. Sam Hunter patted the horse's shoulder and swung himself into the saddle.

'He looks good enough,' he allowed, 'but looks mean nothing, do they?'

The horse, standing at seventeen hands, looked magnificent. Ears pricked, he snorted impatiently as he waited for a signal to move.

'Sam! You know as well as I do that he's by far the finest animal in Fairbanks. I got him for a good price, too.'

'I don't doubt it,' he muttered.

'Take him out for an hour,' she suggested, 'and then we can discuss it over lunch.'

Despite being in the saddle, Sam was reluctant to make a deal.

'I swore many years ago never to buy anything from you, Amelia. The idiot who bought that stove from you in Dawson must rue the day–'

'Nonsense, he was desperate for a stove.'

'Ah, but I'm not desperate for a horse.'

'Then I'll have to find someone who is.' She grinned up at him. 'You won't find a better animal, and you can afford to pay top price.'

'Just as you can afford to let him go for a reasonable price,' he retorted, laughing as he urged the animal to a trot.

Smiling to herself, Amelia watched them move off, horse and rider in complete accord.

When they were out of sight, Amelia walked back to the hotel.

She had been spending a lot of time with Sam Hunter lately. He'd had a house built in Fairbanks and was in the process of setting up a business. That it would be a success, she had no doubt. There was little Sam didn't know about designing and building boats.

There was little he didn't know about

horses, too. He was looking for something special, and she knew they didn't come any better than Caesar.

Later that morning, when Sam joined her at the hotel for lunch, Amelia could tell that he was eager to make a good deal. So was she. This was going to be fun!

First, they ordered their food. While they waited, they talked of all sorts of things – except the horse – but, as soon as their food arrived, a glint came into Sam's eyes.

'Name your price,' he said at last, adding a dry, 'and I may pay you half of it.'

Amelia spluttered with laughter.

'Here I am, giving you a free lunch, and you talk as if I'd cheat you!'

'Where you're concerned, Amelia, there's no such thing as a free lunch.'

Amelia gazed across the table at him and marvelled at just how much she loved him. Gone were the days when she had felt awkward in his company. Now, they were easy with each other. They had a past and they were comfortable with it.

'Of course,' Sam said amiably, 'to hurry this deal along, I could offer you the price you paid for him.'

'You could,' she agreed, grinning, 'if you knew what that price was.'

He leaned forward to whisper.

'A word of advice, my dear. Never tell your son how much you paid for something.'

'What?' Amelia was horrified. 'Jack told you?'

Grinning from ear to ear, Sam nodded.

'We've just walked here together.'

'I bet you wheedled it out of him!'

Sam laughed.

'I didn't even have to ask him.'

Amelia supposed she shouldn't be surprised. Jack idolised Sam and spent as much time as he could with him. He spent hours at the boatyard, 'helping' as he liked to call it.

'I might have lied,' she pointed out.

'Lie to your son? Never.'

No, she would never do that.

'So what did you think of Caesar?' she asked eagerly.

'You're right. He's the finest animal in Fairbanks. And yes, you got him at a good price.' Smiling, he shook his head. 'Everyone says you have the Midas touch, and I believe they're right.'

'No,' she argued softly. 'I've been penniless too many times for that.'

'But not any more.' Sam patted her hand in a reassuring way. He knew just how much security meant to her.

'Have you heard from your brother yet?'

'Yesterday,' she told him happily. 'I'm in the process of transferring funds.' She laid down her knife and fork. 'Isn't it wonderful that I'm able to help? I couldn't bear to think of the orphanage closing. I just wish Matron was there to see it,' she added.

'She can rest in peace now,' Sam said.

'Yes.'

'So what are the plans?' he asked.

'The two nearby buildings are being bought,' she told him. 'I remember those, they're huge. At least, they're huge in my memory. They're being turned into school buildings and the orphanage itself is being completely modernised. There will be a new kitchen and dining-room, and the dorm-itories are being expanded.'

She laughed suddenly.

'How Ivy has done all this, I'll never know. Of course, she's changed a lot over the years,' she added thoughtfully. 'I was always telling her she was too shy for her own good. Now, here she is taking on politicians. Whatever must Jimmy think?'

Sam smiled.

'I'm sure he's very proud of her.'

'Oh, he is. I just wish I could see them—' She broke off.

She could see them any time she wanted. As a wealthy woman with a staff more than capable of managing the business in her absence, she could go to Liverpool when-ever she chose.

'I will visit Liverpool. Soon,' she said vaguely.

It was Bella who had pointed out that

there was nothing to stop her visiting her old home. Just as it was Bella who had guessed the reason for her reluctance.

The truth was, she didn't want to leave Fairbanks at the moment. She would miss Sam too much. Over the years, in ways she hadn't even noticed at the time, he had somehow become everything to her. Nowadays, she didn't feel quite whole if he was away from her.

She looked up and caught him gazing at her in a way that took her breath away.

He smiled at her.

'What are you thinking?'

'About going home,' she said softly, and the way his face fell warmed her heart. 'Only for a visit,' she added quickly. 'This is home now.'

His relief was evident.

'I don't suppose you would care to act as chaperone to a woman and her two children?' she asked, breath suspended.

'I might be persuaded.'

She smiled at that.

'Thank you.'

'It will depend on the price I have to pay for this horse,' he added, and she hooted with laughter.

'There you go again – sounding as if you think I might cheat you!'

Sam smiled, but he was silent for a long time. Then he reached for her hand.

'Do you have any idea how much I love you?'

She gazed down at their hands, fascinated by how well they fitted.

'Yes, Sam,' she said, looking up at him. 'Yes, I truly believe I do.'

June 1909, Fairbanks

If Bella could have sung all night, Amelia could have danced until dawn. In her wildest dreams, she had never imagined it was possible to know such complete happiness.

'You know Bella's never forgiven you for not allowing her to sing at the hotel's grand opening?' Sam murmured.

'I know.' Amelia laughed at the memory. 'She would have been a bundle of nerves, though, so she should be grateful to me.'

'Ha!'

'She can be very contrary. I had to beg her to sing this evening,' she told him, 'and this is far more important. That was merely to celebrate the opening of the hotel. This is to celebrate – us.'

As they moved around the dance floor as husband and wife, Amelia could hardly believe it. Nor could she believe how right it felt.

When she had married Miles, she had loved him with all the passion and naïveté of youth. On marrying George, she had been fond of him and grateful, but it was only later that she had learned to love him. And it was much later, long after he was killed, that she learned to forgive him for cheating Miles out of their boarding-house.

But the love she felt for Sam had been built slowly and carefully on the strongest of foundations. It was a love born out of respect, trust, friendship and admiration.

Bella sang the last few notes and Amelia and Sam slowed to a stop on the dance floor.

'Our guests are looking to leave,' Sam murmured in her ear, taking her hand in his.

'Of course.'

Standing side by side, Sam's arm resting on her waist, they said their goodbyes, thanked their guests for making their wedding day such a happy occasion and accepted yet more congratulations and good wishes.

'We'll be off now,' Bella said, hugging Amelia tight. She had to wipe another tear from her eye. 'You've made me happier than you'll ever know,' she added. 'To think that my dearest friends are married–' She shook her head at the wonder of it. 'Sam will make you so happy, Mel.'

'I know, Bella, I know. And thank you.' Amelia squeezed her friend tight. 'Thank you for everything.'

When Bella and her family left, it was time to persuade Jack and Victoria to go to their beds. Not an easy task. The children were over-excited. Jack couldn't quite believe that the man he worshipped above all others was now his step-father, and Victoria was only content when she was being carried in Sam's arms.

When, at last, Amelia and Sam were in their bedroom, Amelia was far too happy to waste time sleeping. She sat at their window and gazed out. At this time of year, Fairbanks didn't see darkness and she could gaze at the town spread around her.

'Amelia Hunter,' she murmured, trying out her new name. 'Mrs Amelia Hunter. Actually, that sounds quite grand.'

'Then it's as well I persuaded you to marry me,' Sam replied with amusement.

Amelia laughed at that. She had gone to great lengths to explain to him that she didn't want to marry a third time, that she was perfectly happy with things as they were, that she was too independent a woman for marriage and that she didn't think she was at all suited to marriage and that she didn't want to risk spoiling their friendship. Sam had quietly, and surprisingly easily, worn down each argument in turn.

Here I am, she thought, the happiest woman alive.

'I should be packing,' she told him. In less than forty eight hours, they would be setting off on their honeymoon.

'There will be plenty of time for that tomorrow. And whilst we're on the subject,' Sam added grimly, 'I really don't see the need to take that trunk with us.' The object in question lay in the corner of the bedroom and he eyed it darkly.

Amelia spluttered with laughter at his expression.

'I've told you, Sam. Everywhere I go, that trunk goes. I've explained that a hundred times.'

'Yes, you've explained, but I still don't see the need to take the confounded thing on our honeymoon.' He saw the steely glint in her eyes and smiled. 'But I'll accept defeat,' he told her, 'and I'm sure it won't be the last time I do that.'

'Oh, Sam,' she said earnestly, 'I'll be a good wife to you, I promise. Really, you'll find me very easy to live with and I'll–'

'Pah!' He roared with laughter. 'Easy to live with? You?' He sat beside her at the window. 'But that's fine. I enjoy a challenge, my love.'

She grinned at him.

'Then we're very well suited.'

She slipped her arm through his and hugged him close.

August 1909, Liverpool

The city was baking beneath a blazing sun and Ivy was pleased when they reached the

335

sanctuary of the park and blessed shade. She liked the summer as well as the next person, but this was too much. The air was heavy and humid, and everyone agreed that a good thunderstorm was needed to cool things down.

'We'll be complaining when the ice is thick on the ground,' James said, guessing at her thoughts.

She smiled at the truth of that.

The children, walking on ahead, didn't seem to notice the heat. Martha and Albert walked with their heads bent, hatching some plot no doubt, while Lizzie trailed behind them, lost in a world of her own.

Ivy's heart thrilled at the sight of them. It took all her powers to persuade Albert to make himself presentable but, today, even he looked smart. Ivy had always loved Sundays when the five of them could wear their best clothes and enjoy the afternoon together.

'Perhaps we'll hear from Amelia this week,' she remarked.

'It's high time,' James agreed.

That was an understatement, but Ivy refused to worry about it. She guessed that Amelia's next letter would be full of excuses about lack of time. It would also be filled with news.

'When I write back,' Ivy said with satisfaction, 'I can send her the photograph of the children.'

'She'll marvel at how grown-up the twins are. Mind you,' James added, shaking his head, 'I marvel at that. I can't believe the years have passed so quickly.'

Ivy couldn't either. It seemed no time at all since they had stood side by side in the church and vowed to love each other until death parted them. And what an easy task that was, she thought.

'They've been good years, haven't they, Jimmy?'

James smiled, and patted her hand.

'The best, love. We're very lucky.'

'We are.'

Ivy wouldn't have swapped her life with anyone. Her husband and children brought her more happiness than she had ever dreamed possible. People could keep their riches and their fancy houses.

They left the park and headed for home. Ivy would be relieved when they got there, too. It was cooler inside than out today.

Thinking about it later, it was odd how they all stopped – even Albert – at the sight that met them as they rounded the corner.

A couple and two children were standing there and it took a moment to realise that the woman was hammering on their door.

'Who on earth–?'

Ivy's heart skipped a couple of beats. The auburn hair that shimmered in the sunlight.

337

That tall, erect carriage. No. Surely, it couldn't be! The heat must be taking its toll.

The woman turned then and spotted them.

'Oh, my! It's–' But Ivy's throat had tightened and she couldn't force out another word.

Instead, she ran, only coming to a stop a few feet from the woman.

'Is it really you?' She hardly dared to believe it possible.

'Well, of course it's me! Who did you think it was?'

Ivy shrieked with laughter at Amelia's response, and then the two of them were hugging the breath from each other's bodies and dancing a circle in the street, their faces wet with tears of joy.

Then James was there, and there were more hugs and more tears.

The children, Jack and Victoria, Ivy would have known anywhere. It was the man who aroused Ivy's curiosity. Incredibly tall and very handsome, he stood watching the proceedings with amused patience.

Then, even before Amelia announced proudly, 'This is my husband,' she realised who he was.

'You'll be Sam Hunter,' she said happily.

Amelia and Sam looked at each other in amazement.

'How did you know?' Amelia demanded,

and Ivy had to laugh at the expression on her face. If there was one thing Amelia hated, it was having her surprises ruined.

'I remember one of your letters,' Ivy explained. 'It must have been written – oh, ten years ago now. It was the first you sent us from Dawson, remember? We wanted to know that you were safe and well, and all you wrote about was the handsome river boat pilot who'd taken you there.'

'Really?' Sam looked exceedingly pleased on hearing this.

'For heaven' sake, Ivy!' Amelia burst out laughing. 'You do exaggerate so. I'm sure I merely mentioned him in passing.'

It was pandemonium, Ivy thought, her face still wet with tears as she finally shooed everyone inside.

Lizzie, as was often the case with strangers, was trying to hide behind her father.

'Now then, Lizzie,' Amelia said, reaching out to her, 'you can't possibly be shy. I'm your aunt Amelia and I know all about you, and surely you've heard about Jack and Victoria, haven't you?'

Lizzie nodded shyly.

'Good. Then come here and tell me what you've been doing today.'

Amelia took Lizzie by the hand and sat at the kitchen table, listening to Lizzie tell her every last detail of their day.

Their kitchen was tiny at the best of times,

but with four extra, especially when one was her sister-in-law, there wasn't room to move. Given the chance, Ivy would have ushered them into the parlour.

'My, you're a real chatterbox!' Amelia told Lizzie with amusement.

Ivy had to chuckle. It served Amelia right. Once Lizzie started talking, there was no stopping her.

But wasn't it typical of Amelia to arrive without warning? Typical to get married without telling them, too. What on earth was she going to give them to eat, Ivy wondered.

'What's amused you?' Amelia wanted to know, spotting the expression on Ivy's face.

'I was wondering how I could be worrying about feeding you all when it's so wonderful to see you. I often thought—' Again, her throat tightened on myriad emotions. 'I often thought I'd never see you again,' she confessed.

'Don't you remember when I left?' Amelia said gently. 'I promised I'd soon visit.'

'Soon visit?' Ivy spluttered. 'Mel, that was twenty years ago!'

'Amelia has a tendency to get wrapped up in things,' Sam put in. 'A quiet life doesn't seem to agree with her.'

Ivy laughed.

'That's true enough, Sam.'

'As for feeding us,' Amelia said, 'you'll do no such thing. A table's already booked at the hotel. A table for nine and it will be wonderful!'

'Hotel? Which hotel?' Ivy was horrified. 'With these three?' she demanded, nodding at the children. 'Besides, what do you expect us to wear? We're not used to going to–'

'Ivy,' Amelia said, shaking her head. 'You all look wonderful just as you are. And we'll threaten all five children with dire consequences if they dare to misbehave. Now, do stop fussing.'

'She's right,' Sam said gently. 'We'll have a wonderful time. I've so been looking forward to meeting you all.'

What a lovely man, Ivy thought. He really meant it. He was so in love with Amelia that he wanted to know them, too.

Who wouldn't fall in love with her, Ivy thought fondly. The years hadn't marked her at all. She was as attractive and as full of vitality and fun as she had been all those years ago.

Ivy had to bite her bottom lip. This was too much to take in and, if she wasn't careful, she would be in floods of tears again.

'So what do you think of Liverpool, Sam?'

'I love the weather!'

Amelia smiled at that. It was true that the weather had been kind to them. Each day, they had been blessed with warm sunshine and unbroken blue skies.

'I love your family, too,' he added.

Amelia, careful not to damage the flowers she was carrying, slipped her arm through his as they walked, alone for once, along the much-changed quayside.

'I knew you would.'

The feeling was mutual, Amelia thought fondly. At first, James had been a little in awe of Sam, but Sam had soon put him at his ease. Now, they would chat for hours as if they had known each other all their lives.

Ivy, she knew, had taken to Sam immediately. Amelia's nephew and nieces adored him as much as Jack and Victoria did.

'You'll miss them all when we return,' Sam pointed out.

'Yes,' she agreed, 'but my life is in Fairbanks now, just as theirs is here.'

'Do you think they'll visit?'

'Yes. Yes, I do. Oh, Ivy will worry about everything – the journey, the children – but yes, they'll come. James is very keen and Ivy will do anything to make him happy.'

James and Ivy were the perfect couple, she mused. She had known from the start that they might have been made for each other, but this was the first time she'd seen them as a comfortable married couple.

Sam nodded at the sea.

'The weather's turning.'

She followed his gaze to see a huge, black cloud heading their way. Amelia had warned him that it would probably rain every day, but this was their sixth day and there had been no hint of it. This cloud looked ominous, though.

'We'd better get a move on, Sam.'

They weren't dressed for a downpour and, besides, Amelia didn't want her flowers to receive a soaking. Fifteen minutes later, the first spot fell.

'Make a run for it,' Amelia said, laughing. 'We can shelter in the church.'

By the time they reached the building and slammed the heavy wooden door shut behind them, Amelia was breathless with laughter. Fortunately, they weren't too wet and, more importantly, the flowers weren't damaged.

'It'll soon pass,' Sam said, shaking rain droplets from his hair.

'I hope so.'

Amelia was busy looking around her at a church that seemed so much smaller than she remembered.

'I used to come here every Sunday,' she confided to Sam, 'and I would have sworn that the roof was at least twice as high. It's nothing like I remember it.'

Her gaze went to the stained-glass window that was directly behind the pulpit.

'But I can tell you,' she added with a grin, 'that there are forty-three pieces of red in that window.'

Sam laughed.

'Daydreaming, Amelia?'

'Oh, yes. There were times when I believed the sermons would last for ever! The poor man must have despaired of me. It's a wonder Matron didn't, too.' She ran a light finger over the flowers. 'But she never did.'

They walked around the church and then Amelia slid into the front pew.

'I remember the family that used to have this pew,' she murmured. 'There were two daughters who thought themselves very grand. They were about the same age as Ivy and me. I used to embarrass Ivy by poking my tongue at them when no-one was looking.'

Sam rolled his eyes in a look of mock horror.

'I had no idea I'd married such a shameful woman.'

'There was another lady,' she remembered. 'I never saw her in church, but she was beautiful. I first saw her when we were walking here from the orphanage. She waited patiently while Matron hurried us all past. She had a lovely smile. I only saw her half a dozen times, but I remember vowing to Ivy that, one day, I, too, would wear fine clothes like hers. The first time I saw her was the day I asked Matron for my trunk,' she recalled, 'and I was determined to fill that trunk with beautiful clothes.'

'And what,' Sam asked, 'has persuaded you to give your precious trunk to James and Ivy?'

'Firstly, it's always belonged to James as much as me–'

'Which would account for nothing,' Sam put in dryly.

'Secondly,' Amelia went on, her lips twitching with humour at his remark, 'because it still contains all the gold sweepings from the boarding-house.'

Sam's eyes widened.

'James won't accept what he sees as charity,' Amelia explained, 'so, when we've gone, I'll write and suggest they have the gold valued and either treat themselves or keep it for a rainy day.'

'Thirdly,' she continued, before he could comment, 'I think Ivy would like it as a reminder of our childhood.'

'I'm sure she would,' Sam agreed.

'And lastly, I no longer have a need for it.'

'But I thought it had to follow you everywhere?'

'No more.' She touched his face. 'I have all I want or need – more than I ever dreamed of, Sam.'

Sam put her flowers aside, held her close and kissed her. When he pulled back to look at her, she saw her love reflected back in him.

After a few moments, Sam handed her the flowers and helped her to her feet.

'The rain has stopped, my love.'

When they stepped outside, the sky was a watery blue and, once again, the sun was shining.

'I think it's this way,' Amelia said, leading Sam between old gravestones. Near the old yew, Ivy had said, and there it was: ELIZABETH VICTORIA JOHNSON.

Amelia felt a sharp pricking sensation at the back of her eyes as she read the simple inscription that ended, so very aptly, *Loved and Remembered Always.*

She arranged her flowers – in purest white – at the foot of the stone. As she knelt, she felt Sam's hand on her shoulder and she reached for it, squeezing it tight. Memories flooded her mind. Memories of a loving, kind, wise woman to whom Amelia owed everything.

'Amelia,' Sam whispered. 'Look!'

She stood and looked to where he pointed.

'Oh, Sam–'

Too choked to speak, Amelia simply gazed at the shimmering rainbow.

As Amelia stood behind the tall, wooden desk, she saw more than a hundred faces of all shapes and sizes and various degrees of interest staring back at her. Most of the faces belonged to children, but a few adults – orphanage staff and local dignitaries – also waited for her to speak.

Despite having been awake for most of the night thinking about her speech, she didn't know where to start.

Ivy, who had arranged this, had dismissed her concerns.

'Simply tell them your story, Mel. Prove to the children that St Joseph's can be a stepping stone to anything. Convince the adults to come up with more funding.'

What a daunting task, Amelia thought now. Strangely, it was returning to the orphanage that had shown her, more forcibly than anything, just what she had made of her life.

Towards the back room, a young girl with her dark hair in long, thick plaits was playing with the hem of her skirt, daydreaming. That was exactly what Amelia would have been doing at the same age. She would have been dreaming of security, of living in a grand house and wearing fine clothes.

Now, Amelia had all that she'd dreamed of and more. As a child, though, her big ideas had been ridiculed by the other children.

Another girl, one with a round face framed by curls the colour of carrots, couldn't take her eyes off Amelia. The girl was taking in every detail of Amelia's dress and shoes. In years to come, Amelia thought, that girl will remember me. She'll remember the wealthy woman in her splendid clothes who had been introduced as their benefactor before telling them her story.

What a story it was! Even as a child, when reaching out and grasping the rainbow had seemed possible, Amelia hadn't imagined she would make one of the worst journey imaginable to search for gold in the inhospitable Yukon territory.

It was strange to be back at the orphanage. The place had changed little over the years. Amelia, having been granted the grand tour, had marvelled at how familiar it felt, and how many memories had rushed back both to touch and amuse her.

Soon, however, it would change drastically, and the main improvements would be due to the determination of people like Ivy and the funding from people like Amelia. If only Matron could have been here, she would have been so proud.

No longer would children sleep in over-crowded rooms. No longer would they eat cold food simply because it was so far from the kitchen to the dining-room. With the purchase of the two adjoining buildings, they would have space in which to learn and to play.

People were waiting for her to speak, Amelia realised with a jolt. She took a deep breath.

'It's a privilege and a pleasure to be invited here today,' she began.

She spoke of the plans for the buildings, and she gave credit to all those who had worked hard to make St Joseph's what it was. She spoke of Matron and of Ivy.

Yet, she knew what the children wanted to hear was her own story. They wanted to know how a girl who had nothing came to grow into the smart, self-assured woman standing before them.

'For me,' she told them, 'it all began on February the fourteenth, eighteen seventy-three when my twin brother, James–' she nodded at James who shuffled, embarrassed, in his seat next to Ivy's '–and I were left at the gates to this orphanage. We'd been wrapped in blankets and put in a huge, wooden chest. Oh, it was a fine chest with brass handles, but it was little defence against the bitterly cold winds...'

Amelia warmed to her own story. Hers was a tale filled with love and loss, triumph and despair. She had left Liverpool for an unknown life in Seattle. She had walked until her feet bled on the infamous Chilkoot Pass. She had started businesses, made them successful, only to lose them. She had married and been widowed. She had been imprisoned and charged with the murder of her second husband. Yet, her life had been blessed with good sense, a strength of

349

character and the determination to succeed that was the legacy of St Joseph's.

At the back of the room sat Sam. As Amelia spoke, she glanced his way and was warmed by the smile he gave her as he winked.

Yes, my life has been a very special one, Amelia thought, as the children of St Joseph's hung on her every word. But how much more exciting it is to know that the best is yet to come!

The publishers hope that this book has given you enjoyable reading. Large Print Books are especially designed to be as easy to see and hold as possible. If you wish a complete list of our books please ask at your local library or write directly to:

Dales Large Print Books
Magna House, Long Preston,
Skipton, North Yorkshire.
BD23 4ND